He Was Out for Revenge.

"Didn't your mother ever teach you that gentlemen don't brag about—"

"I've never claimed to be a gentleman," Ty interrupted, shutting her up. "There's something you don't understand about ball players, Dani. We believe in revenge. And you and I . . . The joke made Mike and me even, but I owe you one, Dani."

BROOKE HASTINGS

is that rare individual who can combine many careers and excel in all of them. In addition to her writing she is active in California politics and community affairs, while she maintains a home for her husband of fourteen years and their two children. *Rough Diamond* is her second Silhouette Special Edition.

Dear Reader:

During the last year, many of you have written to Silhouette telling us what you like best about Silhouette Romances and, more recently, about Silhouette Special Editions. You've also told us what else you'd like to read from Silhouette. With your comments and suggestions in mind, we've developed SILHOUETTE DESIRE.

SILHOUETTE DESIREs will be on sale this June, and each month we'll bring you four new DESIREs written by some of your favorite authors—Stephanie James, Diana Palmer, Rita Clay, Suzanne Simms and many more.

SILHOUETTE DESIREs may not be for everyone, but they are for those readers who want a more sensual, provocative romance. The heroines are slightly older—women who are actively involved in their careers and the world around them. If you want to experience all the excitement, passion and joy of falling in love, then SILHOUETTE DESIRE is for you.

I'd appreciate any thoughts you'd like to share with us on new SILHOUETTE DESIRE, and I invite you to write to us at the address below:

Karen Solem
Editor-in-Chief
Silhouette Books
P.O. Box 769
New York, N.Y. 10019

BROOKE HASTINGS
Rough Diamond

Silhouette Special Edition
Published by Silhouette Books New York
America's Publisher of Contemporary Romance

For Dave, who would have liked to be Mike

 SILHOUETTE BOOKS, a Simon & Schuster Division of
GULF & WESTERN CORPORATION
1230 Avenue of the Americas, New York, N.Y. 10020

ISBN: 0-671-53521-8

First Silhouette Books printing May, 1982

10 9 8 7 6 5 4 3 2 1

Map by Tony Ferrara

SILHOUETTE, SILHOUETTE SPECIAL EDITION
and colophon are trademarks of Simon & Schuster.

America's Publisher of Contemporary Romance

Printed in the U.S.A.

Other Silhouette Books by Brooke Hastings

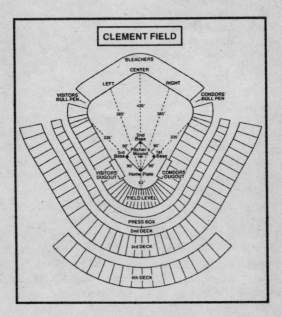

CLEMENT FIELD

Chapter One

". . . are meeting with the president here in Paris today, in order to resolve problems related to the recent entry of Greece into the Common Market." Danielle, her eyes still closed, reached out a hand and groped for the volume control on her clock-radio. The announcer didn't have to scream the news at her—not when she'd stayed out until one o'clock the night before.

She had just made contact with the proper dial when he continued, "We have a late bulletin from Los Angeles. Producer George Korman, who was rushed to the University of California Medical Center two hours ago, is dead of a heart attack."

Dani's hand twitched, then dropped back to the bed. "Mr. Korman, fifty-eight years old, was best known for his film *Parallel Universe*. The movie and its two sequels, along with his many other investments, made him one of the wealthiest men in Hollywood. He was a master at staging publicity stunts and movie spectacles, and a self-confessed sports addict who owned an American baseball team, the California Condors. Mr. Korman was married four times: to automobile heiress Claire Templeton, French dancer Brigitte Ronsard, and American actresses Laura Storm and Viveca Swensen. Miss Swensen was at his side when he died."

The announcer started to read the weather forecast, but Dani didn't hear him. Disjointed images and flashes of competing emotions preempted her attention.

Her father on a movie set. He couldn't be dead. He was too young, too energetic. His heart condition wasn't serious—he had told her it wasn't. Had he lied to her? Oh, God. He must have.

Viveca by his bedside. Lord, what a charming performance she must be giving. The stricken wife, the bereft widow. Her current lovers could take turns consoling her.

The money. Millions and millions of dollars of it. She was buried in it, suffocating. The image faded.

She was flying on the Concorde, giving orders to a legion of men in business suits. Daddy, I'm only twenty-five years old, she thought. You weren't supposed to die—not so soon.

She rocked forward onto her knees, her head in her hands. Why couldn't they have been closer? Why had he rejected her all those years ago? She scolded herself. It was no use to blame him. Did you blame an earthquake or a tornado for the pain it left in its wake?

She rubbed away her tears. Love him for what he was, she told herself. Fairy tales are for children. Her expression turned dreamy, wistful. Her father had belonged to another age. Flamboyant, eccentric, extravagant, brilliant—wherever he went, he attracted attention. He could juggle five projects simultaneously, and never lose track of a single detail. He was wonderful at friendship . . . and very, very poor at loving.

He had never been much of a parent to Dani, but she had been no more immune to his charm and intelligence than the rest of the world. Eventually she had accepted the fact that although she was his only child, she would be granted no more of his time than anyone else. And like everyone else, she would miss him.

Her eyes were dry as she got out of bed, pulled on a robe, and walked toward the kitchen. She knew about grief. It turned you numb, made you physically sick, caused an enduring pain that faded much too gradually. She felt regret, sadness, an aching sense of loss. But not grief.

Her Aunt Jeanne was already dressed, sitting at the maple table in the dinette, reading the morning paper and drinking black coffee. "We have a busy day today," she said in French, looking up from the front page. "Madame Rousseau is coming in for a fitting at . . ." She paused, taking in the somber look in her niece's eyes, and the unnatural paleness of her face. "Darling, what on earth is the matter?"

"I was listening to the news. My father—he had a heart attack—he's dead." She stared at Jeanne, thinking, You're the one who's always been there.

"Je t'aime, Tante Jeanne," Dani murmured, then knelt by her aunt's chair, and dropped her head into the older woman's lap. As she cried, Jeanne's fingers stroked her hair, and Jeanne's voice offered soothing words of solace.

The tears gave way to talk. Jeanne guided Dani into the living room and sat her down on the couch. The room had a tranquil effect on Dani, as always. It was filled with memorabilia and objets d'art which Jeanne had acquired on buying trips for her boutique, or which wealthy clients had given her as gifts. An exquisite antique lace tablecloth graced a round, inlaid end table; a carved wooden tiger from Asia was curled up next to a row of books; a lovely, pastoral landscape by a Dutch artist hung on one wall.

They reminisced about George Korman, but the conversation was oddly impersonal. Eventually, though, Dani was able to share her feelings with her aunt. "It isn't like it was with Mama. It doesn't hurt the same way, Aunt Jeanne."

Dani's mother, a beautiful, raven-haired dancer named Brigitte Ronsard, had met producer George Korman during an audition for a minor role in one of his films. They were married after a whirlwind courtship and divorced seven years later when Dani was six.

After the break-up, Brigitte had taken Dani to Las Vegas, where she took back her maiden name, and resumed her career as a dancer. George Korman had many faults as a father, but shirking his financial obligations was not one of them. He bought them their house in Las Vegas and sent enough money each month so that Brigitte could work when and where she pleased.

For the first five years after the divorce, until Dani was eleven, her mother's sister Jeanne had lived with them, helping to care for her. Jeanne worked for several of the hotels, designing everything from the costumes in production numbers to the uniforms of the cocktail waitresses in the casinos. The three formed an unusually close-knit little family during those years, but once Dani was old enough to be on her own in the evenings, Jeanne returned to Paris to start her own business.

Dani had chosen to move in with her father after Brigitte was killed in an accident. She was only thirteen at the time, and she felt as though her world had been capriciously smashed to pieces. George Korman had been a rather distant figure to her, a man she had seen for only two or three weekends a year. But he was her only surviving parent, and she had a great need to feel closer to him.

At first she was achingly lonely, going to bed each night in the frilly pink and white bedroom of her father's house and crying into the pillow. But after a few months, she began to adjust. Her father's house-keeper was a kind, motherly woman and tried her best to be a substitute for Brigitte Ronsard. As for George Korman, Dani coped as best she could when her hopes went unfulfilled. She learned that he worked long hours, sometimes in countries halfway around the world. Even when they were together, he seemed puzzled by what to do with her. She was too old for a steady diet of Disneyland and Knott's Berry Farm, and too young to treat as an adult.

His fourth marriage, to a twenty-two-year-old ingenue named Viveca Swensen, destroyed whatever contentment Dani had managed to find. She wasn't surprised by Viveca's hostility; her father's third wife had been equally unfriendly during Dani's occasional visits to Los Angeles. Stepmothers, she postulated, were by their very nature a trial. One could hardly fault them for disliking the offspring of another wife, especially when a picture of that earlier family graced the husband's desk.

Dani had inherited Brigitte's dark brows and wavy hair, warm brown eyes, and saucy nose. When she laughed, her eyes sent out a mischievous sparkle which everyone but Viveca found enchanting, and when she teased, her mouth pouted with an impish-ness which charmed the most jaded of men. She owed only her height to her father. George Korman had been some two inches shorter than Dani's 5'10" mother, and Dani herself had stopped growing at 5'4".

Dani knew it would be useless to complain to her father about Viveca's constant, if clandestine, attacks. He would simply have ordered the two of them to get along with each other, and then escaped to the site of his most distant film set. Since she thought him unaware of Viveca's actions, she took it as a rejection when he sent her off to Paris to spend the summer with his former sister-in-law, Jeanne Ronsard. In time, Dani acknowledged that she would be happier with Jeanne, and except for two years of college in Boston, had lived with her ever since.

Dani tried to explain to Jeanne why she felt the way she did. "It's just that there was nothing even remotely parental about him, Aunt Jeanne. I suppose I came to think of him as a special sort of friend, more than anything else."

"Your papa was like a wonderful uncle, darling," Jeanne replied. "You mustn't feel guilty about your feelings."

"I don't. Not really." Dani paused, thinking that George Korman had really only been able to relate to her once she was an adult. When she was still a teenager, he had sometimes visited her when business took him to Paris, perhaps twice a year. He had offered no advance notice, but simply swooped down on the apartment like some whirling dervish, carting Dani off to the Louvre, or Versailles, or some other suitably cultural place. He would sit with a movie script or company report while she walked around.

After Dani returned to Paris from Boston and

completed her degree at the University of Paris, these educational excursions gave way to weekend jaunts to the playgrounds and capitals of Europe. In between the parties and screenings and meetings, her father began to schedule occasional meals with Dani. She was twenty-two when she learned that she was his principal heir, and now she paid close attention when he spoke of his business interests, and reacted with enthusiasm when he regaled her with the triumphs of his baseball team. She, in turn, would tell him about her job as the manager of Jeanne's boutique, sometimes asking his advice about problems she had. But neither confided anything personal.

"Being with Daddy was like visiting a fantasy world. The way he lived and the people he worked with—none of them seemed real to me." Dani glanced at the grandfather clock, which was sounding nine o'clock. "It's only midnight in California, Aunt Jeanne. Viveca must still be awake. Do you think I should try to get hold of her?"

The expression on Jeanne Ronsard's face conveyed her opinion of Viveca Swensen more eloquently than mere epithets would have. "It is her place to call you, darling. I would not waste my time talking with her. Get in touch with your father's attorneys; they will know what to do."

"I'll wait until it's morning in California," Dani agreed. "Go ahead to the shop, Aunt Jeanne. I'll take the day off, if that's all right. I want to walk around, visit some of the places I used to go to with him. Maybe I'll look through his letters."

At first Jeanne refused, but a little further coaxing convinced her that Dani genuinely wished to be alone. During the next few hours, Dani meandered through the Bois de Boulogne and its surrounding neighborhoods. Her mood was sober, pensive, even tearful at times, but there was no agony, none of the twisting bereavement she had felt when her mother died.

She and her father had been so different that it was hard for her to think of herself as his daughter. Although completely bilingual, Dani supposed that her outlook was primarily French. She and Jeanne lived comfortably but conservatively. Dani's friends tended to be intellectual, articulate, and well-mannered.

George Korman's notions of enjoyment—boisterous parties, outrageous practical jokes, extravagant living—were completely alien to her. On occasion she had found herself caught up in his world, but as she had told her aunt, she regarded those instances as temporary, if amusing, aberrations.

Once back in the apartment, Dani turned to her father's letters. The term was actually a misnomer. George Korman's communications seldom exceeded half a dozen sentences, often typed by one of his secretaries and beginning with the words, "Mr. Korman asked me to send this to you." The messages would be stapled to magazine or newspaper articles: a review of one of his movies, a piece on one of his business enterprises, an article on a subject he thought she should study. He would often underscore a phrase here and there, adding a word of agreement or ridicule.

Dani had saved all his correspondence, storing it in neat stacks in the bottom drawer of her dresser. She took out the entire drawer, carried it into the living room, and set it down on the oriental carpet. Then she began to reread the notes in chronological order, rifling through the accompanying articles. His interests had certainly been catholic, but then, he was a brilliant man.

The most recent message, which had arrived only a few days before, was scrawled in his own handwriting. The note was clipped to an article from a top sports weekly—the magazine's annual World Series wrap-up, which this year concerned the Condors' victory over the New York Yankees.

"Dani," it read. "I like these boys almost as much as I like actresses. Am I slowing down? Winning the Series is as good as winning an Oscar. And a lot less work. G.K."

Dani, busy with work and interested in baseball because it pleased her father, had not yet read the article. Now she did so, and found it to be an early valentine to the Condors, especially to a pitcher named Ty Morgan. He was responsible for two out of his team's four victories, giving up only two runs in seventeen innings. Even Dani knew that such a performance was outstanding. The sportswriters obviously agreed, because they had voted him the most valuable player of the Series.

Several paragraphs at the end of the article were devoted to the question of whether the pitcher would be playing for the Condors next season. The author pointed out that Ty Morgan had played out his option this year, and although he was expected to re-sign with the Condors, he would certainly become a free agent if no agreement were reached within the next few weeks.

Dani was not knowledgeable about the technicalities of free agency, but it was obvious from the article that several owners were itching to negotiate with the pitcher. "Winfield gets one and a half million a year plus a cost of living increase," Morgan was quoted as saying. "I don't see why I should take less." George Korman had scribbled in the margin, "He has a point!"

No one could accuse her father of holding a grudge, Dani told herself. She grimaced in distaste as she recalled a previous article about Ty Morgan, one that George Korman had most assuredly *not* sent her!

She had been in college in Boston at the time, in accordance with her late father's wishes. The month was October, and the Condors were in New York, again playing the Yankees in the World Series. After his team's victory, George had flown back to Los Angeles on business, but Viveca had stayed behind to join in the celebration.

Dani could still see her roommate running in with a newspaper to show her a picture of her stepmother, hanging on Ty Morgan's arm. They had been photographed leaving the city's most "in" disco together, Viveca quoted as cooing, "We thought we'd continue the party back at my hotel." Obviously they were more than "just good friends," and Dani had been appalled that one of her father's ball players would conduct an open affair with the owner's wife. It was one thing to know their marriage was less than perfect, another to see such graphic proof of it.

Judging from the current close-up of Ty Morgan, her father's arm draped around his shoulder, age had only added to his attractiveness. His uniform and hair were soaked with champagne, yet he projected satisfied self-assurance and a magnetic virility. For the first time that day, Dani smiled, amused by the notion of "owning" such a macho specimen.

She sobered quickly. Suppose he hadn't signed yet? Her father had played a major role in contract negotiations with his star players, but she lacked the experience to do so. George Korman had often railed against the irresponsibility and ignorance of some of his fellow owners. Given her own lack of knowledge, she should probably sell the team to somebody who would run it correctly.

Fortunately, such decisions were in the future. Dani laid the article atop all the others and returned the drawer to her dresser. For the next twenty minutes she prowled around the apartment, straightening cushions and knickknacks that were already perfectly placed. Then she put in the call she had been waiting all day to make.

Her father had given her the number of his lawyer, Edward Reed, Sr., after an earlier scare with his heart. "He'll always know how to reach me," her father had told her. "You can depend on him in an emergency."

"Good morning," the receptionist chirped. "Reed, Schultz, Decatur, and Clemson."

"This is George Korman's daugher Danielle, in Paris." Dani's voice was husky but firm. "May I speak to Mr. Reed?"

"He tried to call you late last night, Miss Ronsard," the woman replied, "but there was no answer. We're all very sorry about your father. I'll put you right through to Mr. Reed."

Edward Reed, Sr., earned full marks for thoroughness, Dani thought as she waited. She was not surprised that the man knew of her existence; as her father's personal attorney, he would have drafted the will. But the "Miss Ronsard" impressed her. Her father had obviously mentioned that she used her mother's maiden name, but "Danielle Patrice Korman" was still her legal name, the name in the will, and the one most people would have remembered.

"Miss Ronsard, this is Edward Reed." The attorney's voice was deep and smooth, like a radio announcer's. "We'll all miss your father. He was the kind of friend you could count on. And absolutely unique. Even with all my Hollywood clients, I've never run across anyone quite like him. I'm sorry."

Dani thanked Edward Reed for his condolences. It was ironic; given the breadth of her father's business interests, the attorney and his colleagues had probably seen more of him than she had.

Edward Reed continued in a kind but matter-of-fact voice. "The funeral is Thursday morning, Miss Ronsard. We booked two seats on TWA's noon flight to Los Angeles tomorrow. The return tickets are open; you can make your own arrangements when you pick them up at the airport. I'd like to suggest that you stay through Saturday morning, although there's no need for your aunt to do so." He named one of the most exclusive hotels in Beverly Hills, where a suite awaited them. "We hope you'll be comfortable there."

"Yes, thank you." Dani felt disoriented. To her father, nonstop flights halfway across the world and posh hotel suites were expected comforts, but she was not so blasé. "The money . . ." she began.

"We'll pay for everything at this end. This must have been a difficult day for you, so I won't take any more of your time. I'll fill you in on arrangements at the airport."

"You'll meet me? How will I recognize . . ."

"I'll recognize *you,*" the attorney interrupted gently. "I hear you look just like your mother, minus about six inches in height. She was a beautiful lady in every way, Miss Ronsard, and if I hadn't been a happily married man, I think I might have fallen in love with her myself."

"You knew her?" Dani asked.

"I've been your father's personal attorney for twenty-two years. I handled the divorce. There are things I'd like to tell you about him, and about his feelings for you."

"And I'd like to hear them," Dani replied. "I'll make time when I'm in California. Thank you, Mr. Reed."

Jeanne returned home as they were exchanging good-byes. Dani repeated the conversation to her, adding, "He's so well organized, it's intimidating. But he sounded very nice."

"To an heiress, of course he sounded nice." Jeanne's smile took the sting from her words.

"About your coming to the funeral, Aunt Jeanne." Dani paused, trying to find tactful words for a painful subject. "I know you're very busy, and given the way you felt about my father . . ."

"I think you misunderstand my point of view, *ma chère.* George made his own rules. In many ways he was a wonderful man, but as a husband, he was hopeless, and as a father, only slightly better. Of course I hold him responsible for hurting your mother very badly, but that is not the same as hating him for it. Oddly enough, I believe he considered her the great love of his life. His affairs were trivial diversions. Perhaps it is a shame that Brigitte could not tolerate them, but she was not made that way. And *he,* it would seem, was incapable of fidelity. I will certainly come to pay my respects, and also to meet this attorney. Your interests are involved, after all. But I will leave immediately after the funeral."

Dani answered that there would be time to speak to Edward Reed on Wednesday. As far as her "interests" were concerned, inheriting her father's money was a troubling complication in her life. Even if she remained only a figurehead, there would be reports to read and meetings to attend. She loved Paris above all cities, and was dismayed by the prospect of spending a substantial amount of time in Los Angeles.

Jeanne didn't pursue the subject, either then or during the long and tiring flight to California. After they passed through Customs, Dani looked around at the people meeting the flight. She spotted Edward Reed even before he smiled in recognition.

He was handsome and fit-looking, with graying blond hair and blue eyes. His fifty-odd years had added strength and virility to a face that might have been merely pleasant in his youth. She knew he was George Korman's confidant because of the way his expertly tailored pinstriped suit hung on his 5'11" frame, and because of his air of self-contained confidence. George Korman would be remembered not only for his creativity but for his business acumen, and the people who worked for him were sharp as sharks. Edward Reed, Dani decided, was not the type of man who made mistakes.

"You're very like your mother," he said as they shook hands, "and even more like your aunt."

It was a remark Dani had heard many times. Like Dani, Jeanne was several inches shorter than Brigitte and had inherited the same chocolate eyes, dark hair, and gamine features. She looked far younger than her forty-seven years, and radiated a chic and elegance that were typically French.

"I'm usually taken for Aunt Jeanne's daughter," Dani confirmed. She was not so weary that she failed to notice the way Edward Reed's gaze had flickered over her aunt's body and face. Admiration was the usual male reaction to Jeanne Ronsard; she had long ago lost count of her rejected suitors.

But Edward was very much the efficient attorney

as he drove them to their hotel. The funeral would be held at ten o'clock on Thursday, he said, and a reception for George Korman's friends and colleagues would take place at two o'clock the following afternoon at Viveca's house. He had urged Dani to remain in California until Saturday so that she might attend.

Dani had no desire to set foot in the Beverly Hills home that her father had shared with Viveca, but she recognized that Edward Reed must have a reason for wanting her to do so. If he knew enough to book her into a hotel, he knew that she and Viveca didn't get along.

Their suite consisted of a sitting room, two bedrooms, and two baths. A silver bowl of fresh flowers sat on the round dining table, adding a touch of warmth to the restrained blue color scheme of the five rooms. Edward stayed just long enough to set up a lunch meeting for the next afternoon, then left the two women to recuperate from jet lag.

"You are in good hands," Jeanne announced when they were alone. "I thought that we could trust his judgment when you told me he had arranged the divorce, because your father was very generous. But I wanted to meet him first. You should do as he says."

Dani concurred with Jeanne's assessment. At this point, Edward Reed knew more about her situation than she herself did.

Viveca Swensen phoned the next morning, breathily contrite over her failure to contact Dani earlier. She excused herself on the grounds that she was overcome with grief due to the death of her "darling George." In spite of this apology, she evinced no desire to see Dani, who responded with the proper show of polite concern and thought privately that she had underestimated her stepmother's abilities as an actress.

Viveca's romances were front-page news in all the tabloids, and if her father had also been less than faithful, at least he had been more discreet. Dani didn't pretend to understand what had kept the two of them together for eleven years. It seemed to her that Hollywood was as alien a planet as the one in her father's movie *Parallel Universe*. In neither place did the normal laws of human existence apply.

By the time Edward Reed knocked on the door of the suite the next day, Dani felt less disoriented and more capable of discussing her affairs. Lunch was served by a uniformed waiter in the sitting room; when he finished ladling out the cream of asparagus soup, Edward dismissed him and then apologized to Dani for intruding on her privacy so soon after her father's death.

"I don't want to rush or upset you, Miss Ronsard, but your father wasn't an ordinary man, and there are things we should discuss before you return to Paris."

"These endless 'Miss Ronsards' are becoming confusing," Jeanne observed with a smile. "Please call us Jeanne and Dani, and we will call you Edouard, if we may." She pronounced the name in the French manner, her accent wholly charming.

"Thank you, Jeanne." Edward looked at Dani. "You're aware that you're your father's major heir?" His mind was obviously fixed on business today. He betrayed no response to Jeanne's intrinsic allure, but then, given the wedding ring on his finger, he had no right to do so.

"Yes," Dani answered. "He told me a few years ago. I just never thought . . ." She was unable to continue. The rest of the sentence, however, was self-evident.

Edward placed a comforting hand over hers, then removed it. "Honey, it was inevitable. He ignored his doctor's advice, ran around the world like a nineteen-year-old, and didn't know the meaning of the word 'vacation.' But he lived exactly the way he wanted to, loved almost every minute of his fifty-eight years, and died with very little pain. He and Viveca were at my house when it happened, and I don't think he expected to live through it. You know George—he never asked for anything, he just gave orders. Before he lost consciousness, he told me to look after you. And he told Viveca to have a party, invite all his friends, and spend a few hours remembering him. I'll go into that in a few minutes, but first I want to make sure you understand your situation."

Dani helped herself to some seafood salad and a French roll, but doubted she would eat very much of it. Talking about her father's death had upset her. So had the mysterious reference to her "situation."

With Dani silent, Jeanne quickly took over. "Yes, go on, Edouard."

"Are you aware that your father and stepmother signed a prenuptial agreement, Dani?"

She nodded. "Daddy mentioned it when he told me about the will. But he never gave me any details."

"I'll begin with their marriage, then." Edward refilled his glass with wine, as if preparing for a long siege, and leaned back in his chair. "As you know, Viveca was your father's fourth wife. George was aware that he wasn't particularly successful at marriage, but you were only a child at the time, and he felt that a live-in arrangement would be improper. I advised him that if he must get married again, the least he could do was to protect himself financially. California is a community property state. Normally, each party in a divorce receives half of the property accumulated during the marriage. I pointed out to George that Viveca had a great deal to gain by marrying him, whereas the reverse was certainly not true. The result was a prenuptial agreement, which Viveca had no choice but to sign. It was far from one-sided. In exchange for starring her in two motion pictures, she agreed to accept certain stated assets in the event of a divorce, or of George's death."

He paused to sip some wine, then continued. "Viveca is a beautiful woman, but there are hundreds like her in Hollywood. She would never have been selected for the lead in two major productions without George, and she knew it. I think she figured that once they were married, she would be able to convince him to modify the agreement, but the reverse happened. Those two films established her reputation as a cooperative actress with a nice talent for comedy, and gave her financial independence. In view of that, George saw no reason to change a thing. After the first few years, I doubt that they made each other happy, but neither of them had any motivation to seek a divorce. They lived separate lives."

"Most people would say that Viveca has done very well for herself," Jeanne remarked. "She was nothing when he married her. What has she inherited?"

"Only the house in Beverly Hills and five percent of Galaxy Films, George's production company. It comes to millions of dollars, but that's a minor amount compared to the total estate. George left twenty million dollars to the foundation he endowed six years ago to support the arts. With the exception of a few minor bequests, Dani gets the rest."

Dani knew he was studying her, gauging her reaction, but none of this was news to her. "How much money is involved?" she asked, not really caring.

"George's real estate company, Korman Properties, holds a major interest in two suburban shopping centers and four downtown office buildings as well as vacation property in Hawaii and California. He owned forty percent of Galaxy Films, with the remaining sixty percent divided between two other partners. His corporate investments—stocks, money market funds, and so on—are relatively modest in comparison to everything else. Finally, he owned the Condors, which is one of the most profitable franchises in the country. My son Teddy is the team's corporate attorney—he's in San Francisco for a trial this week, or I would have brought him along. You'll eventually receive a complete accounting, Dani, but if you want a rough estimate . . ." He proceeded to name a figure so high that Dani found it impossible to comprehend.

"I suppose you'd better tell me where we go from here, Edward." She shook her head, picturing herself in Paris and all those assets in California, wondering if such an arrangement would be workable. "I consider myself a good businesswoman—I've managed Jeanne's boutique for three years—but I wouldn't know where to begin."

"Your father had a great deal of confidence in you, Dani," Edward assured her, eating between sentences. "His wives were conveniences, hopefully pleasant ones, but you were his only child, and that put you into a special category. We both know that

George wasn't good at family relationships, but I'm sure he loved you, in his way. Even more important, he approved of you. He considered you to be sensible and well-brought-up, and insofar as he cared what would happen to his money when he died, he decided you were a fit heir. Otherwise, I think he would have changed the will and left everything to the foundation."

He paused for a moment, helping himself to some coffee. "Your father liked to run the show, Dani, and it's reflected in the terms of the will."

"Indeed?" Jeanne said. "Please enlighten us, Edouard."

"George was sentimental about the Condors. He didn't want them to end up as part of a big conglomerate, so Dani can't sell the franchise for five years unless it loses money. He had a reciprocal agreement with his partners in Galaxy Films, stating that if one of them died, the heirs of the deceased would sell out to the remaining partners. We'll be happy to handle that for Dani; she may want to use the cash for inheritance taxes and executors' fees. Most important, Dani, your father intended you to take a personal interest in his investments. I know he's talked business to you from time to time, but still, there was no way to force you to do what he wanted. So he did the next best thing. Under the conditions of the will, you have to move to Los Angeles to inherit, and remain here for at least the next five years."

For a few moments, Dani said nothing. She was neither stupid nor naive, and supposed that she had been unconsciously steeling herself to accept such a move since she learned of her father's death. What she resented was his method of imposing his wishes on her. "It would serve him right if I refused," she said under her breath.

The comment was loud enough for Edward to hear. "If you do, everything goes to Viveca," was his laconic response.

"That devil!" In spite of the ejaculation, Dani felt genuine admiration for her father's wiliness. "What a mind he had, to think up something like that. He knew . . ." She stopped in mid-sentence, her face slightly flushed. She had been raised to value discretion and civility. A Ronsard did not air family grievances in front of strangers.

But Edward Reed was not in the least bit fazed. "Of course he did. He also knew how Viveca felt. She decided that you were all that stood in the way of a young and affluent widowhood. If she got you out of the house, your relationship with your father would become so distant that he would change the will."

His face became sympathetic. "George sent you to Paris for two reasons, honey, and neither had anything to do with not caring about you. The first was Viveca's hostility, but he would have handled that if it hadn't been for the second reason: he knew he wasn't much of a father. He was afraid that you would wind up as everyone's worst stereotype of the spoiled Beverly Hills brat, all glitter and designer labels, with no sense of responsibility and no goals in life. It's ironic," he added, "how badly Viveca miscalculated. You might have seen just as little of your father in Beverly Hills as in Paris, and wound up hating him for ignoring you. Believe me, your relationship was much warmer with thousands of miles between you."

Edward tossed his napkin on the table and tipped

his chair back on two legs. "So who gets the money, Dani? You or Viveca?" His expression gave no hint of his emotional state, but Dani suspected he was secretly amused by her show of irritation.

In reality, her annoyance had waned. Gratitude mixed with a little guilt had taken over. Dani had always considered her dispatch to Paris a rejection, and now Edward had made it clear to her that it was nothing of the sort. At the time, Jeanne had tried to explain, but Dani supposed she had been too immature to accept her father's failings as human ones. Now she could.

"Darling?" Jeanne prompted.

It was not Dani's nature to rush into decisions—especially not into important ones. "How much time do I have to make up my mind?" she asked.

"Until the baseball winter meetings next month. I'll check the dates for you. The other National League owners will have to approve your ownership of the team. And, uh, by the way, Dani, try not to be too appalled by the party on Friday. I imagine Viveca will try to out-Hollywood Hollywood."

Dani stared at him, suspicious of the glint in his eye. A smile was pulling at a corner of his mouth as he continued cheerfully. "Los Angeles is a terrible place, Dani. Tinseltown. Crude. Obsessed with status and money. You'll hate it here. At least, by Friday night, you'll think you will."

Her thought processes were working at less than peak efficiency today, but she was not so dim-witted that she didn't grasp the point Edward Reed was making. "You're telling me that she knows the terms of the will, and wants me to be so horrified I'll refuse to move."

The attorney's half-smile faded into mock solemnity. "Your stepmother isn't rapacious, Dani. But what woman could resist the Condors? Twenty-five healthy, young . . ."

"Yes, her own private stud farm!" Dani's voice had snapped right along with her temper. If she blushed, it was not out of regret for the ribald comment, which Viveca fully deserved, but because she had permitted the woman's machinations to goad her. She hated to lose control of herself.

"I see you're not all sweet French pastry, honey, you have some of your father's California citrus in you," Edward teased. "I take it you've made your decision."

She had, and there was no reason not to admit it. "I would have moved anyway if it were necessary, but if my father wanted to prod me, he succeeded. What do I do now?"

"Until the will is probated, very little. George has capable people handling his money, but legally, any major decisions will have to be deferred until his heir approves them. The only exception is the Condors. Trades and contract negotiations are already in the works; if you don't deal now, you don't deal at all. In theory, the team's g.m.—general manager—has the temporary authority to make all necessary decisions in a situation like this, but in practice, he'll want to talk to you first. It's your money and your ball club, and you happen to have a very expensive problem on your hands."

"The pitcher who wants a million and a half dollars a year?" Dani guessed. She noted Edward's surprise and explained, "My father sent me an article about him. I thought it seemed like an outrageous amount of money to demand. Why should we pay it?"

Edward grinned at her. "Other than the fact that a few million Condors fans will lynch you if you don't sign him, you mean? Your g.m., Mack Harmon, will be at Viveca's on Friday. He's a very savvy guy, been around baseball all his life. I'll introduce you to him and let *him* explain it."

So much for selling the team, Dani thought when Edward had left. Not only *couldn't* she sell it, it appeared that she was destined to play a far more active role than she had ever imagined was plausible. Had the Condors been solely a business, this wouldn't have troubled her. She understood balance sheets and cost/benefit analyses. What bewildered her were athletes' egos and motivations, fans' demands and reactions. Little wonder the team had been her father's favorite toy! With so many psychological factors to juggle, there was no limit to the entertainment he must have derived.

Chapter Two

$\mathcal{A}$ newspaper reporter, unable to resist the obvious metaphor, would write that funeral services for George Korman played to a packed house. A world-famous minister conducted the service, and eulogies were delivered by a former vice president of the United States, a two-time Oscar-winning actress, and one of the partners in Galaxy Films. The ladies and gentlemen of the press, aggressive in recording the event for posterity, contributed to an atmosphere which Dani found more appropriate to a Hollywood opening than a solemn rite of passage.

When they arrived, Edward settled Jeanne into a pew, then escorted Dani to a spacious side room where Viveca Swensen was holding court. The platinum blonde actress was wearing a veiled pillbox hat and a clinging black silk dress that accentuated her fair skin and famous curves. Dani, dressed in a simple navy knit with white collar and cuffs, thought that at thirty-three, Viveca was more beautiful than ever. Certainly she played the role of grieving widow to the hilt, an impressive performance, given her farce of a marriage.

"You *will* come to the house tomorrow, won't you, Deedee darling?" she asked, the tremor in her voice underscoring her bravery in keeping control of her precarious composure.

Dani had loathed the nickname Deedee from the moment Viveca had come up with it. As she remembered, it had something to do with an "adorable little French poodle" of the same name, a pet Viveca had had as a child. She claimed that Dani reminded her of the animal.

"Of course," she answered, forcing a smile to her lips. "It's kind of you to invite me."

"You'll want to see how much everyone loved your father, dear. Naturally, I won't embarrass you by announcing who you are. Most of them don't even know you exist."

Dani ignored the poison behind Viveca's understanding tone, as she pecked her stepmother on the cheek. She could think of no civil reply to such a barbed statement, and wouldn't degrade herself by resorting to retaliatory sarcasm. The courtesy call was over; now she wanted only to escape.

She glanced to her right, looking for Edward, but Viveca's attention had already been captured by some newcomer. She was smiling tragically, holding out her arms like a bereft little girl, and Dani automatically looked over her shoulder, curious about the recipient of this poignant greeting.

Cool, gray eyes and over six feet of power intercepted her stare. She recognized Ty Morgan immediately, acknowledging that he was even more devastating in the flesh than in his magazine photographs. His dark blue suit, beautifully cut, accentuated his height and superb physical condition. The sun had tanned his skin and streaked his hair with blond, making him look as much like a movie star as an athlete. For a moment, his eyes met Dani's, showing no reaction; then he turned his attention back to Viveca. As Dani walked away,

Viveca flung herself into his arms, whimpering, "Oh, Ty!"

Dani felt physically ill. What kind of city was this, where a man strolled baldly into a solemn gathering and enfolded his mistress in his arms, oblivious to her husband's death and the bereavement of others? Mercifully, Edward noticed her standing alone and walked to her side. After a brief glance at her face—pale and distressed—he followed the direction of her gaze. Viveca's head was leaning against Ty's shoulder, his hand rhythmically caressing her back.

"That isn't what it looks like," he said quietly. "Ty and your father were friends. He's not the type of man who sleeps with other men's wives."

"Anymore, you mean." Somehow the words slipped out.

Edward put a comforting arm around Dani's shoulder, leading her from the room. "It's ancient history, honey. Don't let it upset you."

They rejoined Jeanne and waited for the service to begin. As the eulogists spoke, their genuine admiration and love for her father touched Dani deeply. In light of Viveca's hypocrisy, such sincerity made the following day's reception difficult to face. Only Dani's pride convinced her to go. Having re-experienced Viveca's sweet-faced hostility, Dani was determined to show the woman that she was no longer a defenseless thirteen-year-old, who would burst into tears and run away at the first sarcastic word.

Jeanne was leaving for New York on an afternoon flight with a connection to Paris that evening, and had left her suitcase in the trunk of Edward Reed's Continental. The attorney, due to meet a client for lunch, had arranged for a taxi to take her to the airport. As Jeanne thanked him for his help and climbed into the cab, Dani impulsively decided to go along for the ride. Once she would have fretted about the extra money this would cost her, but not anymore. She supposed she was thinking like an heiress already.

Back at the hotel, Dani stripped off her dress and climbed into bed. Her exhaustion, she recognized, was mental as well as physical. For the last four days, the loss of her father and its implications for her future had occupied her constantly, until she couldn't bear to think about it anymore.

She slept for over three hours. When she woke, she swore that she would put the future out of her mind. For at least one evening, she was going to forget about moving to California, forget about her inheritance, and simply relax. Nothing would be permitted to interfere.

Step one was a long hot soak in the tub. Step two was a prime-rib dinner which she ate in her suite. And step three was a television movie, a stylish murder mystery some fifteen years old which had been produced by her father. It was one of Dani's personal favorites.

She was soon caught up in the story. Only the increasingly frequent commercial breaks distracted her, and when yet another toothpaste ad started to run, she went into the bathroom to get herself a glass of water.

She curled up on the couch again, staring at the television screen. The camera was panning a city block, the names on the stores written in what Dani thought were Japanese characters. A man dressed in Western clothing—blue shirt with the sleeves rolled up, tan slacks, his longish hair windblown—was walking toward the viewer on the busy sidewalk. Dani groaned aloud. Lord, the man was positively ubiquitous! Here she wanted to relax, and *he* had to intrude on her privacy and remind her of things best forgotten.

He walked into a sporting goods store, picked up several cans of tennis balls, and brought them to the counter. He smiled into the camera. "I'm recognized everywhere in California," he said, "and almost everywhere in the rest of the country. But here in Japan it's been a little different. No one keeps my personal check for a souvenir. No one buys me dinner to thank me for the hundred-dollar-World-Series bet he won. And no one invites me to spend the weekend at her beach house. That's why I carry a WorldBank card."

He handed the card to the salesgirl just as an adorable Japanese child, dressed in a kimono, toddled up to him. She clutched a pencil and paper in her hands. "May I have your autograph, Mr. Morgan?" she lisped in careful English.

He crouched down on his haunches and obliged, then stood up again. As he took the card back from the salesgirl and held it up, he winked at the camera, as if to say, "So maybe I was a bit too modest!" Then he uttered the obligatory, "When you travel with WorldBank, you never travel alone," while his name —James Tyler Morgan, Jr.—was typed out for the benefit of that segment of the American audience which, Dani thought sourly, had presumably been hiding in a cave for the last few years and was unaware of his identity.

On television, Ty Morgan exuded an aura of macho charm, all the more potent for a slight lack of smoothness which hinted at tough arrogance, or perhaps even danger. Dani admitted to herself that she found the rough edges physically attractive; one eventually tired of European playboys with their manicured haircuts and continental clothing.

For all their outward differences, however, Ty Morgan had at least one thing in common with those men: the Viveca Swensens of the world shared their beds.

Edward Reed picked Dani up at 2:30 the next day and drove her to Viveca's house. They arrived to find both sides of the long driveway lined with expensive automobiles, the overflow spilling out past the wrought iron gates along both sides of the street. Edward entrusted his car to a waiting attendant and escorted Dani into the house, which was much larger than the one she had lived briefly in as a teenager.

Her eyes swept across a sea of expensively clad bodies, which ebbed and flowed through the marble-floored foyer and living room beyond. Some of her stepmother's guests were seated on brocade-covered couches; others stood in small groups, talking; still others were sprawled right down on the Persian carpet. Uniformed waitresses circulated with snacks and drinks, and served out more substantial fare from buffet tables in the living and dining rooms. Judging from the amount of smoke in the air, those present subscribed to the Los Angeles admonishment: Don't breathe it if you can't see it. Dani recognized more than a few of these people, although she had actually met almost none of them.

"I'd like to wander around on my own a bit," she told Edward. A light flashed, causing her to blink. More reporters, more photographers. "I don't want to speak to them," she said.

"Then we won't mention who you are. No one knows you except Viveca, and she's not about to give up center stage." A middle-aged woman was waving at the attorney, and he excused himself to say hello.

Dani threaded her way through the crowd to the bar to ask for a glass of wine, and accepted an assortment of hors d'oeuvres from a passing waitress. Rather than looking for someone to talk to, she eavesdropped quite openly on the conversations around her. Between the shop talk and gossip, people were reminiscing about George Korman: the movies he had produced, the publicity stunts he had engineered, the ball club he had made into a winner.

The familiar feeling of unreality enveloped her. These people seemed to belong only in front of a camera, or perhaps behind it. They didn't do everyday things like go to the dentist, or run to the bakery for bread, or take their dogs to the vet. They had maids and chauffeurs and cooks, and probably perfect teeth as well.

Real or not, they talked up a storm and smoked to match. Dani looked over several heads to the patio, and determined to make her escape. En route she passed Ty Morgan. A redhead and a blonde stood next to him, gazing adoringly into his eyes as he held forth about heaven only knew what. WorldBank, Dani thought with a roll of her eyes.

There were fewer people outside, most of them seated at tables adjacent to the swimming pool, some standing here and there on the redwood deck. Edward Reed was talking to a man and woman, the latter of whom Dani recognized as Diana Kendall. They had met briefly, during the filming of one of her father's movies. Dani almost never asked for introductions, but she admired Diana's way with a song, and had wanted to tell her so. The dusky-skinned actress/singer was sinuously beautiful, her exotic features the gift of both African and European forebears. Her magnificent ebony hair, usually worn flowing down her back, was pinned into a neat bun today. She wore a beige suit with a slitted skirt, the styling similar to Dani's own dark brown outfit. Unlike some of her stepmother's other guests, Dani decided, Diana Kendall had class.

The man standing next to her, black like the actress herself, was tall and broad-shouldered, his build that of a football player. A neatly trimmed beard and mustache gave his handsome face a slightly ferocious look. Dani thought that she had seen him before, but couldn't place where.

She approached the group, slipping off her jacket and slinging it over one arm as she walked. The long-sleeved blouse underneath was beige silk with a stripe woven into the material.

Edward greeted her with a smile and started to introduce her to the couple by his side. "Dani, this is Diana Kendall and Mike Jones. Diana is—well, Diana. And Mike is the first-string catcher for the Condors. In real life, to quote the gossip columnists, they're Mr. and Mrs. Mike, Diana—meet Dani Ronsard, a friend of mine from Paris."

As they shook hands, Dani realized why Mike Jones had looked familiar. She had seen his picture in the same article that had extolled Ty Morgan's exploits. Like his teammate, he was one of the game's true superstars, a man who delivered thirty or more home runs and a .300 batting average year after year.

She was about to congratulate him on his part in the Condors' successful season when Diana said in a puzzled voice, "You look familiar. Have we met?"

Dani scarcely had time to react before the actress

was smiling her satisfaction. "I recognize you now. We met about a year ago, when I was making *Intermission* for your father. I loved working for him. We'll all miss him, Miss Ronsard. Our business could use more like him."

It took Mike Jones a moment to grasp what his wife meant, and then he added his own condolences. Even while Dani murmured, "Thank you," she was wondering how to keep them quiet.

Edward Reed solved the problem quite easily. "You're going to keep this to yourselves, okay?" he said bluntly. "Dani's not broadcasting who she is. Every reporter in the place would be after her."

"Of course," Diana agreed immediately.

"No way," Mike said at the same time. He added in a sly drawl, "Then again, Edward, if you trade me some information, I might be persuaded to keep quiet."

The attorney grinned, shaking his head. "You're unscrupulous, Jones. You want to know what everyone in this damn town is asking, don't you?"

Mike Jones, his arms now crossed in front of him, nodded. "You've got it, Edward. Is she the new boss?"

"Pending approval of the other owners, she is. That makes five of us who know that for a fact, and the fifth is back in Paris by now."

"I won't tell a soul," the catcher promised with a wink.

It seemed an appropriate time to insert a compliment on Mike's contributions to the team. Dani did so, admitting that, as a Parisian, she had a lot to learn about the game. For a few more minutes they reminisced about some of her father's more colorful maneuvers as owner of the Condors, until Edward interrupted, "I just noticed Mack get up from a table down there." He motioned toward the lawn. "I'm going to take Dani over to meet him."

"You're going to blow her cover, honey," Diana teased.

"Not by telling Mack, I won't. If there was no such phrase as close-mouthed, they would have invented it to describe him."

They walked around the kidney-shaped swimming pool and on past a redwood spa, continuing down a short flight of steps onto the wide back lawn. Dani smiled wistfully when she noticed the putting green to the left.

Had her hyperactive father ever taken the time to play a full eighteen holes of golf? She doubted it. He had probably remained on the course of the exclusive country club near his home just long enough to conclude some business deal with a fellow golfer, then hurried off to his studio in Glendale, or his office on Wilshire Boulevard, or his ballpark in Orange County.

Several round tables had been placed on the lawn, and were shaded from the autumn sun by large yellow and orange umbrellas. The colors were those of the Condors. Edward helped Dani into a seat at an empty table, then excused himself and walked over to a man who had been standing quietly awaiting their arrival. He was older than the attorney, his gray hair closely cropped, his build rangy and substantial. He and Edward shook hands, exchanged several sentences, and then returned to Dani's table and sat down.

"Dani, meet Mack Harmon, the Condors' general manager. You won't find a better one in the game," Edward said.

"It's a pleasure to meet you, Miss Ronsard. I'm only sorry about the circumstances."

"So am I, Mack, but I'm glad we'll have a chance to talk," Dani replied. "And please, make that 'Dani.' We're going to be seeing a lot of each other, and I know my father was 'George' to everyone in the organization. I only hope every year will be as successful as last year."

"When you work for an owner like George Korman, winning comes easy," Mack replied in a soft, southern drawl. "The players loved him. He wasn't the sort to chew them out, and he was always a soft touch in salary negotiations."

Dani was about to confess her relative ignorance of the game when she spotted her stepmother sashaying across the lawn. Viveca was swathed in dove gray wool today, the V-neck of her dress presumably providing air conditioning against the day's atypical heat.

"Edward, I'm going to steal you away." Dani noticed that she had finally reverted to the girlishly breathy voice that was one of her strongest assets as a sex goddess. "Have a nice chat with Mack, Deedee darling," she added to Dani, whose contemptuous look belied the smile on her lips.

"Viveca's always called me that," she explained to the puzzled Mack Harmon. "I really don't know why." She added this little bit of mendacity to smooth an awkward situation. It was obvious to her that Mack had picked up on the dislike between her and her stepmother.

"Edward was telling me you live in Paris," Mack remarked, tactfully changing the subject.

"That's right. After my mother died, I lived with my father for almost a year, but it wasn't . . . it didn't work out very well," Dani said. "So I went to Paris to live with my Aunt Jeanne, my mother's sister. She's a wonderful designer; she owns her own boutique, and I manage it for her."

"Did you see your father very often?" The question was not meant to be probing, Dani sensed. People in Los Angeles were informal, and Mack was merely making polite conversation.

"Actually, I saw more of him when I moved to Paris than I did when I was living in Las Vegas with my mother. He used to come visit me a few times a year. And then, when I finished school, he started sending me plane tickets—to London, Rome, Cannes, wherever he was going to be. I couldn't always go, and when I did, I wound up spending a lot of time in museums, but I was a fine arts major in college, so I didn't mind. We usually managed a lunch or dinner together; he loved to talk about the Condors, Mack."

The general manager nodded and smiled. "He was a fan, all right. And a pleasure to work for, unlike some I've known. He'd have his say, Dani, but then he'd let you get on with the job."

"I'll try to live up to that," Dani said. "My father . . ." A gust of laughter from a nearby table attracted her attention, and she interrupted herself to look to her right, seeking the source of the sound. She found that it came from Mike Jones and Ty Morgan, who were seated on either side of Diana Kendall.

"My father," she continued, "could be pretty scathing about some of his fellow owners. Having grown up in France, I'm no expert on baseball, although I *did* try to follow the Condors so I wouldn't sound too ignorant when Daddy talked about some player or specific game. If Edward told you the terms of the will"—she paused, waiting for Mack's confirmation—"then you understand that my father wanted me to be personally involved with the team. But it's going to take some educating to turn me into a decent owner."

She pointed in the general direction of Ty, Mike, and Diana. "Those are two of my star players with Diana Kendall, aren't they?"

Mack was obviously pleased by her show of interest. "You've got the best battery in baseball there, Dani. And as of next year, probably the most expensive."

"Battery?" she repeated. Perhaps her English was rusty, but as far as she knew, a battery was something that went in a flashlight, portable radio, or a car.

"A pitcher and a catcher. They're called a battery," Mack explained patiently. "Mike Jones—real name, Marshall Jones—is the catcher. He led the National League in home runs and runs batted in last year, and had the fourth highest batting average. He also won the M.V.P.—uh, that's Most Valuable Player award, given every year by the Baseball Writers' Association. He's a street-smart, easygoing sort of fellow, real good at settling down jumpy young pitchers. You wouldn't want to tangle with him when he loses his temper, though."

Dani could believe it. The catcher had removed his jacket, and his broad shoulders stretched the fabric of the blue shirt he wore. "If I were a man, I'd think twice about flirting with Diana Kendall," she remarked with a smile. "And Ty?"

"His real name . . ."

". . . is James Tyler Morgan, Jr.," Dani recited,

trying to keep the acid out of her voice. "I know that because I saw his WorldBank commercial on TV last night."

"Your father used to kid him about it. George told him he was getting so rich from endorsements he should pitch for free, but Ty wouldn't buy it. Said he was such a celebrity that George should give him a bonus for bringing the fans into the park. He has a right to his big ego; I'd say he's the best pitcher in the major leagues, and I'm not the only one who thinks so. For two out of the last four years, he's walked off with the Cy Young Award—that's also given by the baseball writers, to the best pitcher in each league. Three years ago, they voted him the M.V.P., and that almost never goes to a pitcher. I'll warn you now—he's a free agent, and it's going to cost a bundle to hold on to him, but he's got the best mechanics in the business, which means he should have a lot of good years left in him."

For the moment, Dani ignored Mack Harmon's baseball jargon, more interested in the subject of money. "I read about him in an article my father sent me. Are you really going to pay him a million and a half a year?"

"Not if I can help it. But Ty's the hottest piece of talent on the free-agent market, and he knows it. He'll be thirty-one next month. Assuming he doesn't hurt himself again, he should pitch outstanding ball for another six or seven years, maybe longer. That's where the mechanics comes into it. Pitching is the most unnatural motion in sports, Dani. It's real rough on a man's elbow and shoulder, and no one who pitches for any length of time has the full use of his arm when he retires. But if a man has good mechanics . . ." He paused, noticing Dani's rather confused expression. "I guess you don't know what that means."

Dani shook her head. "You're right. I thought a mechanic was someone who fixes cars."

"Not in baseball." Mack laughed. "Mechanics means how a pitcher moves his body when he throws the ball. The motion is always basically the same. He'll kick his front leg forward and rock back on his rear foot. Meanwhile he's bringing his arm back as far as he can. When he springs forward to throw, he puts the power of his whole body into the pitch. His arm-speed goes as high as 700 miles an hour. Ty's fast ball has been clocked at 98 miles an hour—we use a radar gun. Throwing that hard puts a terrible strain on a pitcher's elbow and shoulder, but if he moves the right way—what we call good mechanics —it's less of a strain. Everything being equal, he's going to have a longer career. Still, you have to remember that a pitcher throws about a hundred pitches a game, plus another hundred in warm-ups. He works out on most of his days off, too, and over ten or fifteen seasons, it slowly tears apart his joints."

It sounded brutal to Dani. "I can see why throwing correctly would help, then," she said. "But there must be more to winning than that."

"You're right. Athletic ability is a factor, but a pitcher can have all the talent in the world, and if he doesn't have concentration and confidence, he's never going to win ball games. When Ty steps out on the field, they could be fighting World War III in the stands and he wouldn't notice it. His mind is on throwing the ball. As for confidence," the general manager gave a quick wink, "nobody ever accused him of being too humble."

Privately, Dani asked herself why this paragon of pitching talent would willingly subject his body to the crippling abuse Mack Harmon had described. Money, she supposed. "How much did Ty and Mike earn last year?" she asked.

"Mike is thirty-four years old. He's in the middle of a four-year $2.8 million contract right now. Ty earned half a million last year, but like I told you, he's a free agent this year and that puts him in a good position to get himself a whole lot more. It's going to be your club, Dani, and your money. Ty is a big favorite with the fans, and an important factor in the team's success, but no one player is indispensable. What do you want me to do?"

Dani shook her head. "I don't have the knowledge to offer an opinion, Mack. Do what you think is best."

"Just between us, he's probably worth what he's asking. Your father would have paid it. I'll do whatever I can to sign him, within reason. And I appreciate the vote of confidence, Dani."

She started to get up, and Mack quickly followed suit, helping her out of her seat. "Would you like to come up to the house with me?" she invited. "I'd like a cold drink."

"Sounds good," Mack agreed.

Their route took them past Ty, Diana, and Mike, who called out in a teasing voice, "Who's the beautiful lady, Mack?"

Dani checked an incipient smile, appreciating Mike's sense of humor. If he wanted to pretend that they had not yet met, that was fine with her.

"Her name is Dani Ronsard, and she lives in Paris," Mack said. "I was telling her about your mechanics, Ty."

"And she's still awake?" The pitcher laughed.

Dani knew she shouldn't snub a man who was her team's most outstanding asset, but when she thought of the intimate way this conceited lothario had comforted Viveca Swensen, her outraged sensibilities outflanked her common sense. She gave him a frigid look and replied, "The technical side of it was very interesting, Mr. Morgan, but then, the movements of a champion race horse are equally so."

She proceeded to studiously ignore the pitcher, tossing a glowing smile at his teammate. "Mr. Harmon was telling me that you won the M.V.P. this year, Mike. Congratulations."

Dani was only too aware of the individual reactions to her rudeness. Mack Harmon, standing slightly in front of her, had stiffened, perhaps in disapproval, perhaps in puzzlement. Ty Morgan had a lazy smile on his face, as though her set-down had for some reason amused him. As for Diana and Mike, they had instinctively sought each other's eyes, exchanging a surprised look, and then schooled their features into pleasantly bland expressions which gave away nothing.

Even before Mike Jones thanked her for her compliment, Dani felt her face reddening. She eased herself away from the now unwelcome confrontation with a somewhat breathless, "I'm parched, Mack. Let's get up to the house."

If Mack Harmon was curious about her reaction to Ty Morgan, he was much too well-mannered to question her. Besides, she was his boss.

Finding the situation awkward, Dani remarked, "It must be hard to run a ball club in a city like Los Angeles. Do the sportswriters second-guess you all the time?"

"All the time," Mack agreed, evidently relieved by her innocuous question. "Of course, as g.m., my main responsibility is the business end of the franchise; I oversee the Condors' minor league teams, arrange trades, handle contract negotiations, and so on. The field manager—the fellow out in the dugout every day—gets most of the flack. His name is Marv Richardson. The reporters are always telling him about all the mistakes he supposedly makes, in spite of the pennants he's won. And when a player's having problems on the field, they're a regular bunch of piranhas. You learn to live with it or you quit. I'll see if I can find Marv if you want to meet him today."

Dani shook her head. "It would be hard to find anybody in that mob, but thanks anyway."

The words turned out to be prophetic. The living room was even more crowded than before, with the overflow spilling into most of the downstairs rooms. The reason for this crush of bodies was immediately apparent: some of Hollywood's most glamorous figures had worked for George Korman, and they were dazzling storytellers. Her father had wanted them to spend the afternoon remembering him and his achievements, and they were honoring that request by spinning out recollections of their encounters with the exuberant producer.

One actress spoke of filming, in a small town in eastern California, a movie concerning a run-down traveling circus. George had descended on them from Los Angeles, taken one look at the animals, and announced that they were all wrong: they were too sleek, he said, too fat. The result was a nationwide search, reported at length by the media, to procure more suitable-looking livestock. The producer eventually donated a large sum of money to a zoo in the Midwest in exchange for the use of their animals, but he had already received ten times that amount in free publicity.

A director contributed his recollections of working with an actress known for being as difficult as she was beautiful. Six weeks into the production, she announced that she was two months' pregnant, a condition she apparently felt gave her the right to be even more of a prima donna. She developed culinary whims impossible to satisfy in the Asian jungle. Afraid that her demands would wreck the film by stalling production until her pregnancy showed, the harried director put in a frantic SOS to George in Hollywood.

"He was a magician. Conjured up everything from Polish sausage to Russian caviar to French pastries. We ran into some nasty weather—the Red Cross couldn't get their medical helicopters in with supplies, but George got Alicia her cheesecake."

After a time, Dani found herself joining in the laughter. George Korman had possessed a giant ego and he had wanted to be remembered forever. Dani had seldom shared in his wacky, frenetic, uproarious and ultimately triumphant life, but others had. Somehow, she felt, he was hearing the respect and affection which poured out of those whose lives he had touched. And if he was, he was loving every minute of it.

Chapter Three

The afternoon wore on. Dani, eventually weary of inside jokes and Hollywood war stories, edged her way out of the living room. She found herself in a wide hallway, next to the open door of a game room. Several jacketless men were smoking cigars, drinking whiskey, and shooting billiards. Fragments of conversation reached her ears; they were apparently discussing George Korman's last movie. Dani assumed they were connected with his production company, Galaxy Films.

Beyond the game room was a library. Dani walked inside to skim the books on the shelves, and found that most of them concerned some aspect of show business. Her father had collected everything from technical works on filmmaking to movie stars' autobiographies, and she wondered if he had found the time to read any of them.

There was a powder room across the hall. She slipped inside to freshen her makeup, and then peeked into the adjacent office. Loose sheets of paper and dog-eared file folders were strewn carelessly atop the desk, as though waiting for George Korman's attention.

A screening room occupied the far end of the house. Standing in the doorway, Dani looked at the blown-up image of actor Jason Wilder. He was sitting next to a lizardlike creature, the two of them piloting a space ship through a mind-numbing display of images and lights. The film was, of course, *Parallel Universe,* the first of a smash-hit, Oscar-winning trilogy.

Since Dani had seen each of the three movies several times, she decided to go back to her father's office to sit down. She turned, almost colliding with the husky frame of Mike Jones, who was walking in the opposite direction, a can of beer in one hand.

He reached out his free hand to steady her, asking if she was all right.

"Yes. Fine. But we've got to stop meeting this way," Dani stage-whispered as Mike released her.

He laughed, asking her what she thought of the party. As if by mutual agreement, they started back toward the living room, walking into George Korman's office and sitting down on the leather couch. Mike had flipped the door shut behind them.

Dani had been drawn to Mike immediately, perhaps because of his sly sense of humor, and felt very much at ease with him. "To tell you the truth," she said, "when Edward Reed first told me about this, I thought I'd have a very negative reaction. It seemed bizarre, even tasteless. But listening to people talk about my father, I realize that this is just what he wanted. I wish I'd been more like him, more a part of his world—that I could go out there and tell a story about him, as a tribute to his paternity, I suppose. But I'm no actress. Those Oscar-winners are a tough act to follow."

"I don't know about that," Mike drawled. "You gave a pretty good performance out on the lawn. I was beginning to wonder if you remembered meeting me half an hour before." He paused to sip his beer, stared straight ahead for a few moments, and then shrugged. "I'll tell you, Dani, I've had just enough of this stuff"—he wiggled the can of beer— "to ask you about something that may be none of my business. Why did you hand Ty such a set-down? You have something against left-handed pitchers?"

Dani was taken aback by his directness. She had no intention of offering either explanations or apologies, so she maintained what she hoped was an intimidating silence. Surely he would take the hint.

He did no such thing. "Ty Morgan is my closest friend on the team," he persisted in a calm voice, "and he's also a guy you shouldn't make an enemy of. He doesn't know who you are yet, but when he finds out, he's going to figure the job isn't worth it if the owner's going to hassle him. He'll sign somewhere else, and I don't want that to happen."

Dani felt herself redden. Oh, Lord, she thought, I've made a mess of this. Why couldn't I have smiled very sweetly and congratulated him on his blasted Cy Young Award? Aloud, she murmured, "I lost my temper over something . . . personal. I'd rather not discuss it."

"Viveca Swensen?" Mike asked.

Dani stared at him. "How could you . . . how did you figure *that* out?"

"I didn't. Diana did. Only a woman could come up with something like that." His tone said that the female of the species was utterly incomprehensible to him.

By now Dani was concentrating on her lap. People just didn't act this way in Paris. They respected your privacy and expected the same in return.

"Hey, look, Dani," Mike said. "I don't know exactly what you heard about that, and I really don't want to embarrass you, but you have to understand that it was a long time ago, and Ty was just a green kid. Your father never held it against him."

"I saw them at the funeral together," Dani mumbled, unwilling to accept his explanation. "The way he was holding her . . ." She stopped, feeling she had said quite enough.

"And you think he's involved with her again?" Mike asked, incredulous. "Hell, you should have seen her with *me!* There's nothing between them, believe me."

Dani's instincts about people's honesty were usually accurate, and she felt Mike was telling her the truth. As for Ty Morgan, perhaps she would revise her opinion.

Mike settled back against the cushions, frowning. Dani watched, puzzled, as he cocked his head to one side, squinted as if lost in thought, and then smiled slowly. Why did he look so delighted with himself?

For the moment, curiosity was her primary emotion. "What *are* you thinking about, Mike?" she asked.

"I'm going to tell you a little story about Ty and your father," he answered, twisting his body to face her. One arm was stretched along the back of the couch, and the other periodically conveyed the can of beer to his lips.

"Once upon a time there was a famous pitcher who decided to play a practical joke on an equally famous catcher. He managed to talk the catcher's boss and the catcher's wife into helping him. The boss—"

"A famous producer," Dani interrupted with a smile.

"Right." Mike winked. "He told the catcher that Hollywood was just holding its breath, waiting for him. But he'd have to shoot a screen test, just to make sure. Now the catcher was a modest guy; he had a lot of doubts. So he asked the pitcher, who he thought was his buddy, whether he should do it. 'Sure,' the pitcher said. 'Look at all those football players who are actors now.' And he asked his wife . . ."

"A famous actress," both of them said together.

". . . whether he should do it. 'Sure,' she said. 'It's only a screen test. Esther Moore is the female lead in that picture. She's my friend; she'll take *good* care of you.'"

It was just like her father, Dani thought with amusement, to set up an elaborate but phony screen test, all for the pleasure of a good laugh. "So what happened?" she asked.

"When I showed up at the studio, Esther was in a double bed," Mike said, switching to the first person. "Lights and cameras all around. She had on a body stocking that made her look like she was wearing almost nothing. Your father booms out, 'Okay, Marshall, take off your clothes!' I look at Diana, who shrugs. 'All in a day's work, honey,' she says. So your father and I negotiate. In the end, I strip off my shirt and get into bed. And this beautiful lady starts rubbing my back, just like Diana isn't standing there and watching. 'Relax, baby,' she says."

By now Dani was laughing. "Where was Ty? Hiding under the bed?"

"Behind a two-way mirror, and if you think they stopped there, you underestimate the treachery of these people. Your father directed the test. He kept yelling things like, 'More emotion, Marshall. More passion. You haven't seen Esther in weeks and you're hungry for her. Star-r-r-v-i-n-g.'" Mike Jones imitated George Korman perfectly, Dani noticed with a giggle.

"Diana's friend had her hands all over me. I was so embarrassed I felt like bolting out of the bed, or maybe ducking under the covers. By the time I left, I never wanted to see the inside of a movie studio again. Around a week later, on my thirty-fourth birthday, your father shows up at the ball park and says he has some films of opposing hitters and pitchers he wants to show us."

"And it was the 'screen test,'" Dani guessed. "Did everyone sit around and watch it?"

"Twice," Mike admitted. "And no one laughed louder than Morgan, damn him. I've wanted to get back at the guy for the last six months, and I think I've just worked out how. I'll need your help, though. You know that tribute to your father you mentioned? He would have approved of this."

But when Dani asked Mike what he had in mind, he shook his head. "I'll leave the details up to you. Just wait in here for the next half-hour—and make sure you're alone." He walked to the sliding glass door and opened it a few inches. "Keep an ear open," he said with a wink, then sauntered out of the room.

Dani followed him, turned the lock, and returned to the couch. Obviously she was meant to "accidentally" overhear a conversation. But why?

A covered walkway ran parallel to the back of the house, about two yards from where Dani was sitting. If she looked behind her, she could watch people strolling by, their forms partially concealed by the gauzy curtains on the floor-to-ceiling windows.

She stretched out on the couch, her head cradled against a suede-covered pillow, and thought about her conversation with Mike Jones. Perhaps her dislike of Viveca had caused her to overreact to an incident best forgotten. Only a few days before, she recalled, Aunt Jeanne had characterized her father's affairs as "trivial diversions" to him. She supposed that that was the way men viewed such things—as unimportant, easily dismissed.

As for the scene at her father's funeral, Mike was quite right to imply that Viveca had a habit of flinging herself into the arms of the nearest available male, particularly if he happened to be young and handsome. Ty's caress, which had appeared to be a romantic one, could have been meant only to comfort.

Not that she gave the man credit for turning down what so many women were eager to offer a celebrity —she didn't. But taking advantage of proffered favors was really no great sin. She had no respect for shallow playboys, but had always managed to be civil to them.

She was only half-listening to the conversations of passersby when she picked up the deep voice of Mike Jones.

". . . not to worry, Kenny. If Mack says he won't trade you, he won't trade you. You helped us a lot in September and October."

"It's just that Judy—my wife—is pregnant, and she doesn't want to move. I thought I had a lot of confidence, but I want to be a starter next year, and the competition on this team has me psyched out. I mean, I can't even believe that the world's best pitcher and catcher are standing here and talking to me."

Dani peeked around the arm of the couch, then curled up again. There were only three of them out there: Mike, Ty, and an awestruck rookie.

"Kenny, if I ever get rid of Mitch Ellison," Ty drawled, "I'm going to make you my agent. Stop worrying. You throw as hard as I do. Your curve is pretty wild, but so was mine at your age. You should learn a slider. Take it easy this winter, stay in shape, and I'll help you when we get to Florida, right?"

"Yeah, thanks." The young pitcher's voice was husky with gratitude. Ty's offer *had* been generous, Dani thought, upscaling her opinion another notch.

"What happens to the team?" Kenny asked, sounding more composed. "Is Viveca Swensen going to be the new owner?"

"No one seems to know," Ty answered. "Viveca told me that the will is ambiguous. She thinks it's a good possibility."

Dani hissed a French epithet. "A good possibility," was it? Viveca could think again!

"You became a free agent just in time." Mike's tone was meant to goad. "You know Viveca, Ty. She might have wanted a few special services put into your contract."

"I'm getting too old for that kind of stuff. Need all my strength for pitching," Ty answered lazily. He didn't sound at all embarrassed by the ribbing he was receiving from his teammate as a result of that past indiscretion.

"The baseball Annies—they drive my wife crazy," Kenny said. "I told her I don't fool around, but she wouldn't believe me."

"Yeah, pregnant women," Mike inserted.

"Anyway, I finally managed to convince her that all of them were hanging around the bull pen waiting for you, Ty."

"Not all of them. There was a little French chick with Mack," Mike Jones informed Kenny. "He brought her over to our table and introduced her. She sure gave Ty the brush. Liked me a whole lot better, but Diana was around."

"She was just trying to get my attention," Ty Morgan retorted. "Women do it all the time."

Dani's ears had perked up at the reference to herself—"little French chick," indeed! She would have a few choice words with Marshall Jones over that one! As for Ty Morgan's egotistical explanation for her coldness, the man's success with women had obviously warped his capacity for common sense. How could he have mistaken her put-down for some sort of sexual come-on?

"She *had* your attention, Morgan," Mike needled. "With a shape like that, all she had to do was stand there."

"Face wasn't half-bad either," Ty admitted. Dani could all but hear the grin on his face. "But it's been a tough season. I'm going to Tahoe on Monday, then to the Caribbean for a few weeks."

Where you'll play with women instead of baseballs, Dani thought acidly.

Apparently their bantering conversation puzzled the younger pitcher, Kenny Whoever-he-was. "Who are you guys talking about?" he asked. "Some actress?"

"Don't know. Mack said she lived in Paris, but she sounded like Beverly Hills to me," Mike drawled. "Maybe she's some kind of starlet—one of the boss's protégées."

Dani suppressed a giggle. The man's sense of humor was absolutely outrageous. He was utterly shameless, to tease her like that, knowing there was no way she could retaliate.

"I don't think so. I saw her kiss Viveca at the funeral," Ty answered.

So he remembered seeing her. Dani was rather surprised. By now she understood that Mike was setting Ty up for something—but what?

"If I wasn't so hung up on Diana, I would ask that lady out to dinner," Mike mused. "It was really something, Kenny. She couldn't take her eyes off me. Never even noticed Morgan."

"Come off it, Mike. You heard the dig about a Thoroughbred race horse. It was a come-on," Ty insisted. "She wants to go to bed with me. I was supposed to get annoyed about being compared with an animal and try to prove to her what a great human being I am. But there are better ways to spend an evening."

"Put your money where your mouth is, Morgan," Mike Jones challenged his teammate. "Five hundred bucks says you're wrong. She'll never let you into her room, much less near her bed."

"You've got to be kidding. I'm not . . ."

"So forget it. Only next time, don't start shooting off your mouth about how irresistible you are."

There was a decided lull in the conversation. Dani was almost holding her breath, wondering if Ty would fall into the trap Mike was setting. Finally he answered, "It's an interesting proposition, Mike. It would be easy to take your money, but the stakes are just too crass. Make it a thousand dollar donation to the team's high school athletic fund, and I'll spend the night with her."

Dani was amused in spite of herself. She wanted to be annoyed at Ty's incredible conceit, but how could you do anything but laugh when a man turned down five hundred dollars for himself, but agreed to sell his body for double that amount to charity? She'd handled a lot of wolves in her time, and didn't doubt her ability to teach the egotistical pitcher a well-deserved lesson. After the practical joke he had played on Mike Jones, he could hardly take offense at his own comeuppance.

Now Mike was speaking again. "You're on, buddy. How about you, Kenny? Joining the action?"

"Can't afford to, even for charity. I don't make the kind of money you guys do. Hey, speaking of money—do you think contract negotiations are going to wait 'til there's a new owner?"

"Probably," Ty said. "By which time, Mack will forget the twenty-six games I won last year, and the fact that my E.R.A. was lower than any other starting pitcher's."

"I have faith in you, baby." Mike laughed. "You'll remind him. And if you don't, the sportswriters will."

Two more team members joined the group, and the players began to discuss the previous season's triumphs. Dani had no interest in last summer's baseball games, and her attention drifted away from the conversation. Then she heard Ty Morgan speaking again, his voice more emotional than at any time in the last half-hour, and she couldn't help listening to what he was saying.

"I'm telling you, I'll remember that pitch as long as I live. Worst slider I ever threw. Hardly broke at all, just sailed over the plate. The minute Parker hit it, I knew it was in the seats for a home run. He lapped it up like a hot fudge sundae, and bam, the score is two-zip and there goes the ball game."

The man was certainly a perfectionist, Dani thought. Of course, he was paid a very handsome sum each year to make good pitches, not bad ones—to win games, not lose them. She wondered if his competitiveness was typical of star athletes.

"Just don't let it happen again," Mike kidded.

"There are a lot of guys in the minors who are after your job."

Eventually the group of athletes left in search of liquid refreshment. Dani could only admire Mike's performance; in spite of that screen test, he had a real talent for acting! Now it was her turn. She had to see that Ty lost the bet, and in a manner calculated to cause him some embarrassment. That meant setting him up for the alleged conquest—and then walking out on him. Her plane left the next morning, so she would need some place to spend the night after stranding him. Perhaps she would take a taxi to another hotel.

It occurred to her that the situation was potentially explosive; one could only push a man so far before turning him off became dangerous. As for wounding Ty's ego, she was certain it was quite impervious. She would have to take care, but that didn't preclude enjoying herself.

Dani was mentally scripting the coming encounter with Ty Morgan when a light knock on the door intruded on scene two. She gathered up her purse and turned the lock to find Mike Jones standing in front of her.

He held up a hotel room key, then dropped it into her purse. "Compliments of Diana. She found out your hotel from Edward, then drove over and picked this up."

"Tell her our minds work the same way," Dani said with a wink. "I was going to go some place else for the night, but staying in the same hotel is even funnier." She paused, giving him a disapproving look. "Of course, after those cracks of yours about my being a 'little French chick' or one of the boss's 'protégées,' I just might pull a doublecross, Mr. Jones."

"Don't say that!" Mike pretended to be horrified. "I don't want to put Ty down, but when we're on the road, it gets pretty crowded with three of us in the room."

"Three?"

"Yeah. Me, Ty, and Ty's ego."

Dani smiled at the gibe, thinking that Mike Jones's ego could probably rival Ty Morgan's any day of the week. "You'll just have to see how it turns out, won't you?" she teased.

They returned to the living room some five minutes apart. People were already drifting out to their Rollses and Mercedes and Porsches. It was dark out now; Hollywood's unusual farewell to George Korman had steamed along for some four hours, and was finally running out of fuel. Dani got herself a soda and waited for the inevitable pick-up attempt. When she felt a hand on her shoulder, she slowly turned around, expecting to see Ty Morgan. Instead, she found herself face to face with Edward Reed.

"We'll probate the will as soon as possible, Dani," he told her. "I don't anticipate any problems. I'll be in touch, probably in a month or so."

"I can't leave Paris until the Christmas season is over. Jeanne will need my help."

Edward said he understood that. "When the time comes, we'll do everything we can to help you get settled out here. By the way, Dani," he continued with a smile, "Diana and then Ty came up to me maybe five minutes apart to tell me he's giving you a lift to your hotel. I know you didn't want to be introduced around today, but don't you think you should tell Morgan you own him?"

"Absolutely not." Dani shook her head gravely. "Mike Jones would never forgive me."

"And Diana wanted to know where you were

staying." Only moments after this pensive statement, a twinkle appeared in Edward Reed's eyes. Obviously his agile mind had made the proper connections. "It sounds as though I'd better warn you that Ty was cross-examining me about you. I told him you were a distant relative, but I don't think he believed me." He gave her a slow wink. "You know what your father used to say, Dani. Don't sleep with the help. And in this case, the help might be tough to handle. Have fun, but watch yourself." He turned her around and gave her a gentle shove in the opposite direction, straight toward Ty Morgan.

He studied her body every step of the way. By the time they were face to face, Dani could cheerfully have picked up the dregs of the goose liver pâté from the marble-topped credenza and dumped the whole mess, limp garnishes and all, on top of his head. Instead, she smiled up at him.

"I hear you're taking me back to my hotel," she said, trying to sound pleased by the prospect.

She could tell nothing from the bland expression which had clicked into place on his face. "That's right," he said. "Are you ready to leave?"

Dani considered looking for Viveca in order to say good-bye, but decided against it. One or the other of them was bound to lose her temper, saying something that would sabotage the whole gag. She nodded her agreement.

They waited at the end of the flagstone path while a young man fetched Ty Morgan's car. As he flipped the keys to the pitcher, he asked, "Are you going to play for the Condors next year?"

"Could be. Re-entry draft was yesterday. There are a few different clubs I want to talk to, and one of them may make me an offer I can't refuse. L.A. or New York would be best, for endorsement money."

He opened the passenger door of his wine-colored Jaguar and helped Dani inside. Her hotel was located only a few miles from George Korman's mansion, and within minutes they had pulled up in front of a uniformed attendant.

Dani didn't want to make it suspiciously easy for the egotistical pitcher, although he was so overly confident that he probably *expected* women to fall into his arms. "Thank you for the lift, Mr. Morgan," she said, her hand on the door handle.

"Have dinner with me," he countered.

"I'm really not hungry." She flashed him a dismissive little smile.

"A drink, then."

"No, thank you." Dani turned back toward the door, slightly puzzled by his apathetic manner. For a man intent on seduction, he exhibited a definite lack of charm. As she pulled at the handle, she noticed that two cars had driven up behind them, their drivers presumably impatient to go inside.

Ty Morgan ignored her refusal. By the time Dani had maneuvered herself out of the bucket seat and closed the car door, he had already handed his keys to the attendant and walked around to her, taking her arm to lead her into the hotel. She planned to continue her cool rejection, but as it turned out, she had no opportunity to do so.

The lobby was quite busy. Some of the people simply stared. A few shouted out expressions of admiration, "Great Series, Ty!" or "Great season!" The most aggressive of them fumbled for pieces of paper and pens, which were shoved into his hands for autographs.

So the TV commercial hadn't exaggerated the extent of the man's celebrity, Dani thought. Surely he would be ingenious enough to catch up with her if she gave him the slip. She left him surrounded by a crowd of fans, patiently signing his name. He made absolutely no attempt to stop her as she walked off toward the elevator.

Back in her bedroom, she gathered up most of her cosmetics, emptied the dresser drawers, and hastily repacked her small suitcase, placing it in the closet of the adjoining sitting room. She left only a single garment unpacked—a white silk nightgown, seductive in spite of its innocent color. Delicate lace insets covered the breasts, tapering into a V which ended just below the waist. This exquisite piece of froth had been designed by Jeanne, who had given it to Dani as a twenty-fourth birthday present. Now she draped it provocatively across the bed.

She sat down at the dressing table and began to loosen her long hair from its businesslike style. As usual, she had pulled it back from her face and gathered it into a bun atop her head, silky bangs just reaching the tops of her brows. When her hair was brushed out, the dark, wavy strands floated below her shoulders, making her look enticingly fragile and even more beautiful.

She had just finished freshening her lipstick when she heard two sharp knocks on the door. She went to answer it, thinking that she certainly couldn't fault the man's timing.

"Yes? What is it?" she called out.

"Room service," was the reply.

No room service waiter had ever possessed such a seductive drawl. Fighting the urge to smile, Dani opened the door. Ty Morgan stood before her, tray in hand, a pristine white napkin draped over his right arm. A bottle of wine, the label turned downward, was nestled in a silver ice bucket. Judging from the shape of the two glasses on the tray, it was probably champagne

Dani frowned, pretending to wrestle with her supposedly sensible inclinations for a few moments. Then she opened the door wider and admitted him. "I really shouldn't let you in," she murmured in a sultry voice.

"Yes you should." His eyes scanned the sitting room, and continued through the door of the bedroom beyond. They came to rest on the nightgown, which was just within view as it lay on the bed. He proceeded to scan Dani's body as well, starting with her now shoeless feet and ending at the mane of hair framing her face. "This is much better than a public restaurant. Nobody around to ask me for autographs."

"Fame and success can be such a bore," she sighed.

"Actually, they recognize me from the TV game shows and the WorldBank commercial," Ty said nonchalantly. "It's been especially bad since the Series, but give the fans a few weeks and they'll be talking about nothing but football. *Sic transit gloria mundi.*"

Bemused by an athlete who quoted Latin to her, Dani watched him set the tray down on the dining table and uncork the champagne. It was Dom Perignon. "In your honor," he informed her.

"I'm only half-French," Dani said. "My father was American."

"Was?"

"My parents are both gone now. I live in Paris with my aunt." She took the glass of champagne he held out to her. Considering the cost of the bottle, perhaps Ty planned to write it off as a charitable deduction. Dani took a quick sip to hide her amusement.

"You came all the way from Paris for George Korman's funeral?"

Dani delivered her prepared answer to the question. "No. I happened to be in Los Angeles on business. Miss Swensen is a good customer of my aunt's—she owns a boutique in Paris—so I went to the funeral to pay my respects. She invited me to come to the house today, too."

"Edward Reed told me you were a relative."

"In a way, through my mother's family. One of Mr. Korman's ex-wives is a relative of mine, actually."

"You seemed to be pretty friendly with Mack Harmon. Where did you meet him?"

Goodness, the man was persistent with his questions! "He's a charming man. Edward Reed introduced us. And before you ask, I met Edward in Paris last year. Viveca suggested that he stop into the boutique to shop. He said he wanted to buy his wife a present." Dani was astonished at the glibness with which she tossed off these lines.

"Eleanor Reed died two years ago," Ty answered evenly.

Whoops! Thinking quickly, Dani flashed him a smile and shrugged. "Perhaps I misunderstood. Now that you mention it, I think he chose a black nightgown. It must have been for a . . . friend."

"That doesn't sound like Edward Reed. He's pretty straight."

It was impossible to tell how suspicious Ty was; his bland tone gave away nothing. Dani knew it would be a strategic error to plead further confusion. The best defense was a good offense, in both senses of the word.

"My aunt doesn't design *lurid* clothing, Mr. Morgan," she sniffed. "The gown was beautiful and tasteful. I have no idea who he gave it to, but I'm sure she loved it."

"Cool down. Nobody accused your aunt of anything," he drawled.

At least he hadn't thrown another question at her. Content with the silence, Dani sipped her champagne. Ty Morgan was unlike any man she had ever met. He radiated a bored self-confidence, as if women had long ago ceased to excite him, but there was something else besides. Not calmness, precisely. Control, as if he wasn't devoid of emotions at all, but simply kept them well under wraps. She couldn't imagine him losing his temper, or doubling over with laughter. His strongest shows of feeling seemed to be reserved for recollections of rotten pitches he had made.

She studied his features, wondering if any woman had ever heard his mouth whisper passionate endearments, or seen his eyes glazed over with sexual hunger. She doubted it. He was even better looking up close, with that blond-streaked hair and those unexpected light gray eyes of his. Tiny lines trailed off from the corner of each eye, this sign of maturity more appealing than mere boyish handsomeness. His dark suit was much too well-tailored for any bulging muscles to stretch the fabric, but Dani supposed that his body was as hard as the baseballs he threw. His tough virility had a disturbing physical effect on her, an effect she tried to ignore. With over six feet of lithe power behind each pitch, it wasn't surprising that he was a superb athlete.

Only one feature seemed out of place on his face, and that was his nose. It was too sculptured, too perfect. Dani's eye was quick to detect the hand of a skilled plastic surgeon; many of Jeanne's customers had availed themselves of such services. She was aghast at the notion that a healthy man like Ty Morgan had been so vain as to have a nose job.

"You're staring," he said softly. "Is that a good sign?"

Provoked by the phony caress in his voice, Dani decided to take him down a peg. "It's your nose," she said in a sweetly sarcastic voice. "Wasn't it pretty enough to begin with?"

"It was fine to begin with." If his bored tone was any clue, her sarcasm hadn't pricked him in the slightest. "But at spring training eight years ago, a batter laced into one of my fast balls and smashed it right up the middle. I put my hand up and started to duck, but the ball caught me in the face anyway. It broke my nose, splintered the bones around my eyes, and left me with a concussion. Fortunately I got some very fancy medical care, or it would have ended my career. I was out for the rest of the season, but I came back a year later. That accident cost me two years out of my major league career, but all in all I was damn lucky. A little bit in either direction, and I would have been left half-blind."

Dani's cheeks were flushed with embarrassment. She had certainly misjudged the man, at least in regard to his vanity. "I had no idea pitching was so dangerous," she said.

"It was a freak accident. If I had been older, more experienced, maybe I would have gotten out of the way in time. And maybe I wouldn't have."

He was, Dani realized, utterly matter-of-fact about an incident which must have been both painful and traumatic. "I was pretty wild as a kid," he continued. "Some days I never knew where my fast ball would wind up."

"But now you do," Dani said.

"Sure. George Korman didn't pay me half a million bucks last year to throw wild pitches." He put his glass on the table and walked into the bedroom. Dani followed, uncharacteristically nervous about his intentions. He reminded her of a panther getting ready to spring.

He picked up the nightgown, ran its gossamer length through his fingers, and tossed it back on top of the covers. "And you didn't let me into your room to listen to me talk about baseball. Let's go to bed."

Talk about fast balls! Dani was caught totally off guard by the abruptness of his proposition. If he had followed the usual male pattern, he would have stroked her hair or told her that she was beautiful, then geared up for a full-blown seduction. Instead, he apparently wanted to get the whole thing over with, and Dani had to check the impulse to throw him out on the spot. Mike Jones, she decided, had had no idea what he was asking of her!

"I've heard ball players have a lot of women," she said, wanting to stall him a little.

"We do. *If* we want them. They proposition us from the stands, hang around our hotels, and even call up to our rooms. Once I found one in my bed. Personally, I got tired of that scene after my first few years in the majors."

"Then why play it now?" Dani asked him.

"Because you're very beautiful, Dani. And because I've wanted to make love to you from the moment I met you," he answered huskily.

You miserable liar! Dani thought to herself. You're here because of a ridiculous bet, despite that well-acted note of passion in your voice! Her feminine ego was a little bit injured by his lack of interest—even fortune hunters had more enthusiasm for the stalk than Ty Morgan did.

His indifference provoked her into modifying her original scenario. "Ty," she purred, walking to within inches of him, "in France we do things a little more slowly. It was warm at the Kormans', don't you think? Why don't you take a shower and cool off?" She reached out a hand and ran teasing fingers down his cheek. "It will take me a few minutes to take off my makeup, and then I'll join you, *cheri.*"

He caught her hand and turned the palm to his mouth, nuzzling it for several seconds before he released it. "Is that French enough for you?" he murmured teasingly. "They're big on hand-kissing, right?"

Dani took a step backward. Why had the man turned on the charm *now?* And why had her body reacted to it?

When Ty took a step forward and tipped her chin up with his finger and thumb, Dani began to panic. The boredom had disappeared from his face, to be replaced by open desire. She hadn't planned on this. He brushed his lips against her mouth, then slowly pulled her into his arms.

"You're rushing . . ." she began to protest, stiffening in resistance.

"I never rush," he interrupted. "Relax, Dani." He lowered his head to kiss her, and she had no choice but to cooperate. If she continued to resist, he would start cross-examining her about why she had let him into the room in the first place. And if she confessed that the whole thing was a practical joke that was getting out of hand, the wretched man would probably rib her about it until the day he retired. So she allowed him to part her lips, and when his tongue began to slowly probe her mouth, she slid her arms around his waist and kissed him back.

He certainly knew how to arouse a woman. His hands were gently rubbing her back, and his mouth had wandered to her neck, nuzzling just below her ear in a way that left her whole body aching. He toyed with her lips until they opened once again, then took unhurried possession.

Dani felt flushed with heat, her heart pounding rapidly, and yet she found it impossible to react naturally. She was aware of every movement she made, like an actress who wants to make sure that her body is arching just sensuously enough, that her mouth looks beautiful for the camera. As aroused as she was, there was somehow no emotion in her response.

After what seemed like ages, Ty broke off the embrace. Dani avoided his gaze, knowing how uncertain she must look.

"I'm not the only one in this room with good mechanics," he drawled. "What's the matter, Dani?"

She didn't pretend to misunderstand the gibe, but ignored it in favor of the succeeding question. "I'm a little tired," she mumbled. "Jet lag . . ." Walking over to the dressing table, she sat down and began to brush her hair. It gave her something to do with her hands, and some time to recover her composure.

"Have you been to bed with a lot of ball players?" Ty asked, sitting down on the bed. Dani could see his body, reflected in the mirror in front of her.

In twenty-five years, no man had dared question her about her past. Edward Reed was right. Ty was proving difficult to handle. She had to wrap up this little love scene, and fast.

When she didn't immediately answer, he went on, "Look, if you want me to leave, I'll leave. Or eat first. Or talk. Or whatever. But I can't read your mind."

First charm, now decency. It was altogether too much! Some of Dani's confidence began to return. As Ty had assured her, he was not the type of man who rushed a lady into bed. So where was her spirit? When Mike Jones was dying of embarrassment in Esther Moore's arms, had George Korman stopped the gag? She must have inherited at least *some* of her father's talent for practical jokes. This was no time to back out.

With a renewed sense of humor and purpose, Dani shook her head. She set down the brush, swung around on the bench, and smiled. "I haven't been to bed with any ball players, Ty. Actually, I collect French royalty. Barons, counts, that sort of thing."

"You're putting me on," he answered.

"Yes," Dani admitted. "You were on your way to the shower, remember, darling?"

"What are you, some kind of water fetishist?" he shot back.

"You'll find out, won't you?" Dani prayed that he wouldn't argue the point.

He stood up. "Okay, Dani," he said. "For tonight, you're the boss."

It was all she could do not to burst out laughing. Ty took off his jacket, tossing it onto the bed. Dani turned back to the mirror and slowly—very slowly—applied cleansing cream to her face. She resolutely ignored what was going on behind her.

As soon as she heard the shower running, she snatched up her nightgown and few remaining cosmetics and threw them into her suitcase. Then she pulled out the note she had written while waiting for Ty to show up at her door, and placed it on the dressing table. "Better luck with the next bet," it read.

Finally, she gathered up all of his clothing, bundling everything but his wallet into a large shopping bag, and tiptoed out of the suite. The room Diana Kendall had rented for her was only one flight down. It was a simple matter to arrange for the clothes to be cleaned, pressed and returned to the suite. She didn't want Ty to suffer *too* much, after all.

An hour later, Dani was lying in bed, reliving her evening's work. She was surprised by the sense of satisfaction she felt. Her father would have loved this if he could have seen it, but that was only part of the reason for her mood. She had always considered herself a Ronsard—practical, sensible, conservative —but had learned that she also possessed a streak of the Korman unconventionality. She had lost someone very special to her, but part of him lived on in her. And that pleased her very much.

Chapter Four

*E*arly on Sunday morning, Dani's taxicab dropped her off in front of the three-story apartment house where she lived with Jeanne. After eleven years in Paris, she usually took the understated charm of this thirty-year-old building for granted. Designed by the French architect August Perret, it overlooked the Bois de Boulogne in the quietly fashionable sixteenth arrondissement.

Now, after three days amid the nouveau riche glitter of Beverly Hills, Dani found renewed pleasure in the clean, classic lines of the concrete residence, with its many windows, wrought-iron balconies and surrounding gardens. Viveca Swensen's mansion might proclaim its own splendor and importance, but Dani considered it garish rather than beautiful. She had come back to Paris only to realize how wrenching it would be to leave again.

Jeanne was still asleep, and it was not until late morning that she and Dani sat down over coffee and fresh croissants to talk. Dani willingly satisfied her aunt's curiosity about the guests and food at Viveca's party, but hesitated before admitting that she had snubbed one of her players, and why.

Jeanne knew nothing of Ty Morgan's affair with Viveca Swensen, and not much more than that about American baseball. Dani tried to explain the extent of Ty's stardom, but got nowhere with talk of earned run averages and games won. Finally she mentioned the WorldBank commercial and the way he was mobbed in public, and Jeanne smiled her comprehension.

Expecting disapproval from her no-nonsense aunt, Dani was surprised when Jeanne giggled through her entire account of the events leading up to Ty's visit to her hotel room, and his subsequent trip to the shower.

"Your papa would be pleased," she announced. "Perhaps this move will do you good, Danielle. You have always been a serious child, but too much so since you broke your engagement to Paul. You work too hard and play far too little, and I have been selfish enough to allow it. I will miss you horribly, darling, but it is best that you learn to be on your own."

Dani saw the justice in this viewpoint, but felt the remedy rather extreme. She could have adapted easily to living by herself in Paris, with family and friends close by; independence in an alien city thousands of miles away was something else again. She wasn't the sort of woman who underestimated her own resources, but the change ahead was so total that even a chameleon would have found it difficult.

Only five and a half weeks remained before Christmas, and the boutique was increasingly busy as December wore on. Dani's memories of her father, at first primarily poignant, were increasingly lighthearted. She had spent so little time with him throughout her life that she could appreciate their relationship without being devastated by its termination. As for her inheritance, she resolutely dismissed it from her mind. Her energies went into such tasks as hiring and training her replacement, tracking down missing shipments, getting the books into shape for the year-end audit, and making sure that Jeanne's designer originals were sewn and delivered in time for holiday parties.

For the most part, Dani handled these responsibilities with a determined calmness that soothed even the most volatile suppliers. In her more harried moments, however, she would marvel that, before she had become Jeanne's business manager, her aunt had attended to all these administrative details, and had somehow managed to find the time to design clothing and go on buying trips as well.

Jeanne's success in building the boutique from a crowded little shop in an unfashionable location into an elegant establishment on Avenue Victor Hugo owed nothing to either luck or accident. Not only was Jeanne organized and decisive, she seemed to have an almost eerie talent for anticipating the future whims of fashionable women. Her frenetic pace over the last fourteen years would have exhausted many younger women.

Sometimes Dani told herself that the business was Jeanne's truest love, and that no man could hope to compete. Her aunt had never elaborated on her reasons for avoiding marriage beyond stating that it was an institution created by tyrannical men to rob women of their independence, but Dani suspected that Brigitte Ronsard's experience with George Korman had reinforced Jeanne's innate reluctance to commit herself. The older she became, the less inclined she was to change anything about her lifestyle. Most men were threatened by her success, and those who risked proposals invariably wanted her to cut back on business so as to be a proper hostess, housekeeper, helpmeet, and sometimes even stepmother. Jeanne saw no reason to give in to their demands.

Edward Reed's secretary phoned during the hectic week before Christmas to ask Dani if she could meet with the attorney in Paris that weekend. Given the holiday rush, Dani asked if the matter might be handled other than in person. It was soon clear to her, however, that the answer was no. Given the length of the trip Edward was determined to make, Dani felt the least she could do was to invite him for Sunday dinner.

For the first hour of his visit, everyone concentrated on Jeanne's cooking: seafood crêpes, roast duck, sautéed potatoes and asparagus, and an array of cheeses for dessert. They talked about Jeanne's work as a designer, and of Dani's responsibilities as her business manager.

Afterward, they retired to the living room for a second cup of coffee and some serious conversation. "This is obviously a busy time of year for both of you," Edward said as he sat down. "I appreciate your having me in your charming home, Jeanne, and preparing such a superb meal for me."

"It was my pleasure, Edouard," Jeanne replied. "But you did not travel all the way to Paris to make small talk and offer me pretty compliments. You are busy also, yes?"

As he helped himself to coffee, Edward explained that his firm had a dozen other attorneys who could cover for him while he was away. He had scheduled two other meetings while in Paris, but his primary reason for coming was to see Dani.

"Don't forget," he told her, "that I promised your father I would look after you. I wanted to see how you were doing."

"Just fine. If I can survive Jeanne's customers, Los

Angeles will be . . . a piece of cake." Dani smiled at her use of the Americanism.

"Then we'll get down to business. First, I want you to know that we're through probate. Viveca made some noises about filing a legal challenge, but the will had a clause that if she filed and lost, she would get nothing. She's much too practical to throw away her inheritance when she has no real chance of winning."

"I don't want to feud with her; I wish she'd let the past alone." The move to Los Angeles would be difficult enough without contending with a wrathful Viveca Swensen, Dani thought.

She had already noticed Edward Reed's perceptiveness; now he easily deduced the motivation for her comment. "Viveca won't give you any trouble, Dani," he assured her. "Your position is too powerful. Living in Paris, I don't suppose you really grasp the amount of money you'll control and the influence it gives you, but Viveca does."

"I am glad to hear it," Jeanne said with a smile.

Dani wondered if her aunt had noticed the way Edward Reed's eyes kept straying in her direction. Perhaps it was the resemblance between Jeanne and Brigitte that drew his attention, but more likely her aunt's vivaciousness and elegance were the attraction.

He opened up his briefcase and pulled out a file folder, placing several copies each of two documents on the coffee table in front of them. Red *X*'s had been penciled in next to the signature lines. "I have some papers with me for you to sign," he said to Dani. "The first document gives me power of attorney until you move to Los Angeles. If you're at all uncomfortable about having me represent you, I suggest—"

"No, that would be fine," she broke in. "I'd like you and your partners to handle things just the way you did when my father was alive."

"Thank you, Dani. Your ownership of the Condors was approved without any problems, and now that it's official we'll need the second document. It authorizes Mack Harmon to proceed with negotiations on salaries and trades, and to attend to other business as necessary. Please sign your legal name on these, Dani."

As she flipped through the pages to locate all the signature lines, Edward continued, "A local business group approached me about sponsoring a dinner-dance to introduce you to the players and other people associated with the organization." He reached into the inside pocket of his jacket and pulled out a black leather appointment book. "I told them to go ahead, and they scheduled it for January 16th. That's a Saturday night. Can I tell them you'll be there?"

"Do I have a choice?" Dani asked, setting down the pen. "After all, I seem to be the guest of honor."

Edward shook his head. "No choice at all. My son will take you—he's looking forward to meeting you. He'll probably be the one who picks you up at the airport; just let us know the date and time. By the way, one of my assistants is looking at houses for you; she found a beachfront cottage south of the city that I think you'll like. It's closer to your ball park than your office, but for the time being, it should do."

"Yes. Thank you," Dani replied. Her ball park? Her office? Her beachfront cottage? Did he expect her to turn into a tycoon the instant she set foot in California?

She watched, somewhat dazed, as Edward conjured up two more folders and a book out of his seemingly slim leather briefcase and laid them on the table. "I brought along your homework," he said.

Good grief, what now? The book was entitled *Baseball Rules and Strategy*, and judging by its size, she would be reading it for weeks. She picked up one folder and thumbed through its contents. The enclosed material concerned the team's personnel; there were photos of the players, coaches and executives, summaries of their careers, and even information on their families and backgrounds. The other folder contained detailed information about the business aspects of the franchise.

"Mack put that material together for you," Edward explained. "Most owners take a personal as well as a business interest in their ball clubs, Dani. While the athletes consider themselves professionals with a job to do, they're also human beings, and they appreciate praise from the boss. Like your father used to say, there are owners who drive everyone crazy because they're frustrated managers who second-guess every decision. You'll find that your people will value your interest and enthusiasm."

"And noninterference," Dani teased. "Now I understand my role—resident mother hen!" That, at least, was something she could smile about.

"When you aren't playing practical jokes, you mean?" Edward shot back. "Everyone connected with the Condors has heard about that by now, you know. They're calling you your father's daughter."

"And Ty Morgan?" Jeanne laughed. "What is he calling her?"

"She'll find out when she sees him. I imagine he'll be there on the 16th."

Edward gathered up the documents Dani had signed and packed them into his briefcase. "Before you leave," Jeanne said, "there is another matter I would like to discuss with you, Edouard."

"Of course."

Her aunt, Dani noticed, was smiling at Edward Reed in the most entrancing manner. Although Jeanne could be extremely flirtatious when she wished to be, she was invariably brisk and direct when it came to business. What was she up to?

"I am going to open a second boutique, I think in Beverly Hills. I will need some help."

It was the first Dani had heard of the scheme. "Since when is this?" she asked.

"Since I learned you would be moving to California, *ma chère*," Jeanne informed her. "Now I have decided to go ahead, and I will need help in choosing a location, selecting merchandise, and so on."

Edward Reed promised to look into the matter, and said he hoped Jeanne would get in touch with him when she required the services of an attorney. "Please let me take you out to dinner when you come to the States," he added.

Jeanne smiled and said she would look forward to it, and soon afterward, the attorney took his leave.

"You know he's smitten with you," Dani said. "He's a widower, too."

"So you told me. He will help me all the more, and become the perfect escort in Los Angeles. Smitten men have their uses, don't you agree?"

Dani studied her aunt's placid expression, and realized that she was actually serious. "I certainly *don't* agree, Aunt Jeanne! You're absolutely shameless, and one of these days you're going to meet a man you can't wrap around your little finger. I only hope I'm there to watch."

"What? After forty-seven years of doing exactly as I please?" Jeanne shook her head. "Not me, *ma petite.* Truly, Edouard is a very attractive man, but I am too old to change. Now you, on the other hand . . ."

Dani held up a hand in surrender, laughing. "Touché!" Then she picked up the book Edward had left for her, and began to skim the table of contents.

Shortly after New Year's, Dani and Jeanne joined a group of Ronsard relations at St. Gervaise, a ski resort located in the Mont Blanc area of the French Alps. For several years now the Ronsard clan had gathered there to ski, romp in the snow with their children, and hold a delayed Christmas celebration. Dani had always taken full advantage of this annual opportunity to unwind from the madness of the holiday season, and during the week they spent in the mountains she gradually accepted the imminent move to California. Her adult cousins teased her about being a millionairess, and her aunt presented her with a collection of designer originals as a Christmas present, but otherwise everyone treated her as they always had.

The snow was excellent for so early in the season. Dani skied all but the most difficult slopes, enjoying the relative peace and solitude. In the past she had always taken along a special book or two to read during quiet evenings, but this year she had packed away Edward Reed's "homework."

The four days after she returned to Paris were spent in a frenzy of packing and last-minute good-byes. Some three weeks after her meeting with Edward, Dani was once again flying to Los Angeles. Her farewell to Jeanne had been an emotional one, but she looked forward to a promised February visit.

Meeting Teddy Reed caused a reassuring flash of déjà vu. Just as she had immediately spotted Edward a few months earlier, she knew at once that the blond-haired, blue-eyed man in the three-piece pin-striped suit was his son. The family resemblance was obvious, and he broadcast the same aura of self-assurance and competence. His handsome features, lacking the strength of maturity, brought to mind an overage California surfer. Dani wondered how many courtroom opponents had been lulled into complacency by that.

It was raining as they swung onto the freeway, heading south, parallel to the coast. Traffic was heavy, the large American cars weaving impatiently from lane to lane. Dani had been fearless when driving her Fiat through the streets of Paris, but the thought of tackling the Los Angeles freeway system terrified her. When she said so, Teddy blithely assured her that she would get used to it.

Their destination was near the oceanside community of Newport Beach, some fifty miles south of the airport. As they drove, Teddy briefed her on the pending sale of her late father's interest in Galaxy Films, as well as on matters relating to the Condors. His presentation was well-organized and concise, confirming Dani's earlier impression of competence. Before he left, he made arrangements to take her to the banquet on Saturday night, as Edward had mentioned he would.

Her house, all weathered redwood and glass, sat on a gentle rise. The beach was just outside the back door, down a short flight of wooden steps. Edward Reed had leased it with an option to buy, but the owner was asking an enormous amount of money, especially in view of how small the house was. There were only two bedrooms, two baths, a utility room, a living room with dining area, and a nice-sized kitchen. But for Dani, it was a case of love at first sight. The warm wood interiors were cozy and welcoming, although the institutional-looking contemporary furniture would have to go. The view of the Pacific Ocean from the picture window in the living room was both superb and soothing. She could hear the surf from her bedroom. True, the house was rather far from downtown Los Angeles, but that was actually something of an asset. It was also far from Beverly Hills and Viveca Swensen.

Over the next four days, Dani settled into her new home. She shopped for staples, read, cooked, walked along the beach, and let her body accustom itself to California time. She also acquired a California driver's license, using a mid-sized American car which was waiting in her garage when she arrived. Edward had bought it subject to her approval; he had left a note on the front seat to the effect that she might wish to trade it in for a more luxurious model in the future. In fact, Dani was happy with the Chevy. It handled easily and got good mileage.

Her phone was installed on Friday afternoon, and she immediately placed a call to Jeanne. Unfortunately, far from soothing her loneliness, the sound of her aunt's voice only increased it.

By Saturday, Dani was bored with her own company and eager to go out. Teddy was far more informal that evening than when they had first met, his appreciation of Dani's appearance only too obvious. She was wearing one of the gowns Jeanne had given her for Christmas, a stunning original made of white matte jersey, with a shirred bodice and softly draped, handkerchief-hemmed skirt. Two triple rhinestone spaghetti straps were gathered at the shoulder and fanned out over the bodice to the waist, which was also banded in rhinestones. With her dark hair falling to her shoulders and a subtle application of makeup, Dani managed to look both sensual and innocent at once.

She and Teddy were among the first to arrive at the downtown hotel where the banquet was being held. Although their conversation as they drove to the city ' ad concerned nothing more personal than the tourist attractions in the Los Angeles area, he took her arm in a proprietorial gesture as they walked into the room. Dani had asked that they come early; she felt that it would be a gracious gesture on her part to greet the team's supporters and employees as they entered the plush ballroom.

Several of the evening's sponsors, prosperous middle-aged businessmen who advertised their products on local broadcasts of the Condors' games, stood talking with Mack Harmon, and a second man whom Teddy introduced to Dani as the field manager, Marv Richardson.

"I've been reading through all the material you sent," Dani said to Mack, "and I feel like tonight is the final exam. I'm ready, except that I can't remember which league uses the lower strike zone, and I'm not sure I understand when you're supposed to bunt. Let's see now . . . Teddy filled me in on all the trades, so I'm an expert on that, although"—she winked at him—"I think I've got the three Lopez brothers mixed up."

Marv and Mack were grinning at her by now, and Dani grinned back. "Aren't I lucky," she sighed, "to have the two of you running things for me?"

They glanced at each other in such ill-disguised relief that Dani couldn't resist teasing, "Did you think that in just two months I'd turn into some interfering, ignorant female who would drive you slowly insane?"

"No. No, of course not." The laughing disclaimer came from Mack. "Can I get you a drink, Dani?"

"I'll walk over to the bar with you." The catering staff had just finished setting out the hors d'oeuvres, and everyone was homing in on a buffet table adjacent to the bar. While the bartender poured Dani a glass of wine, Mack introduced her to his wife Lillian and Marv's wife Kay. Many of the guests were arriving now, and Dani was grateful for her success in learning who everyone was, even if some of the rules continued to elude her. She managed to keep the players straight—and without a scorecard.

"The prawns are delicious," Kay Richardson remarked. "Do try one."

Dani obligingly impaled a prawn on a plastic toothpick, dipped it into the thick reddish sauce, and nibbled at it. It *was* good—crisp, and the sauce pleasantly tangy.

"Oh! Your dress, Miss Ronsard!" Kay exclaimed.

Dani glanced down to see a tiny speck of sauce near the waist of her white gown. She wasn't usually so clumsy, but she was on display tonight, and found it difficult to relax. "I think I'll find the ladies' room," she said with a smile, automatically repeating her earlier invitation to use her first name. Even when she laughed or teased, she supposed her manner was still far more formal than her father's had been. It would take time for some of these people to feel at ease with her.

The ladies' room was located at the end of a long, carpeted corridor. Fortunately, Dani was able to remove the stain with a small amount of hand soap and water. She had just left the ladies' room and was on her way back to the ballroom when she spotted Ty Morgan striding down the hall, on his way, she assumed, to the men's room.

Ever since Edward had told her that her role in Mike's practical joke was common knowledge, Dani had wondered what Ty's reaction would be when they met again tonight. He was so very controlled that he might easily act as though nothing had happened.

"Well, look who turned up," he drawled. "Here on business again, are you?"

"How did you guess?" Dani asked, her face just as innocent as his.

"Who did you come with tonight, Dani?"

Certainly he gave no sign of annoyance over her abrupt departure that Friday night over two months before. "Teddy Reed," she said, and then, unable to resist pricking at that irritating composure of his, asked, "Did you get your suit back, Mr. Morgan?"

"It turned out to be a very enjoyable evening— and night," he told her in that same lazy drawl. "It seemed like a shame to let the room go to waste, so I called up . . . uh, a friend. We ordered steak béarnaise and a hundred-dollar bottle of wine to go with it. I don't know who paid the tab—I certainly didn't. They had the suit back in under an hour, by the way. It was thoughtful of you to get it cleaned for me. The last woman who took my clothing tore it off for a souvenir. I felt like a rock star."

The man was infuriating! He didn't even mind that she had walked out on him. It hadn't caused him the mildest inconvenience; on the contrary, he had amused himself at the expense of Edward Reed's law firm. Poor Mike Jones must have been desolated. All that ingenuity wasted, a victim of Ty Morgan's utter unflappability.

"You know, Dani," he went on, "I wouldn't have made the bet if you hadn't given me the cold shoulder. Women do use that routine as a come-on, and it seemed pretty harmless, since I assumed you collected ball players for kicks. I've had one-night stands in a dozen different cities, and believe it or not, I'm tired of being a notch in someone's belt. Even someone as beautiful as you are."

He reached out his left hand, caught a strand of her hair between his thumb and first finger, and casually let his hand slide downward, absentmindedly rubbing his thumb into her bare shoulder. "Actually," he mused, "I was disappointed when you made it too easy. I have to admit, it never occurred to me that you and Mike were setting me up."

Dani found the roughness of his fingers intensely unsettling. The men she dated were students or professionals, and their hands were smooth and manicured, not calloused and masculine like Ty Morgan's. "Would you kindly stop pawing me, Mr. Morgan?" she bristled defensively.

"Only if you stop spitting at me, kitten. The name is Ty—remember?" He dropped his hand back to his side. "I know it's all a shuck, Dani—that Paris sophistication you put on. Or are you going to plead jet lag again?"

Dani was no fonder of condescending teasing than she was of taunting bluntness. Ty's nonchalant tone didn't fool her; he was sticking in the knife, and with all the finesse of an expert. She supposed he had some justification, but that didn't make enduring it any more pleasant.

Since she didn't want to quarrel with the man Mike Jones had called "someone you shouldn't make an enemy of," she decided to defuse the situation with humor. "I don't collect ball players for kicks, if that's what you mean," she said, tossing him a dimpled smile. "Or barons. Or counts."

"And I don't collect actresses," he replied. "Or other men's wives. Especially not my boss's wife."

So Ty Morgan *did* get angry sometimes—at least, Dani assigned that cause to his curt, cold tone. His words made her redden with embarrassment. Obviously Ty and Mike had talked about the reason for her initial snub, but this was hardly the time to discuss it. One didn't stand in public corridors and talk about illicit love affairs. "Let's forget it," Dani said.

"Why should I? You obviously won't. There's an empty conference room down the hall. We're going to spend a few minutes in there, Dani, and get this straightened out."

"If you insist." Dani decided he was the pushiest man she had ever met, but rather than make a scene, she followed him through the corridor into a small room furnished with a rectangular table and ten chairs.

As soon as they were seated, Ty began to talk. His voice was earnest rather than goading now. "I was twenty-five years old, Dani. It was my first year in the majors, my first World Series. Until that October, I was nothing special—just a very promising young pitcher on a club full of first-rate athletes. But I won two games during the Series, including the seventh and final game, and I won *that* with a two-hit shutout. The sportswriters loved it—voted me Series M.V.P. Suddenly I was a celebrity. I went to the most exclusive disco in town with Viveca and a group of other players, and a slew of people you only see in magazines and on movie screens wanted to meet me, pat me on the back, get autographs. That's pretty heady stuff for a kid who grew up in a small town. And when a Hollywood star who's so damn beautiful you can hardly believe it asks you to spend the night with her, you feel like it's Christmas and your birthday combined. I guess I was a little drunk—no, more than a little drunk, to be honest. Your father was always decent to me, and maybe I felt a pang of guilt about what I was doing, but not much of one. Everyone knew that George and Viveca went their separate ways. So I spent the night making love to her, and woke up late the next morning feeling like a—not feeling very good about myself. And that was the end of it. It was a mistake."

A corner of his mouth twitched upward. "An enjoyable mistake, but a mistake nonetheless. There's been nothing between us since then. So do you think you could revise your opinion of me? I've never claimed to be a saint, but I usually steer clear of married women and virgins."

As Dani listened, her self-reproach grew. She was not usually sanctimonious, but she'd certainly acted like a prig in this case. Knowing Ty now, it was hard to picture him as a star-struck rookie seduced by a glamorous older woman, but that was what had happened.

"I owe you an apology," she admitted. "I'll say what I should have said before. Congratulations on your Cy Young Award. And on the Series M.V.P."

He lazed back in his chair, grinning at her. "In a way, I'm glad you didn't. It was a much more interesting encounter. A little tough on my ego, considering the outcome, but interesting, nonetheless."

From any other man, that statement would have been a gentleman's gallantry, but given Ty's insufferable smile and drawling tone, Dani had no doubts about his motives. He knew perfectly well that she'd panicked when he made a pass at her, and was deftly telling her so.

His needling irritated her, so much so that she couldn't check the impulse to tell him off. "You are the only man I've ever met," she said icily, "who would be uncouth enough to bring that up, and not once, but twice. Didn't your mother teach you that a gentleman doesn't brag about—"

"I've never claimed to be a gentleman, either," Ty interrupted, effectively shutting her up. "There's something you don't understand about ball players, Dani. We believe in revenge. When an opposing pitcher throws at one of my teammates on purpose or a second-base man crashes into one of our runners when there's no defensive reason for it, only the pitcher can put a stop to it. I may not always like it, but I guarantee you, when the offending player comes to bat, he's going to have to duck a time or two. I operate the same way in my personal life. The way I figure it, Mike and I are even. But you and I—that's a different story. I owe you one, Dani."

"It wasn't *my* idea!" Lord, the man was impossible! "And besides, you have only yourself to blame. If you didn't think you were God's gift to the entire female sex, you wouldn't have accepted the bet in the first place."

"Maybe you have a point." In spite of the words, Ty didn't sound at all apologetic. He stood up, holding out his left arm, crooked at the elbow, for Dani to take. "I'd better walk you back to the ballroom," he offered, polite for once in his thirty-one years. "I've taken up too much of your time, and everyone must be looking for you by now."

Dani, somewhat mollified, got up and took his arm.

Chapter Five

As they walked back down the hall, Dani's usual good humor returned. She felt a mischievous urge to run her fingers from Ty's forearm to his shoulder, and soon stopped resisting it. She could feel the solid muscles underneath the suit jacket and shirt he wore.

He tilted her a mocking smile and cocked an inquiring eyebrow at her. "I wanted to find out what Daddy paid half a million dollars for last year," she explained with her best wide-eyed look.

"Then you'll have to feel the rest of me, too. It takes training to throw a ball that fast. Of course, you're the owner. That gives you the right to inspect the merchandise any time you want."

"I'll keep it in mind," Dani retorted.

Their entrance did not pass unnoticed. The local paparazzi were waiting just inside the door of the ballroom, positioned so as to photograph arriving celebrities. When Dani strolled in on the arm of her star pitcher, they all but salivated with joy, their electronic flashes bursting into ecstatic action. It didn't take a genius-level IQ to realize that Ty had set this up. Now she knew what he had been doing in that corridor in the first place—looking for her, to bring her back inside.

Several reporters immediately pounced, asking Ty

whether he and Miss Ronsard had been discussing his contract.

"I was explaining some of the finer points of the game to her, fellas. We'll talk money in the next few weeks." He grinned at Dani and smoothly excused himself to say hello to some teammates he hadn't seen since the funeral. Dani coped with the sportswriters' questions as best she could, and felt that she sounded reasonably knowledgeable.

Mercifully, Mack Harmon soon joined her and confirmed her assertion that she wouldn't be involving herself in the business end of the team, at least for the next few months.

"Miss Ronsard!" an aggressive young reporter called out. "You and Ty Morgan seemed pretty friendly. How well do you know him?"

Initially, Dani had been annoyed with Ty for throwing her to this pack of journalistic wolves. But she was pleased with her own performance, and figured that she'd gotten the last laugh. She noticed Ty watching her, waiting for her response.

"Not nearly as well as I'd like to," she said with a wink. The reporter practically panted with glee, and she almost hated to deflate him with her next line. "I mean that in a strictly professional sense, of course. We want Mr. Morgan on the team next year."

At that point, Mack Harmon called a firm halt to the impromptu news conference. Dani spotted Mike Jones and Diana Kendall chatting with a group of George Korman's Hollywood cronies, and walked over to join them. It was the first time she had met such people as an equal, and she found their enthusiastic greetings rather satisfying. At Jeanne's boutique, some of the wealthy customers had treated her like part of the decor.

"Where's Viveca tonight?" Diana asked, resuming the shop talk.

"Haven't you heard what's going on with her picture?" The counter-question came from a producer.

When Diana shook her head, explaining that she and Mike had just returned from shooting on location in Europe, the producer told her, "It's half a million over budget and three weeks behind schedule. They canned the director and brought in Charlie Larsen. They've been working six days a week, finishing up the interior shots at the studio." He glanced at his watch. "She'll probably show up after dinner."

Viveca Swensen was just about the last person in the world whom Dani wanted to see. She was the widow of the previous owner, however, and as such, her presence was only to be expected. Dani knew she would have trouble tamping down her temper if the scheming actress provoked her, but she would just have to manage it. She wouldn't ignore the woman's saccharine sarcasm; she would simply reply in kind.

"Have you seen the view yet, Dani?" The question came from Mike Jones. Dani stared blankly up at him, her mind still fixed on Viveca Swensen.

"From the top floor," Diana prompted. "All the lights of the city, twinkling right at you. Interested?"

Dani finally got the message. "Yes. Definitely." She was curious about Mike's version of what had happened after she left Ty in the shower. It had finally struck her that for all his nonchalance, Ty was acting like a man who'd been badly stung.

As soon as the three of them were alone in the elevator, Mike started to talk. "I wish I had it on film, Dani. Even Ty admits you were great. He called me to bring him something to wear . . ."

"So Mike played dumb," Diana picked up the story. "By the time we got to the hotel, Ty had his suit back. We didn't want to stop by your room—we thought you might be asleep—so we . . ."

"Wait a minute," Dani interrupted. *"You* were the ones with Ty? He told me that he called up a friend to come over for dinner, and that she spent the night." She paused, recalling his exact words. "Or at least, he said it had been an *enjoyable* night."

"Only someone who liked two-year-olds could say that." Mike was still laughing as he escorted the two women out of the elevator and into the cocktail lounge on the top floor. They sat down at a window-side table.

Dani was utterly lost, as her expression must have shown. "What two-year-old? What are you talking about?"

"We had a steak dinner and spent the night," Diana explained. "Our housekeeper was on vacation, so we brought our little boy with us. Ty was really sweet; he took Jeremy back to his house with him, and we picked him up the next morning."

"He spent the night baby-sitting?" Dani was incredulous. "He had me convinced that one of his girl friends was with him." She stared down at the lights of Los Angeles, which were lovely, even through the haze, and slowly shook her head. "The man should have been an actor."

"Actually, he thought it was pretty funny until I told him you were George's daughter," Mike said. "For some reason that really steamed him, so I reminded him about that screen test of his and he cooled down pretty fast. It didn't take him long to figure out why you put him down in the first place. Did the two of you straighten that out?"

Dani said that they had, but that she suspected Ty wasn't nearly as cool as he pretended about her role in the practical joke.

"No? What makes you think that?" Mike asked.

Ordinarily, Dani would have tactfully changed the subject, but Ty Morgan was beginning to intrigue her. She suspected that his boorishness earlier tonight had been as out of character as it was deliberate. Since Mike was one of his best friends, perhaps he could explain the reasons for it.

"He kept reminding me—almost taunting me—about how outclassed I was," she admitted. "Given his attitude, I'm afraid our business relationship is going to be pretty uncomfortable."

"Outclassed?" Mike repeated. "What do you mean?"

Dani's face, already warm, heated up even further. "He made a pass at me—it came when I didn't expect it—and I panicked," she muttered. "Didn't he tell you . . ."

"Of course not!" The answer came from Diana. "Ty is a gentleman, Dani. He'd never talk about something like that."

So her suspicions were correct. When Mike began to elaborate on Diana's statement, Dani listened intently. "It's hard to figure out just what's in Ty's head sometimes," he said. "Mostly he speaks his mind, but when he's not in a mood to talk, he can give you a poker-faced look and not much else. It's not like him to give someone a hard time without saying why. Something must be eating him, but I'll be damned if I know what it is, and maybe he doesn't either. Just don't take it too seriously."

It was such a steadfast defense that Dani remarked, "You really think a lot of him, don't you?"

The catcher answered with a monosyllabic "Yeah." It was Diana who went on, "It's unusual—a black man and a white man, being that close. Mike gave Ty a lot of help when he started in the majors. Both of them were single, and they used to hang out together. They really hit it off, but it was nothing really deep, just partying and carousing. Then your father introduced me and Mike and we had a lot of conflicts in the beginning. We wouldn't be together if it wasn't for Ty."

"We'll work things out, then," Dani promised.

All of them recognized that the cocktail hour would be over by now, and by unspoken consensus they got up and started toward the elevators. It was obvious to Dani that Ty Morgan was a much more complicated man than she had supposed; to her surprise, she looked forward to their next confrontation. The physical attraction he had for her had been joined by a certain fascination.

Dani was seated at the head table, with Condors general manager Mack Harmon on her right and the lectern and microphone on her left. Mack spent the first two courses filling her in on business affairs relating to the club, and as she listened, she was grateful that Edward Reed had brought those thick folders to Paris for her. At least she understood most of what he was telling her.

"There was a fellow, played shortstop and second base for Montreal, who I signed last month," he said as the prime rib was being served. Dani was beginning to find his soft drawl soporific. "He was a free agent. Cost us a bundle, but he's worth it."

Free agent. She kept hearing that term, but didn't

know how an athlete gained that much-coveted status. "That means he can negotiate with anyone he wants to, right?" she asked.

"More or less. I'll have to back up a bit to explain it," Mack replied. "We've only had free agency since 1976. Before then, there was a paragraph in every baseball contract called the reserve clause, which gave the owners the right to renew a player's contract for an option period of one year, at the same terms. If a ball player didn't like the deal we offered him, he had two choices: he could refuse to sign, hoping for more money, or he could accept what we were willing to pay. He couldn't go to another club."

"Year after year?" Dani asked.

"That's how the owners interpreted it. They said it would ruin the game if players could jump from team to team. Cost everyone a heap of money, and the rich teams would always buy their way to a pennant. During the 1970s we had court cases, an owner lock-out, and player strikes over that clause. First the players' union won the right to submit salary disputes to an independent arbitrator. In 1975 a couple of pitchers played for that one-year option period I told you about, with a signed contract. They claimed they were free to negotiate with other teams the year after, and the arbitrator agreed with them." He gave Dani a slow wink. "The owners fired him, by the way. Said he'd overstepped his authority and took the case to court. That time they lost."

"So a player could go wherever he could earn the most money?"

"They'd love it if they could," Mack laughed. "As it is, salaries have jumped as high as a spooked cat. In the early 1970s, only superstars made $100,000 a year. Now it's less than the major league average. The Players' Association—the union—and the owners negotiated a compromise agreement. It expired after the 1980 season, and in 1981 we had a mid-season players' strike that lasted longer than anyone wanted it to. The issue was compensation—what a club that loses a free agent gets from the club that signs him. They finally worked out a complicated set of rules that I'll explain some other time—when I have a copy of the agreement in front of me. Basically, you should just remember that a player can become a free agent after six years in the majors, and that we have what's called a re-entry draft for all the free agents every November, when clubs choose whom they want to talk to. It creates some extra excitement all through the off-season, and that's fine with me."

"So we decided to talk to this man from the Expos?"

"Along with eight other clubs."

"How many drafted Ty?" Dani wanted to know.

"Only five. We retain the right to negotiate with him. There isn't a team in the major leagues that wouldn't like to own his left arm, but most of them got a bellyache just thinking about the price tag. There was a lot of talent up for grabs this year and the other clubs didn't want to waste one of their draft picks on a lost cause. They knew he wouldn't sign with them."

"Has he given out a definite figure?"

"Not to me. What's floating around is a guaranteed contract for six years at a million and a half a year, with a million-dollar signing bonus up front. Ty left town just after your father's funeral. He hasn't been talking to anyone, but I'll tell you, there are a couple of teams with open checkbooks, just waiting to fill in the zeroes. I spoke with him earlier and we set up a meeting for the week after next."

"You told me how good he is," Dani answered, "but I still don't understand why someone should earn ten million dollars for throwing a baseball."

"For throwing strikes at almost a hundred miles an hour," Mack corrected. "For doing it every fifth day for six straight months for the last six years. But even more important, he brings people into the ball park, and not just when he pitches. Winning creates its own excitement, and stars sell tickets. They also sell beer, peanuts, hot dogs, and fat broadcast contracts. The team makes more from subsidiary rights than any other franchise in the game. Ty knows that. He also knows that he's thirty-one years old, at the peak of his career. Either he makes his money now, or he doesn't make it at all."

Dani had seen all the figures, but never quite understood them until now. "And I used to think baseball was a game." She sighed. "It's been quite an education, Mack."

A five-piece combo played throughout dinner, couples dancing during the breaks between courses. From time to time Dani accepted an invitation, the first from Teddy Reed, the rest from club executives or businessmen. She would have enjoyed dancing with some of the players, but all of them avoided her, perhaps because of her position.

When she finished her entrée, she took matters into her own hands. After all, hadn't Edward lectured her about her role as head cheerleader and den mother? She walked over to one of the round tables near the back, where a group of players were seated with their wives. Her target was Kenny Green, a young pitcher who had joined the team toward the end of the previous season, and the third man, she now realized, in the trio she had overheard at Viveca's party.

"Would you mind if I steal your husband for a few minutes, Mrs. Green?" Dani asked his obviously pregnant wife. Although Judy Green shook her head, she looked distinctly displeased, and Dani realized that she was actually jealous. Good heavens, the pitcher was only a boy, twenty years old, if she remembered his biography correctly.

"Mack . . . Mr. Harmon . . . said that Kenny was one of the newest members of the team, so I thought I'd make him my first victim," Dani explained with a reassuring smile. "Kenny? Are you turning me down?"

Kenny Green glanced at his wife, his face flushed, and he rose. When they reached the dance floor, Dani slipped into his arms and whispered into his ear, "Am I really so intimidating?"

"It's just, well . . ." Further explanation was apparently beyond the young pitcher.

"I *do* know who you are," Dani informed him. "After all, there's only one pitcher on the team named Kenny. But you were an innocent bystander, and the whole thing was only a practical joke. Don't be embarrassed about it."

Dani's breezy attitude loosened him up. "Everyone's talking about it tonight, Miss Ronsard. José Cuevas—he's . . ."

"Yes, the second baseman," Dani inserted.

"Right. He says it's the only time Morgan got sent to the showers when no one had scored!"

Dani laughed and blushed at the same time. The comment Kenny had repeated was innocuous enough, but it struck her that far more ribald double entendres must be circulating tonight. Certainly she would never hear any of them!

She managed to answer with mock sternness, "That's no way to talk about a man who's going to teach you a new pitch. He might withdraw the offer."

Their bantering conversation continued, and was typical of those which followed as Dani danced with other members of the team. She felt every inch the mother hen, particularly with the younger players, and was able to joke and tease while maintaining just enough control and distance to remind them that she was the boss.

As a result, she enjoyed herself on two levels: as a woman and as an employer. The athletes were often amusing and always polite. She supposed that she could thank Mike's practical joke for the fact that they were so accepting of a half-French, female novice for a boss. It pleased Dani that she was able to continue the tradition of laid-back esprit her father had nurtured so brilliantly, and which had made the Condors so unusual and so successful.

The sponsors of the banquet had stinted on nothing, and certainly not on the champagne. By the time the after-dinner speeches rolled around, the guests were on the raucous side of cheerful. They quieted for a pair of nostalgic tributes to George Korman, but erupted into whistles and laughter during team captain Mike Jones's humorous account of the season's highlights. He included a raft of practical jokes perpetrated by the team's more notable pranksters, their identities obvious to the players even if he mentioned no names.

Had somebody really put a hair-spray label on a can of theatrical hair dye and left it in the locker of a teammate who was known for his meticulous concern with his personal appearance? And who was the anonymous pitcher who had finally conceded to an interview with an annoyingly persistent yet prudish woman reporter—and then drawled that he was in a hurry, and that they would have to talk while he showered? The interview had attracted quite an audience, and judging by the smile on Ty Morgan's face, Dani had little doubt just who had been standing there with the soap.

Perhaps these adult men considered themselves hardened professional athletes, but as Dani had learned, sometimes they acted like boys at summer camp. The jokes and pranks served the serious purpose of relieving the tension and fatigue inherent in playing almost every day for six months that built up in twenty-five men fighting to keep or win perhaps fourteen permanent spots in the line-up, and during long, boring road trips and stays in impersonal hotels.

After Mike finished his talk, Mack delivered a very gracious welcome to Dani; then Bill Klemper, the team's public relations director, rose to list the awards received by the club's personnel that season. The first few awards were genuine—Mike's M.V.P. and Ty's Cy Young among them. But Bill quickly strayed to more imaginative tributes, a means of lampooning the peccadilloes of various members of the Condors' organization. Certainly, there was no such thing as the Don Juan Award for off-the-field activities!

As the laughter subsided, Mike Jones rose from his seat and called out, "We've got another one, from the players, Bill."

Bill Klemper motioned him up to the microphone. Dani noticed that he was carrying a brown paper bag, and wondered what was inside. The award he was about to present?

"We've taken a poll here tonight, in order to select the owner we'd most like to be stuck in Cincinnati with. Dani Ronsard was our unanimous choice," he announced with a grin, "and it's my privilege to present her with this token of our esteem."

He tipped the paper bag upside down and dozens of hotel room keys came cascading down in front of Dani. She took the subsequent laughter and applause with good grace; just about everyone at the banquet had come in for his share of ribbing tonight, and there was no reason to make her the exception.

Everyone seemed to expect a speech, and since no one had suggested to Dani that she prepare one, she had to improvise. She got up, adjusted the mike, and shook hands with Mike Jones. "Thank you, Mike," she said solemnly. "This is a very great honor. I'm really touched to have been chosen." She picked up one of the keys; it was from the luxury hotel where they were now dining. Although about half of the players had come in from out of town and were staying at the hotel, the other half lived in the greater Los Angeles area. Someone must have slipped out during the meal and arranged to borrow the rest of these keys from the management.

She looked at her general manager. "Gee, Mack, these keys are all from this hotel." She paused. "This is a very *expensive* hotel, isn't it?"

He nodded. "Sure is, Dani."

"You mean to tell me that I'm paying for these guys"—her hand made an arc, sweeping across the room—"to stay in a fancy place like this? Next time, book them into a rooming house in Oxnard."

When the hoots and shouts of "No way!" had died down, she continued, "I'm very pleased to be here tonight, and I thank all of you for making me feel so welcome. By now all of you know I do things in the tradition of my father"—Dani waited for the laughter to stop—"but I have to warn you that we differ in certain ways. For example, I've spent most of the last eleven years in France, and I was raised to be very careful about money. You like me *now,* but what will you say when you find out about the raises I veto?"

"No one ever gets less than twenty percent a year, boss," someone called out. "That's the way it's done in the majors."

"Thank you for telling me that. I'm certainly lucky to have so many unbiased experts to advise me. I'll look forward to next season." Her dark eyes glowing with amusement, she sat down.

The rest of the evening was devoted to dancing and partying. Viveca Swensen made a dramatic entrance just after the speeches ended, swaying across the room in a low-cut gold lamé wrap dress held up by the flimsiest of straps. The overlapping front panels frequently fell open as she walked, revealing a generous length of shapely leg as she zeroed in on Ty Morgan. Her status as a recent widow was apparently far from her mind as they danced, and if the pitcher objected to the way she was plastering herself against his lanky frame, he wasn't pushing her away.

Dani danced a few more times with Teddy Reed, relaxing in his arms as he told her tales of his more colorful clients. A good percentage of his time, she learned, was spent on Condors business, but many of the routine matters were delegated to an assistant. This arrangement made it possible for him to have a more varied and interesting practice.

Dani found him to be very pleasant company and only reluctantly excused herself to circulate around the room. When she reached Ty's table, she found Viveca seated next to the pitcher, her chair pulled so close that she was practically in his lap. He was talking to Mike Jones, however, and seemed far more interested in some point of Mike's than in making love to the actress.

"How lovely to see you again, Deedee darling," Viveca purred. "Inspecting your assets tonight?"

"I'm getting to know my players, Viveca," Dani said as sweetly as she could. Then she added a dig of her own. "After all, Daddy left *me* the team, didn't he?"

"Of course, dear. Who else would he leave it to?" the actress answered, just as sweetly.

"The will was . . . *ambiguous,* wasn't it, Viveca?" Dani shot back.

"You haven't asked me to dance yet." The interruption came from Ty, who gave Viveca's arm an absentminded pat and stood up. Dani would have accepted this backhanded invitation merely for the pleasure of annoying Viveca, but as it happened, she genuinely wanted to dance with Ty. It would give them a chance to talk.

"Of course," she said, giving him a guileless smile. "I'm dying to find out if you dance as well as you—" she paused dramatically, then concluded with a wink—"pitch."

The number was a romantic ballad, and Dani wasn't surprised when Ty paid her back for her gentle teasing by pulling her almost indecently close against his body. "I *don't* dance as well as I pitch," he murmured into her ear, "but if you're interested in an answer to the other comparison you meant to imply . . ."

He was holding her so intimately that Dani could feel every hard muscle of his powerful body. The hand at the back of her waist drifted upward and began to caress her neck, stroking the skin and playing with a lock of her hair. His lips wandered from her ear to her neck, nuzzling, teasing, exploring. She was even more physically aware of him than she had been two months before, and she couldn't blame it on the champagne. Ty Morgan was a superb masculine specimen, and at the moment he was practically making love to her, right on the crowded dance floor. She wouldn't have been human not to become aroused by it.

Somehow she kept the breathlessness out of her voice as she told him, "You don't have to keep demonstrating, Ty. I thought I'd already conceded you the title of World's Greatest Lover, even though I hear you spent a certain Friday night in the company of a two-year-old boy."

He loosened his hold and looked down at her. There was smug satisfaction in his gaze, telling her he knew exactly how he affected her. Some gentleman! she thought.

"I never said I was with a woman," he said. "You just assumed I was."

"Naturally. You wanted me to think so." She took aim with a dart of her own. "Actually, I'm absolutely astonished that Mike and Diana were able to get into your room. From what you've told me, it's incredible that the door wasn't blocked by the entire female population of North America, trying to beat it down, frenzied to get to you."

Ty merely smiled, replying, "I keep forgetting, *la petite minette française a des griffes.*"

"You speak French?" The words had meant, "The little French pussycat has claws." Apparently the man's talents extended beyond the pitcher's mound and the bedroom.

"French and Spanish. I learned the first in college, and the second from the Latin American guys on the team. We're not all dumb jocks anymore, Dani, especially at contract time."

"I didn't mean . . ."

"Sure you did." And of course, in a way he was right. She did tend to equate athletic ability with less than dazzling intelligence, or at least with a lack of interest in anything but balls and bats.

"Times have changed." Ty went on. "Some college baseball programs offer as much instruction and experience as the minor leagues. Ball players are staying in school longer. All of us know we can't play forever. An education doesn't hurt."

"So why do you do it?" Dani asked, becoming serious now. "I mean, gradually destroy your arm and even risk your life?"

"You're exaggerating the dangers. I'll lose some dexterity in my left arm, but if you love the game, it's worth it. And I do. It feeds both my ego and my bank account. Believe me, I have no intention of getting hurt again, and if the doctor told me I'd become a hopeless cripple, I'd quit."

"And do what?"

"I'll tell you, boss. I'm going to rip you off for so much money, I'll retire a millionaire." He was smiling again, but Dani knew he wasn't really joking.

"I've heard you want ten million over six years. But what will you accept?"

"Show up a week from Tuesday and find out. That's when we meet with Mack Harmon."

The number ended; they moved off the dance floor, pausing in a relatively secluded spot just outside one of the doors to finish up the conversation. "I don't get involved in contract negotiations, Ty. That's Mack's department, just like we told the sportswriters."

"You're going to make an exception in my case. I'll have more details when we get together."

The words, spoken in a soft, even tone, nonetheless constituted an order. No matter why he was provoking her, Dani saw no reason to tolerate it. Because of Ty's value to the team, however, and because of her mixed personal feelings about him, she kept her response low-key and friendly. "Are you asking me or telling me?" she asked with a smile.

She didn't know what sort of answer she had expected—perhaps an apology, perhaps even a good-natured wink, indicating that his show of dominance was nothing more than a put-on. Instead, he frowned and told her, "I was telling you. Damned if I know why. You have a strange effect on me, Dani. I'm always fighting the urge to push you around."

There was no regret in his tone, only a thoughtful bewilderment. Now that he had acknowledged how he was behaving, Dani hoped she could find out why and clear things up. "Why do you suppose that is?" she asked him. "Are you still annoyed about the gag I helped Mike pull?"

He shook his head. "Nope. Mike owed me one, and you helped. Besides, I know you're attracted to me. I could have won the bet."

It was the last straw. Dani had tried her best to get through to him, and now she was fed up. "You have the most awful manners of any man I've met, and probably the biggest ego. I'll grant that maybe you are irresistible to ninety-nine percent of American womanhood, but some of us have the good sense to say no. And even if the reverse were true, if you had any class, you wouldn't keep bringing it up!"

Warming to her subject, she went on, "Mack told me five other clubs drafted you. For all I know, you have the best left arm in the history of organized baseball—"

"I do," he said blithely, smiling at her outburst.

". . . but that doesn't mean we're going to let you blackmail us. You can go talk to the owner of the Yankees for all I care!"

"You want to listen in? It's almost three in the morning in Florida, where he lives, but I'm sure he'd be glad to talk to me," Ty said, by now laughing at her.

His teasing reply only made her angrier. "There's a phone booth down the hall, Mr. Morgan. Go use it!"

He caught her wrist just as she started to stalk back to her seat. "So, okay, I'm sorry. I acted like a pig and you wouldn't have slept with me." He shook his head. "God, you're volatile."

"I'm not!" Dani denied, reclaiming her wrist. "I've dealt with the most aggravating women in all of Europe in my aunt's boutique, and I've never once lost my temper."

He shrugged. "So it must be me. You coming a week from Tuesday, Dani? I really want to talk to you. Please."

"Oh, all right!" This time he made no attempt to stop her as she walked away.

Within moments, a determined smile had replaced the annoyed frown on her face. She made her way to Teddy Reed's table, thinking that Ty's apology was the most graceless she had ever received. She could have kicked herself for letting him needle her into such a burst of fury, but there was no point letting it ruin the rest of her evening.

Teddy immediately invited her to dance, holding her closer than before, but foisting no unwanted intimacies on her. Just as the band finished the number, one of the waiters approached with a slip of paper.

"There's a telephone call for you, Mr. Reed. The operator transferred it to the phone in the kitchen." He handed the note to the attorney. "If you'll follow me . . ."

Teddy, his expression apologetic, excused himself. Dani returned to the dais and sat down next to manager Marv Richardson. She was vainly attempting to decipher the man's baseball lingo when Teddy returned and rescued her. "That was my answering service," he said as he took her aside. "Apparently one of my clients got himself busted on a drunk driving charge. I have to go down to the police station and see what I can do for him. I'll ask my father to take you home." He looked very displeased by the idea.

Dani made appropriately sympathetic noises. By now the party was breaking up, so she sought out Edward Reed herself. Soon they were walking out of the ballroom to his Continental.

As they drove, they talked about the banquet, Edward complimenting Dani on contributing to a successful evening. "You handled things beautifully. I'm impressed, Dani—and your father would have been proud of you."

He went on to mention that he had talked to Jeanne Ronsard that morning. "I heard a rumor that space near Rodeo Drive might become available soon—a possible bankruptcy, still confidential, of course. Jeanne asked me to get in touch with the proper people and feel them out—make a commitment for her if I think I should."

"I hope it works out," Dani replied. "I miss her already, and I can't wait until she visits."

"Neither can I." The statement was accompanied

by a quick glance and a matching wink. "Your aunt is a special kind of lady. Tell me about her. Is there anyone important in her life?"

Dani saw no harm in answering the question. "She has a lot of friends, but no one special."

"She's never been married?"

"No."

"Why not?"

Dani couldn't help but smile at his persistence. "Honestly, Edward, you know I can't answer that. You'll have to ask Jeanne."

"Is she afraid of committing herself?"

Dani kept her mouth firmly shut. Finally Edward said thoughtfully, "Okay, so she doesn't like commitments. She's a businesswoman, independent. She probably avoids anyone she can't push around, because she can't tolerate a guy who makes demands on her. Maybe she saw what happened to your mother and it scared her off."

"What are you, a lawyer or a psychiatrist?" Dani asked in a teasing voice. Although she wouldn't comment on his speculations, she had to acknowledge once again that he was unusually perceptive.

He chose to take her question seriously. "A little of both. It comes in handy in my profession."

For the rest of the trip, he continued his subtle probing, but kept his questions indirect. Dani found herself talking about the years with Jeanne, thinking that if Edward meant to pursue her aunt, there was nothing wrong with giving him a little insight into her character. He was an intelligent, decent man, and best of all, a very eligible bachelor. She wished him all the luck in the world because, knowing Jeanne, he would surely need it.

Chapter Six

For almost a month, Dani had studied baseball in general and the Condors in particular. Her efforts had been rewarded by a successful debut as owner of the club, and she had no false modesty about that achievement. But the initial high of Saturday night was gone by Sunday morning.

She knew she was good with people. Although her role in Jeanne's business was primarily administrative, the salesgirls routinely pulled her out of the back room when difficult customers were in the shop. She had learned to be charming and patient, to do and say the right thing. In retrospect, it seemed to her that her performance on Saturday night was nothing out of the ordinary. She had been practicing for it for years.

So you're a good cheerleader, she told herself. That's not a full-time job. Mack Harmon runs the club, and it's a darn good thing he does. As for Korman Properties, that runs itself too, doesn't it? What can a twenty-five-year-old Parisian with no knowledge of California real estate tell the men in charge?

As Sunday wore on, Dani's restlessness and depression increased. A long walk on the beach failed to improve her mood. She missed Paris and Jeanne keenly.

She decided that she might be happier in California if she felt that her house was truly a home. On Monday she contacted the realtor handling the house and arranged to buy it for the listed price. Normally, Dani liked to bargain, but this time she felt that her need for a sense of security and belonging outweighed the importance of whatever money she might have saved.

Feeling isolated from everything that had once mattered to her and irrelevant to the empire she now controlled, Dani allowed a careless attitude toward money to color her actions for the next week. She shopped in the most expensive furniture and antique stores in Orange County, buying whatever appealed to her. When she came across two antique, hand-loomed Oriental carpets which cost an absolutely outrageous amount of money, she wrote out a check without a murmur of protest. She was uncharacteristically nonchalant about dozens of other purchases, and not particularly excited about how these beautiful new things would look in her home.

By Saturday afternoon, she was even lonelier than she had been a week earlier. She felt guilty about her wild spending spree and depressed over her aimless existence. Material possessions were no substitute for having some purpose in her life. She couldn't see herself making a career out of tennis and shopping, the way so many wealthy California women did.

Teddy Reed had called her earlier in the week to ask her out to dinner that night, and she was looking forward to it. For the past six days, her only human contact had come from salesmen salivating over her bottomless pocketbook. The paparazzi had done their work well. Apparently that picture of her on Ty Morgan's arm had been featured prominently in every local paper, because people seemed to recognize both her name and her face immediately. She was tired of being courted for her bank balance. At least Teddy thought of her as a woman, not a checkbook.

She dressed in a lilac-colored silk shirtwaist with long sleeves and a pleated skirt, the effect both feminine and demure. Teddy took her to a local restaurant featuring continental cuisine, and although Dani politely assured him that the food compared favorably with comparably priced Parisian fare, she crossed her fingers as she said so. Nothing in California could match the best Parisian restaurants, she thought, and instantly reproved herself for being such a culinary snob. In her present mood, she would find fault with everything American.

Since Teddy Reed handled the Condors' legal affairs, Dani wasn't surprised when he raised the subject of Ty Morgan during dinner. "Mitch Ellison called me yesterday," he began. "He's Ty's attorney and agent. I understand that Ty asked you to be present this Tuesday."

"It was more in the nature of an order," Dani informed him. "I wound up losing my temper and telling him off, Teddy. I'm annoyed at myself for letting him provoke me into that."

"Mike told me he was pretty mad about being caught"—Teddy's amused smile turned into a gust of laughter—"with his pants down. Or off, I should say. Not at the time so much as later, when he found out who you were. If he was giving you a hard time, maybe that's why. Did you agree to show up?"

"What choice did I have? Your father once told me that I'd be lynched if we don't sign him. Do you think we could change the topic to something more pleasant, Teddy?"

"In a few seconds, which is as long as it'll take me

to tell you that Ty and Mitch are meeting with Mack at four o'clock, in Mack's office at the stadium. I'll be there, too. I'll give you directions later."

He proceeded to tell Dani about a new French film he had recently seen. As George Korman's daughter, it was logical that she would be interested in movies, as Teddy Reed must have guessed. He was exceptionally charming, and very polished, and it was obvious that he hadn't reached his early thirties without acquiring a good deal of experience with women. Dani genuinely liked him, and wondered if a deeper relationship would develop. It was true that she was in a position to help him professionally, but she doubted he was a fortune hunter.

She continued to talk easily with him as they rode back to her house, and at her door he took her into his arms and kissed her good-night with an expert passion which she found both flattering and enjoyable. But there were no bombs, no fireworks, no bells. Dani was the one who broke off the embrace.

"Thank you for tonight. I enjoyed it," she said.

"Would you like to go out with me again?"

Given her tepid physical response to him, Dani didn't know if it was fair to say yes. "Call me," she suggested.

Teddy shook his head. "Look, Dani, I like you very much. Beyond that, I'm very attracted to you. But you happen to be one of my most important clients. It's important that you feel comfortable with me, that you trust me." He paused, clearly choosing his next words with care. "There's no way you're going to fend me off at night, and want to confide your business problems the next morning. Do you understand what I'm getting at?"

"You mean you'd rather have me as a client than as a girl friend," she answered. She was perversely disappointed that he could be so dispassionate about it.

"What I want is to have it both ways," he said. "And if I had more encouragement from you, I'd probably be stupid enough to try it. As it is, my impression is that you want me for a friend, not a lover, which is probably just as well."

"I guess you're right," Dani admitted. His tactful explanation had restored her good mood. She felt very comfortable with the idea of having Teddy as a friend and legal advisor. He was honest, sensible, and smart, very good recommendations for either of those roles. "Anyway," she added with a smile, "if your father has his way, we'll practically be brother and sister."

"Yes, I've heard all about your aunt," Teddy told her. "Dad's buried himself in his work since Mom died. They were together all their adult lives; they met at seventeen, married at eighteen, and had me a year after that. I think they enjoyed the struggles almost as much as the successes, and I know they were unusually devoted to each other. Jeanne is the first woman he's really mentioned to me, so she must have made some impression on him." He winked at her, the gesture identical to his father's. "Let's plan on a double date when she comes into town. We'll conveniently disappear in the middle."

"Definitely," Dani agreed. Her good-night was accompanied by a peck on the cheek. She felt she had a friend in Teddy Reed, and Los Angeles seemed a warmer place that night.

The Condors' stadium—named Clement Field, after the original owner of the ball club—was located midway between Dani's new home in Newport Beach and metropolitan Los Angeles, on the Orange

County side of the border between that county and neighboring Los Angeles County. Dani pulled into the empty parking lot about half an hour before Ty Morgan was due to arrive, and easily located the private entrance Teddy Reed had told her to use. Somebody, she noticed, had already erected a sign reading "Miss Ronsard" in front of one of the spaces. A uniformed security guard greeted her by name and escorted her to the administrative offices, which were located beneath the third deck of the 54,000-seat stadium.

Mack Harmon's secretary, an attractive woman in her early fifties, immediately re-introduced herself. "I'm Sophie Glenn, Miss Ronsard. We met . . ."

"Of course," Dani interrupted with a smile. "At the dinner two Saturdays ago. Is Mack in?"

Sophie buzzed the general manager, who trotted out of his office and suggested a quick tour of the four-deck stadium. The clubhouse—which included the locker room, training room, lounge and several offices—was eerily quiet and pristine. Dani tried to imagine the entire area filled with half-dressed ballplayers, their equipment and personal effects, but couldn't. Close by there was a separate lounge reserved for the use of the players' wives and families.

The owner's box was located in the narrow second deck, just beside the press box on the first base side of home plate. Mack told Dani that her father had seldom sat there; instead he and his cronies had preferred to watch the games from a field-level box just to the right of the home team dugout. Dani decided that she would follow her father's practice. No doubt she would be able to hear shouts of both congratulations and protest, but she would soon get used to the athletes' less than elegant phraseology.

Mack pointed to the bull pens, where pitchers warmed up before coming into a ballgame. They were located at the opposite end of the park, just to each side of the bleacher seats. They didn't take the time to walk over for a closer look, but instead returned to the administrative offices. After a stop in the press box, which hung down from the edge of the second deck, they returned to the administrative offices. Mack escorted Dani to the V.I.P. lounge down the hall. The room, furnished with comfortable chairs and sofas, contained both a bar and a large-screen television projection system. Mack helped himself to a beer, and asked Dani whether she preferred a mixed drink or something nonalcoholic.

"A soda is fine," she said. "Shouldn't we get back now?"

Mack checked his watch. "You're right. It's just after four o'clock."

Ty Morgan and his agent Mitch Ellison walked into Mack's office ten minutes later. Mitch explained that they had gotten tied up in traffic, not an unusual occurrence in Los Angeles. Dani, wanting to look executive, was wearing a charcoal pinstriped suit and gray blouse, but somehow she hadn't expected similarly formal attire from Ty. She and Mack were already seated on the couch. Ty and Mitch made themselves comfortable in two overstuffed leather armchairs which were grouped around a walnut coffee table opposite the couch. Just as Sophie was taking beverage orders, Teddy Reed appeared, sitting down on the couch next to Dani.

"Scotch on the rocks, Teddy?" Sophie asked.

"You got it, Sophie," he answered with a grin. "Mack, your secretary is a treasure."

The negotiating process around here was certainly a friendly one, Dani thought. The men sipped their drinks and traded shop talk for at least twenty minutes before getting down to business.

"Let's begin with the easy part," Mack started. "We'll go along with a six-year contract, Ty. Naturally the team needs some assurance that if you injure yourself in certain off-the-field activities, we won't . . ."

"Yeah, I know. Just let me see it," Ty interrupted.

Mack handed him a copy of the contract, opened to the appropriate clause.

"No motorcycles, no sportscar racing, no skiing, no sky diving . . ." Ty ticked off. "You want to assign one of your flacks to watch me at the postgame meal? I might injure my arm picking up a roast beef sandwich, right?"

"It's a thought," Mack said solemnly.

"This kind of clause is standard in long-term contracts," Teddy reminded him. "You know that, Ty. Any other team will demand the same thing."

"It's all right with me—as long as you take out the 'no skiing' condition," Ty said.

"You ski all during the off-season," Mack pointed out. "The risk . . ."

Ty cut him off. "I've never had an accident in the twenty-five years I've been skiing."

"Then you're overdue," the general manager retorted. "Your parents live at Tahoe. We know you spend a lot of time up there in the winter. The condition isn't unreasonable."

"I'll think about it. Let's talk money," the pitcher answered.

"All right. What we're offering is five and a half million dollars over a six-year period, with half a million up front. Some of it will be deferred for tax reasons if you want. Teddy and Mitch can work out the details.''

Ty shook his head. "Ten million," he said blandly. "Let's not quibble, Mack. You know I can get that much elsewhere."

Dani almost pointed out that a disagreement of four million dollars wasn't exactly chicken feed, but nobody was paying the slightest attention to her, so she kept her mouth shut.

"You're good, Ty, nobody would argue with that, but there are other pitchers just as good as you, who—"

"No, there aren't," Ty interrupted in a cool tone of voice.

Mack continued without missing a beat, ". . . who have been pitching longer, and who don't make that kind of money." He proceeded to dissect Ty's record, claiming that only three of the last six years had been really outstanding, and that in another two or three years his fast ball would stop overpowering the hitters the way it did now. Since Dani had been told by Mack Harmon on more than one occasion that Ty Morgan was the best pitcher in the game, and that his well-aimed fast balls were the terror of the National League, she wondered just what was going on here.

Ty, however, was not the least bit nonplussed or offended. He merely recited his statistics, pointedly reminding Mack that control and a knowledge of the league's hitters were more important than speed.

The two men exchanged views several more times, basically restating what had been said before. Finally Mack conceded, "All right, Ty. Six even and seven-hundred-fifty thousand up front. No higher."

"One and a quarter a year plus one million," he

answered. "I'm the best in the business and I expect to be paid like it."

There was an uneasy silence, which was broken only when Ty announced, "I want to speak to Dani. Alone."

The other men filed out of the room as soon as Dani nodded her agreement. She knew she looked every inch the self-assured female executive, but Ty's controlled self-confidence put her at a disadvantage. She remembered exactly what had happened the last time they were alone together, and so did he. Besides, they hadn't parted on the friendliest of terms last Saturday night, and given the incomprehensible chip on his shoulder, there was no predicting just what sort of provocation would come her way now.

"I'll be right back," she said, her voice commendably cool. "I just want to get another soda."

Ty straightened his lanky frame and reached out a hand to nudge the can. "This one is almost full," he informed her.

She knew that. She'd been stalling for time, trying to regain the initiative. His not-so-subtle gibe hadn't helped.

"It's a little warm," she answered. "I think I can afford to buy myself a fresh one."

"I'll get it for you," Ty offered. "Funny thing, my beer wasn't warm at all. But then, you've been here longer than I have, haven't you?"

Blast the man, Dani thought as he walked out of the room. Why was she letting him do this to her? It was ridiculous to be nervous. The worst he could do was make another pass, which she would promptly rebuff. Or would she?

Annoyed by her own jumpiness, she rose from the couch and walked over to look at the awards on the sideboard next to Mack's desk. He had been a fine ball player himself, some twenty years ago.

Ty sauntered back into the room, flipped the door closed, and sprawled back on the couch. He stretched his legs out, resting them on the coffee table in front of him.

"Come join me," he invited Dani, who was watching his movements with wary brown eyes.

She stayed right where she was. "Say what you have to say. I'm listening."

"Everyone's down in the lounge, but if you scream loud enough, I'm sure they'd hear you," he said with a grin.

"Why would I scream?"

"Good question. I don't know what you think I plan to do to you, but you sure look terrified, boss."

The drawling reference to her position was intended to goad Dani, as was the reference to her nervousness. Determined to hold her own in the war of wits they seemed to be waging, she shook her head, smiling. "Maybe a little preoccupied, Ty, but definitely not terrified." She walked over to the couch and sat down, careful to put a moderate amount of space between them. She didn't cower into the corner, but she didn't sit right next to him either.

His gaze slid to the can of soda, which was sitting next to a fresh beer to the right of his legs. Dani was on his left. "Do you want me to open that for you?" he asked.

At that moment, a stiff drink would have been far more effective than a carbonated soda, but Dani murmured, "Please." When Ty handed her the can, his fingers briefly brushed against her own, warming her body as though he had just caressed every inch of it. She didn't want to have this wild physical reaction to him—and certainly not when they were about to talk business—and pondered the cause as she sipped her soda.

Some of the attraction lay in his virile masculinity. She thought of him as unpredictable and tough, and thus slightly dangerous. The mixture constantly unbalanced her—and aroused her. She had long ago admitted to herself that he intrigued her. Had his behavior truly lacked refinement, she would have marked him down as a boorish pain in the neck and laughed when he provoked her. But his blunt, tactless comments had been quite deliberate, a means of baiting her into anger and embarrassment. Much to Dani's chagrin, he had frequently succeeded.

She had glimpsed much that was admirable in his character—openness, patience with his fans, a willingness to help his teammates, and even occasional gentleness with her—and her impressions had been confirmed by Mike and Diana. Yet for some reason, he seemed determined to unnerve her, as he was doing now, by staring at her in a way that suggested imminent seduction.

She took another token sip of the soft drink and set it back down on the table, her eyes fixed on the can. Since Ty Morgan had excellent eyesight, he could hardly miss the fact that her hand was trembling. Lord, how he must be enjoying this.

"You want me to make a pass at you and get it over with?" he asked.

The truth was that Dani was in an agony of mixed emotions. If any other man had treated her this way, she would have reduced him to pulp with a few words of well-aimed ridicule. She didn't dare try it with Ty, not when they were alone this way, and when she couldn't trust herself not to respond. She couldn't have faced him afterward.

"I'd rather you didn't," she said. Her voice was soft, but firm.

"Really?" he taunted.

Anger mingled with distress. Dani was sick of this whole game. "For heaven's sake, Ty, what's the point of all this?" she burst out.

"I guess it's the killer instinct." Dani picked up a rueful note in his voice, and looked over at him. "All star athletes have it," he continued, "but that's no excuse for using it here. The truth is, the moment we were alone, that executive image of yours started to crumble, just like I knew it would. And I couldn't resist smashing it to bits. It's called destroying the opposition."

The subsequent silence seemed interminable. Dani stared at the can again, about as uncomfortable as she had ever been in her life. She didn't see herself as "the opposition" or "the enemy." What had she done to merit those labels? She didn't understand Ty Morgan at all. When she felt his hand on her chin, coaxing her to look at him, her whole body jerked in alarm. Their eyes met, hers startled, his sober.

"I was just thinking about what happened Saturday night," he said. Dani had never heard him sound so gentle. "I gave you a very bad time and I'm sorry. You know I'm pretty straightforward."

"That's an understatement," Dani muttered.

"Straightforward." He emphasized the word. "Not crude. At least not usually. But you were right when you said I was still smarting from what happened before. You were right about the size of my ego, too. I didn't want to sleep with you all that

much—not until you started stalling. And then it hit me so hard I was stunned. By the time I got into that shower . . ."

He paused, leaving the sentence incomplete. Dani was astonished by the admission. Stunned? He had seemed so nonchalant, so entirely cool.

"When Mike told me who you were," he went on, "I realized two things. You were the first woman in a very long time who wouldn't have said yes, even if I'd really exerted myself, and you must have laughed all the way back to Paris. I also knew that I was going to be talking to you about my contract. Do you have any idea how that made me feel?"

Dani tried to put herself in his place, but still couldn't understand what he was getting at. "I never meant to be a tease—at least, not much of one, Ty. It was just a gag. It has nothing to do with business. I don't even know what I'm doing here."

"I'll back up a bit. I like to run things, Dani, to be in control. If any other woman had rejected me that way, I could have shrugged it off. It's going to happen to anyone once in a while. But you own the team I want to play for. You seemed to have too much power—on two counts. In a sexual sense, because you would have refused what I wanted, and in a business sense, because you control the purse strings. Maybe all that wouldn't have mattered if I didn't need to ask you for a favor. But I do. So I retaliated by hitting at your weaknesses, making you lose your temper, throwing you off-guard. It was a power play. I just want you to know that it wasn't . . . intentional, in the sense of being planned in advance. It was instinctive, and now that I understand what was going on in my own head, I'm not very proud of it."

Dani needed time to think about the psychological

factors at play here. She couldn't do that right now, but since Ty had been so honest, she wanted him to know that she had listened to what he was saying. "I accept your apology, Ty. I appreciate the explanation. But I guess I'd have to know you a lot better to really understand you. I mean, how much control do you need here? You strike me as one of the most self-assured men I've ever met. You've got more women than you know what to do with, and five other teams just dying to sign you."

"The other women aren't you, and the five other teams aren't the Condors," he answered. "Does that help any?"

Dani began to smile. "You don't just want to run things. You want to run *everything*. Is that it?"

"Let's just say that I have to restrain myself. Before we go on, is the rest of it behind us?"

"Yes, of course," Dani said. The mood in the room was entirely different now. There was no tension, no hostility, only a feeling of cooperation. "This favor you mentioned . . . is that why you wanted me to come today?"

"That's right," he said. "Before the season ended, your father and I discussed my contract for the next few years. I'm not going to play forever. I'd like to be a general manager eventually, but I have to be realistic. Very few men get that opportunity. So I'm looking into other investments. You remember that Mack mentioned my parents up at Tahoe?"

"Yes," Dani said.

"There's a ski area up there I have my eye on. It's not on the market, but the owner is getting pretty old, and I've heard he'd sell if he got the right offer. I'd expand it, put in more lifts and some harder runs, maybe add a first-rate ski school. But I need someone to loan me the money. No institution is going to finance it—not when my career could be ended by one hard-line drive up the middle, or half a dozen other things. Your father agreed to put up most of the money, starting as an equal partner, and gradually selling out to me. He'd have realized a return on the investment, but given how much he could make elsewhere, it amounted to a low-interest loan."

"Of course I'll honor any agreement you had with my father, Ty," Dani answered. "I assume it was tied in with your contract?"

"That's right, but we never discussed specifics. We talked a little one evening last fall, watching football at his house, and agreed that I would play for the Condors if we could work out the details. I became a free agent to protect myself in case we couldn't, but I never had any intention of playing for another team. We were supposed to meet just before the re-entry draft—the day after your father died."

"And you've waited until now because you wanted to speak to me first?" Dani asked.

"Exactly. There was a lot of confusion after George died. Nobody seemed to know what would happen to the team. When I found out from Mike, I decided to sit things out until you got back to the States. It wasn't something I could work out with Mack."

Dani had no experience in negotiating baseball contracts, but she told herself that she was the owner of the Condors, and no one had more authority to make decisions affecting the team. Besides, she had run Jeanne's business for the last three years, and although it was considerably smaller than the Condors, it wasn't exactly the neighborhood lemonade stand.

"I think your salary demand is excessive, Ty. I've seen the figures, and nobody on the team makes close to what you're asking. I'm aware of your contributions, and I know that you wouldn't be the first player to get that kind of money, but I think some of the other owners have acted irresponsibly."

"Under the circumstances, I'm willing to accept less—an even seven million, plus the million-dollar signing bonus. I'm better than guys who earn that much; it's a reasonable figure, Dani."

"You know that the amount of time you've been playing has to be a factor," Dani answered. "Mack's offer is more than fair."

"I'd like to work out a compromise, Dani. Suppose we agree on Mack's figure, with a yearly bonus based on performance to make up the difference."

Dani shook her head. "We're giving you six years, guaranteed. Go to someone else if you want performance incentives, because Mack won't pay them to free agents who are already instant millionaires when they sign."

"You're a tough lady, Dani," Ty said with a grin. "Your father wouldn't have blinked at the eight million bucks."

If the man thought he was going to charm her into an agreement, he was dead wrong. "He had a soft spot for the team. I don't think he really considered it a business, but I do. I'm willing to finance your ski deal. It's a very good package, and you know it."

The pitcher got up. "I'm sorry we can't come to terms. You have to understand that my ego is involved here. I'm the best and I think I should get paid like it. Every time I pitch at Clement Field we sell an extra 10,000 seats. Spread that over fifteen home starts a year, and it comes to a good percentage of the salary you pay me. I'll earn the money,

Dani." He stood, arms folded in front of him, waiting for her reply.

Dani could tell that Ty was ready to walk right out the door. She now understood that the money he wanted was more important psychologically than financially, and strongly suspected that her supposed "power" had something to do with his intransigence. No one doubted that he could make more elsewhere, but the ski deal more than compensated for that.

In terms of actual dollars, they were one and a quarter million apart. That came to over two hundred thousand per year, which would be a very substantial amount to some franchises, but was well within what the Condors could afford to pay. What the team couldn't afford was to have Ty Morgan pitching against it.

"All right, Ty," Dani said after a tense silence. "You've got your eight million dollars. But I want that no-skiing clause in the contract."

"Agreed. Mitch can work out the details with Mack and Teddy." He half-sat, half-leaned against the arm of the couch. "I'll look into the ski deal next time I'm up at Tahoe. Edward Reed and his partner Bob Schultz would be the ones to handle your end of it. They'll protect your interests."

A fluttering sensation was beginning to develop high in Dani's stomach. Mack expected her to stay out of contract negotiations, yet not thirty seconds ago she had made a deal with the Condors' prize pitcher.

She took a deep breath. Now wait a minute, she told herself. You happen to own this team. Both your father and Mack admitted that this guy was worth the ten million he originally asked for. "I'll get in touch with Edward as soon as you have something definite to tell me," she said aloud.

"Fine. By the way, Dani, after the last two contracts, your father's taken me out to dinner to celebrate. Let's continue the tradition."

Dani regarded him suspiciously. There was devilment in those gray eyes of his. She couldn't guess precisely what he had in mind, but was certain that it concerned more of that revenge of his, new beginning or not. "I wouldn't want to argue with tradition, Ty. I'd love to have dinner with you," she told him.

"Take me out," he corrected. "You're a liberated lady, right, boss?"

So he had a little role reversal in mind, did he? Well he wasn't going to embarrass her with that! On the contrary, she might even turn the tables on him.

"About most things," she agreed. "But I'm new to this area. Can you suggest a restaurant?"

"I made the reservation this morning. I do hope that's all right?" he asked, mimicking the tone of a woman who was feigning concern at being overly assertive.

"Of course, sweetheart," Dani tossed off with the proper chauvinist air. Then she laughed. "Come on, million-dollar baby. Let's go find Mack, Teddy, and Mitch."

They located the three men sitting around a card table in the lounge, playing poker. "Do we have any champagne, Mack?" Dani asked. "It's time for a celebration. Ty will be playing for the Condors for the next six years, at seven million even plus one up front, the no-skiing clause to be included in the contract. In addition, my father made a personal commitment on financing for a ski area, and I intend to honor it."

Incredulous stares greeted this blithe announcement. Mitch Ellison frowned. "Damn it, Ty, I could have gotten you ten million, even more elsewhere. Why did you ask me to come if you weren't going to let me do the talking?"

"Baloney, Ellison," Mack retorted. "The owners are tired of shelling out huge salaries to free agents. There are other pitchers."

"Don't give me that. I talked to the Yankees in December. They were willing . . ."

"Gentlemen, the matter is settled," Dani interrupted. "Let's not argue about who could have gotten what from whom." She slipped her arm through Ty's. "And now, if you'll excuse us, I'm taking my star pitcher out to dinner. I suggest that the three of you drink that champagne and start working out the details of the contract."

She winked at Ty and led him out the door.

Chapter Seven

The two of them were still laughing about Mitch's and Mack's squabbling as they approached the stadium exit. "Did you see the look on Mitch Ellison's face?" Dani asked. "I thought he would burst from apoplexy."

"At least the other two had some warning about you," Ty said. "You didn't say a word all the time I was arguing with Mack, and Mitch probably assumed you were . . . a soft, little French pussycat without claws. Where's your car, Dani?"

"Oh, no. It's rush hour. I may be liberated, but not enough to drive in L.A. traffic, Ty Morgan. *You* drive."

"I didn't take my car; Mitch picked me up. I knew I'd be leaving with you."

"So drive my car." Dani pointed to her black Chevy, sitting in the owner's private space. "You were that sure we would come to terms today, were you?"

"Right. I knew you'd be a pushover." Dani shot him a dirty look, which he ignored. "I would have taken six and a half."

"Tell me another fairy-tale, Ty," she invited.

"Seven?"

"Try again."

"Seven and a half. Really," he laughed.

They climbed into the car; Dani inserted a jazz tape into the cassette deck and handed the car keys to Ty. As they drove downtown, he told her about the proposed ski development project and about his childhood in Lake Tahoe. "My father was a minor leaguer when he was in his early twenties, but he never made it to the majors. He became a coach and transferred his athletic ambitions to his children, especially me. I'm the oldest of five. He had me throwing baseballs as soon as I could hold one. Once I wanted to ski in the Olympics, but I'm not that good. I might have made the team, but I wouldn't have won any medals."

Dani burst out laughing; she simply couldn't help it.

"What's so funny?" Ty sounded just a little annoyed.

"What you just said. That you weren't very good. And then you calmly add that you probably would have made it to the Olympics. Most people would say that if you can make your country's Olympic team, you're one of the best in the world."

"Dad didn't raise me to be *one* of the best. He wanted me to be *the* best. And I accepted his point of view. By the time I was sixteen, it was obvious that baseball was my game. But in case it didn't work out, he didn't want me to do what he had to do—finish school at night, and work in a low-paying job during the day. So I went to the University of Southern California, which has a good program, and I figured I'd pitch major league ball as soon as I graduated. The club sent me to the Triple-A farm team instead. That's the highest level in the minor leagues. I was pretty hot-headed as a kid and I made a stink, but they were right. I learned to control my fast ball and started throwing a slider, which is a more effective pitch for me than a curve ball. A good curve will break across to the right or left about twelve to fourteen inches, and drop down at the same time. The problem is that it's unpredictable—I can't 'spot' it . . . throw it exactly where I want to, into a place I know a particular hitter can't reach. It's also relatively slow, which makes it easier to hit. A slider is faster than a curve and it breaks less— about eight inches. Usually it drops very little, but I learned to make mine take a dive at the last moment. It looks like a fast ball when I throw it, and a batter has to swing early to hit a fast ball. If he waits, it's too late. So he starts to swing at the slider thinking it's a fast ball, but the ball veers off and drops down on him instead of coming straight in like he expects."

"So he completely misses it. But you said that with a fast ball, the batter has to swing early. You mean it takes the ball so little time to reach the plate that if the batter waits to see where it's going to go and then starts to swing, he wouldn't be able to bring his bat around in time to hit it?"

"Exactly. The batter only stands about sixty feet from the mound, so a good fast ball takes less than half a second to reach the plate. When you come to spring training, I'll throw you a few pitches. You'll see what I mean."

The thought of standing up there while a hard white object flew at her at nearly a hundred miles an hour lacked any appeal whatsoever. "No way," Dani said. "What if you're in a bad mood that day?"

"Don't worry, boss, I won't hit you," Ty promised.

For the rest of the trip to the city Dani relaxed and listened to the music while Ty coped with the traffic. Their destination was in Beverly Hills, a very posh

French restaurant which Ty claimed had excellent food, even if he preferred steak or lobster himself.

The maître d' greeted him in effusive French, chattering about the World Series while he led them toward a quiet table in a far corner of the room. It was early and the restaurant was almost empty. They received a few surprised looks, but nobody approached with requests for autographs.

When they reached the table, the maître d' pulled out a chair for Dani. She had been anticipating that moment with relish. *"S'il vous plaî, permittez-moi,"* she murmured, brushing his hands away. She stared ingenuously at Ty, who allowed her to seat him. He showed no sign of embarrassment. "Philippe," he instructed the maître d', "give mademoiselle the menu with the prices."

Philippe looked utterly horrified, but complied with Ty's order. As soon as he left the table, Dani said in astonishment, "Do you mean they usually give women a menu without prices? This place is a relic from the past!"

"You wouldn't want me to worry my little head about what this is costing you, would you, Dani?" Ty asked innocently. "You're the gourmet around here. You can order for both of us."

"How do you know I'm a gourmet?"

"You're half-French. The French always make a big deal about food," he answered.

Dani said nothing, but resolved to order the most exotic items on the menu. And if Ty Morgan balked at sweetbreads and squid, that was his problem! She also selected a French cabernet to drink, and when the sommelier began to pour it into Ty's glass for him to taste, blithely informed the man that she would do the honors.

"You're really getting into this, aren't you?" Ty accused. "I don't think I like being a kept man."

"*You* started it. Besides, look what you did to *me* last Saturday night."

He didn't pretend to be puzzled by what she meant. "I *did* warn you, Dani—about taking revenge. I should have known that any daughter of George's would handle the press like she'd been at it all her life."

He paused, grinned, then started to laugh. "Especially that wimp from the *L.A. Chronicle*. When you put on that sexy drawl and told him you wanted to know me better, he looked like he was about to dash to the phone to call the story in. You ruined his night when you qualified the statement."

Dani admitted that although she had initially been irritated with Ty for siccing the press on her, she had soon seen some humor in the situation. She supposed she would have to get used to the idea of talking to reporters, who were sure to request interviews once the season started.

The waiter brought their first course—an herbed pâté made with kidney fat, spinach, lambs' brains and various other meats and seasonings. Although Ty cast a dubious eye at his plate when Dani casually reeled off a list of the ingredients, he made no comment before tasting it.

"So tell me about your childhood," he said. "What was it like, being George's daughter?"

Dani was unusually expansive, a reaction to Ty's earlier openness. She told him about the divorce, the years with her mother and aunt, and the eight months she had spent with her father. She related George's habit of appearing at Jeanne's apartment without notice, and his later practice of sending her airline tickets, not to mention newspaper and magazine articles. Because Ty was still friendly with Viveca, she decided to be tactful and omit any mention of her.

"Hold it a minute," he replied. "Something doesn't add up here. You told me you moved to Paris because George thought you would be happier there. But where does Viveca come into it? Wasn't she married to your father yet?"

"They married a few months after I moved in."

"And you didn't get along," Ty guessed.

"You could say that," Dani agreed.

"So tell me about it."

Dani did. She saw no reason not to, not when Ty had specifically asked about it. The Ronsard dictum of keeping family quarrels within the family was remembered, then dismissed. On some level, she supposed she wanted Ty to know how rapacious and manipulative Viveca could be.

After relating a few examples of the harassment Viveca had inflicted on her, Dani concluded, "I had no idea why she wanted me to feel stupid and ugly, except that I looked like my mother, and she didn't want to be reminded about my father's earlier marriages. I finally found out last November. Viveca and my father had a prenuptial agreement, which I knew about, but didn't really understand."

After briefly outlining the conditions of the document, Dani repeated what Edward Reed had told her. "Viveca figured that if she got rid of me, my father would forget he even had a daughter and change the will. What he did instead was put in a clause that I had to move to L.A. to inherit, and if I refused, Viveca would get everything. He knew how I'd react, but the truth is, I would have moved here even without it."

Ty made no reply. They were on the second course

now, braised sweetbreads served with a cream sauce and mushrooms. He was, Dani noticed, eating it with a minimum of enthusiasm. He had seemed to like it well enough at first, until she had briefly interrupted her life's story to explain just what it was made of. She wondered if his silence reflected a lack of enthusiasm for his meal, or disapproval of her bitterness toward Viveca.

Eventually he set down his fork, his expression registering defeat. "That was terrific," he said with a grimace. "About Viveca, your father's marriage to her hurt you, I can see that. But you have to remember that she was very poor as a kid. She has a hang-up about going hungry and she doesn't think she's really beautiful. She needs constant male attention to feel desirable. She's too unstable and insecure to succeed in a long-term relationship, and she must have perceived you as a tremendous threat, not just because of the money, but because you were George's only child. You were, what, thirteen, fourteen years old?"

"That's right."

"Growing up, becoming a beautiful woman . . . she must have been out of her mind with jealousy. You don't hate someone like that, Dani. You feel sorry for them."

Ordinarily, Dani would have found Ty's capacity for understanding an appealing trait. She knew he was right. But the more sympathetic his words for Viveca, the more irked she became.

"Do *you* feel sorry for her? Is that why you were comforting her at the funeral?" As soon as the words were out, Dani regretted them. They made her sound like a jealous shrew.

"I happen to *like* Viveca." There was no reproach in Ty's voice, but no apology, either. "I know you don't want to hear this, but I'm going to say it anyway. Viveca is fun to be around. She doesn't whine, nag, or give you a hard time. She caters to a man's ego by hanging on every word he says. The only trouble is, any guy with half a brain knows that it's all on the surface. You can't really talk to her. She's only interested in keeping your attention, in making sure you admire her. You can have a good time with a woman like that, but you don't get involved."

Dani couldn't resist the obvious follow-up. "Who *do* you get involved with, Ty?"

He shrugged. "Who knows? Once I would have said, anyone but an entertainer, because celebrity marriages are so hard to pull off. But look at Mike and Diana. You can't make rules."

You certainly can't, Dani thought. If anyone had told her three months ago that she would find herself becoming emotionally involved with an athlete, she would have labeled it absurd. But that was exactly what was happening. She had never talked so openly with a man, and certainly not with Paul Marais, to whom she had been engaged for eight months. But then, no man had ever admitted the things Ty had admitted, frankly discussing the male reaction to rejection, sudden fame, different kinds of women, and even Dani's own superior position.

They were on the main course now. Dani had taken pity on him when ordering, and asked for Tornedos Rossini. Now she was glad. Ty had seemed rather relieved when the steak appeared in front of him.

"Diana was telling me you had a lot to do with her and Mike getting together," she remarked. "What did she mean?"

"Mostly I just listened." There was no false

modesty, no attempt to slough off his contributions. "The fact is, Diana and Mike are unusual people. They're both very stable and they're totally committed to each other. What I helped Mike see was that he *could* compromise and not feel like Diana was running him. His natural inclination was to insist on having his own way, to show her he was the boss, because he felt like the exact opposite. It was hard for him to cope with her stardom. But she's terrific, too. She really understands him."

"Right now, he's a star in his own right, too," Dani said, "but what happens when his career is over?"

"That's for him to decide. I've never met anyone who's better with kids, though. If I were you, I'd try to keep him in the organization—as a manager, or running the minor league operation. It's going to be a tough adjustment for him, because Diana will still be a star when he's through making headlines. But then, it's a tough adjustment for all of us, and the bigger you are, the worse it probably is."

They talked about that for a while, Ty trying to explain how it felt to have a crowd surrounding him, screaming encouragement. When he was getting ready to throw the ball, he shut the noise out. But in between, the cheers could send a kick of adrenaline through his system, and never more so than when he had pitched each of his two no-hitters, and even the opposing fans had rooted for him at the end.

"I don't like to think about giving that up," he admitted. "I plan for the future—make investments and all the rest of it—but I really don't like to think about it."

Over dessert the conversation lightened. A few people had come over to ask for autographs, and when Ty and Dani were once again alone, they started exchanging anecdotes about George Korman. It turned into a friendly contest to see who could come up with the most outrageous story, and both were laughing by the time the waiter approached with the check.

Dani matter-of-factly handed him a credit card, prompting Ty to tell her, "You have a lot of your father in you. After what you pulled at the hotel, and the way you snowed the press, I should have known that taking me out wouldn't bother you. I'll have to be more creative next time."

Dani slipped out of her seat. "I'm getting out of here before you get inspired!" Before Ty could move, she was behind his chair, pulling it out for him.

They continued to trade tales until they reached Ty's Huntington Beach residence. "I take Route 1 to get home, right?" Dani asked.

Ty lazed back and put his arm along the top of her seat. "Aren't you going to walk me to my door and kiss me good-night?" he countered in a needling tone.

With a cheeky smile, Dani got out of the car, walked around to the driver's door, and helped Ty out. So he really meant to continue the game to the very end of the evening, did he? Well, it was all right with her!

"Thank you for a lovely evening, Dani," he said with a broad grin as they reached the door.

Too spirited to let a last-minute attack of cowardice stop her, she stood on tiptoe and slid her arms around his neck. She intended to do no more than brush her lips over his and wish him a friendly good-night. Although earlier that day Ty had told her he was attracted to her, there had been no sign of it during dinner. Besides, his interest and passion had been aroused only when she withdrew. He might prefer the seemingly unattainable to the clearly available. Granted, that didn't gibe with the total impression she had received today, but human beings were often inconsistent.

Somehow, once she had accepted his teasing challenge, her emotions took over from her common sense. She found it impossible to kiss him without longing to provoke some reaction.

It was not Dani's practice to play the role of temptress, but now she stroked his lips persuasively with her own, letting him feel the tip of her tongue rubbing against his mouth. She imagined herself pressing seductively against him, but could not bring herself to go that far. Instead, she trailed her mouth over to his ear, nibbled at the lobe entreatingly, and began to tease his lips again.

To her utter mortification, there was absolutely no response from Ty. He stood perfectly still, hands at his sides, lips closed. At the very least, Dani had expected him to make a joke of her attempted seduction, and she was so humiliated by his stiff rebuff that she wanted to slink off into the night without another word.

Pride forced her to withdraw slowly, masking her devastation with a smile. "Good night, Ty. See you at spring training," she said. Her attempt to sound sophisticated was ruined by the tremor in her voice.

He simply stared into her eyes, unsmiling. Desperately forcing herself to maintain some facsimile of emotional equanimity, Dani turned away from him. She heared a muffled curse as he grabbed her by the wrist and abruptly yanked her back into his arms.

Her first reaction was stunned confusion. Ty Morgan was a very strong man, and she felt the raw power of him as he held her against his muscled length, one hand pressing against the small of her back, the other against her shoulders. He wasted no time on preliminaries, his tongue demanding entry, probing her mouth with a hungry passion that initially astonished her. Where was the even-tempered pitcher, the controlled man who had once remarked, "I never rush."

Within moments, confusion turned to cooperation. Not even Paul had made her feel this way—hot, weak, pliant—or coaxed her body to arch so sensuously. She slid her arms around his neck, her fingers in the crisp long hair which curled well below his collar. When he forced her lips still further apart, his tongue moving deeper and more devouringly, she willingly submitted. He was dominating her senses, but more carefully now, more slowly.

He broke the kiss to nuzzle his way down her neck. Dani tipped her head back, enjoying the aching longing he aroused, eager for him to take her lips again. "Dani . . ." he mumbled hoarsely.

She didn't want him to talk. She caught at his jaw with her right hand, guiding his mouth back to her own. There was an impatient roughness to his kiss now, a harshness to his breathing. She recognized the lack of control. When he started fumbling with the buttons of her coat, she stiffened slightly, her mind racing ahead. Although this intense outpouring of emotion from a man who had been no more than friendly all evening stimulated a passionate response, the bedroom was out. She didn't sleep around. When Ty raised his head, she was already framing a tactful refusal.

"Dani," he said huskily, "we've got to talk."

"Talk?" she repeated blankly, looking up at him. She would have thought that conversation was the last thing on his mind.

Good grief, he was standing there just like before —distant, unsmiling. How could he click off so fast? It was as though nothing had happened between them.

He unlocked the door and motioned her inside the hall. The sound of a television set emanated from a door on the left, toward the rear of the house. Who else was here?

Ty took her arm and led her through the darkened den into the living room. A beautiful young brunette, dressed in a frilly pink bathrobe, was curled up on the couch, watching a basketball game on television. The lamps in the room were off. Dani knew that her face must be stained pink with embarrassment, and was grateful that the TV screen provided so little light. How could she have assumed that a virile male animal like Ty Morgan would live by himself?

He smiled at the girl, who was absentmindedly braiding her waist-length hair into a single plait over one shoulder. "Hi, babe. What's the score?"

"Ninety-four to ninety-three, Lakers, with two minutes to go," she answered. Ty was immediately transfixed by the action on the TV screen. He dropped into a chair and proceeded to ignore both women.

"He's impossible when there's a game on. He'll forget we're here until it's over," the girl said, clicking on a lamp. "You must be Dani Ronsard. You're even prettier than your picture. I'm Jessica."

Dani had no alternative but to sit down next to Jessica, who apparently wasn't the jealous type. "Can I get you something to drink?" she asked.

"No, thank you." Dani wanted only to escape an awkward situation, and as soon as possible.

"I guess you and Ty came to terms, huh?" Jessica asked.

"Yes."

"Hey, Jess. What about me? I want a beer," Ty called out imperiously.

The girl stuck her tongue out at his back. "Yes, sir, superstar," she answered.

She trotted out of the room, presumably to the kitchen refrigerator. A few moments later she was back. "Hey, ace! Catch!" she yelled. She flipped him the beer, a wild toss that almost went sailing over his head into the window behind.

"You must be part of some other family," he said in a disgusted tone. "With an arm like that, you can't possibly be *my* sister!"

"Oh, shut up." She grinned.

His sister? Dani experienced a sensation of almost numbing relief, then realized that she should have picked up on their relationship immediately. Ty hadn't been at all romantic with Jessica.

"Are you a student?" Dani asked.

Jessica nodded. "A senior at U.C.L.A. The girl I used to live with got married two months ago, so I offered to let her have the apartment to share with her husband. I now inflict myself on Ty, who lets me stay as long as I fetch his beer and do his laundry. Anyway, he's hardly been around since I moved in."

"He mentioned he was the oldest of five. Are you the youngest?"

"No. My little brother Greg is seventeen. He's a senior in high school and a football player. I'm the next; I'm twenty-two. Then two more sisters, Christine, who's twenty-eight and a former Olympic skier, and Ellen, who's twenty-six and used to skate with an ice show. Chris is a ski instructor in Colorado and

Ellie is married with two kids. I'm the only non-athlete in the family. Dad once accused Mom of fooling around with the mailman." She giggled. "But I have his gray eyes, just like Ty does."

Now that Jessica mentioned it, Dani remembered Christine Morgan quite vividly. She had won medals in the last two Olympic Games, the only American woman skier to do so.

As for Jessica, as soon as Dani found out that she was Ty's sister, she started to like her. The two were fairly close in age, and Jessica had an appealingly cheerful personality.

"Your brother signed for eight million over six years," Dani informed her. "Are you impressed?"

A groan greeted the question. "He was bad enough to live with *before*," Jessica wailed. "Now he'll be unbearable.

"Conceited, is he?" Dani giggled.

"Conceited? Does California get earthquakes?" Jessica Morgan rolled her eyes. "He thinks he's faster, smarter, and better looking than anybody you can name. It's a good thing he's such a terrible hitter, or we'd never shut him up."

"My little sister," Ty said in a crushing tone, "is prone to exaggeration. I hit .184 last year. Get lost, Jess. I want to talk to Dani."

"*Sure* you do, Ty," Jessica drawled. Just as she reached the doorway, her brother picked up a throw pillow from one of the armchairs and, taking its name literally, heaved it at her, hitting her squarely on the backside.

"Right in the strike zone," he teased. "Just remember, Dani is my boss. Okay?"

"I forgot," Jessica said, and sashayed out of the room.

Ty clicked off the television set and dropped back

into a chair. "Wretched little brat," he said good-naturedly.

"I like your sister. She puts you in your place. And it's nice to meet someone my own age."

It took a long time for Ty to respond, and when he did, the subject of his sister was apparently far from his mind. He had shifted his weight in the chair, so that both legs were sprawled out in front of him, his beer held in both hands. "I had a great time tonight, Dani." His voice was low-pitched, earnest. "I like being with you. I like your sense of humor, the stories you tell, and the way you try to accept your childhood, even though I can see it caused you a lot of pain. I like the vulnerability underneath that Paris sophistication you put on. But I'm not going to make love to you."

The rejection stung, causing Dani to withdraw behind feigned indifference. "Who said I wanted you to?" she asked coolly.

Ty set his beer down on the end table next to his chair. "Don't play games with me, Dani. I'm trying to tell you how I feel. You think it's easy for me to keep my hands off you after what happened outside? It's a good thing Jess is here."

Dani stared at him in confusion. "But you said . . ."

"I meant, I know it's a bad idea. Not that I don't want to. You know damn well I've always wanted to—or almost always. But somewhere in the last few hours, my emotions got involved, and it caught me by surprise. I never expected things to go this far. If you were the type of woman who had casual affairs, I'd be in your bedroom right now. But you aren't." He paused. "Are you?"

"It's none of your business," Dani automatically answered.

"What is this? Some kind of knee-jerk reaction?" Although Ty sounded no more than mildly curious, Dani sensed a seething exasperation in him. "Look, we really talked tonight. I thought you trusted me."

"I do," Dani said. "To a point."

"Why only to a point? Is it just me? Or men in general?"

"Why the cross-examination?" Dani countered. "I'm not asking you about *your* sex life!"

"I never asked you about your sex life. Only about your attitude toward men." He took a long swallow of his beer and then got up out of his chair. "I'm going into the kitchen to get some coffee. Want anything?"

Dani's "No, thank you" was uncharacteristically cool, not because she was angry, but because she was uncomfortable. In spite of an active social life, she had never run across anyone like Ty Morgan. All of her Paris boyfriends had tried to sweet-talk her into bed, frequently on the first date. She doubted whether most of them even knew what the word "straightforward" meant.

Ty was different, and Dani knew it. It was difficult for her to talk about her most intimate feelings, yet he obviously expected an honest answer, and if she couldn't give him one, she should walk out the door.

But when he returned to the living room and sat down on the couch, he didn't resume his interrogation. Instead, he began to talk about himself.

"There were two times I thought I was in love, Dani, but things didn't work out. The traveling this job demands makes it tough on a marriage, tough on a woman who has to be a single parent half the time. And then there's the whole problem of coping with an athlete's ego, his dominating drives, maybe even other women. When I was younger, I wasn't ready to settle down, so the first relationship broke up. Now I am, but she didn't turn out to be the right person." He shrugged, drank some coffee. "Obviously I asked too much of her. I expected her to be self-sufficient, but still drop everything the moment I wanted her. It wasn't very realistic. And you?"

For the first time in her life, Dani found herself eager to explain her feelings. "I was engaged once," she began softly. "Paul was a lawyer—ambitious, bright, interesting to be with. I'm sure he really loved me. I blame myself that it didn't work out. You were right when you said I have a problem trusting men. My parents' marriage broke up because of my father's affairs although, of course, I didn't know it until I grew up. My mother was very badly hurt, and she avoided serious relationships after the divorce. My Aunt Jeanne is the same way. She once said that all men were tyrants, and that marriage was invented by men to rob women of their independence. She may even believe that. It's not that she dislikes men—she goes out all the time—it's just that she almost never lets one get close to her."

"So you're following in their footsteps, is that it?" Ty asked.

Dani shook her head. "No. It's more complicated than that. I've been fending off wolves since my late teens, but that's nothing unusual. It's the money thing, too. When I was twenty-two, my father sent me a plane ticket to come to the Cannes Film Festival. We were having lunch when someone I knew from Paris spotted us. He asked me out as soon as I got back. He'd never even paid any attention to me before. I knew him vaguely from the boutique; he used to shop for his girl friends there.

He thought I was George's mistress, and that appealed to him. Naturally I turned him down, but first I straightened him out about who I was.

"After that, I was in a whole new category to the men I met. They didn't just try to seduce me, they wanted to marry me. You wouldn't believe some of the lines they used. It made me pretty cynical."

"And this guy Paul?"

"He was from a very wealthy family. His parents were really aristocratic; I think they found my background slightly crass, actually. A few months after we got engaged, it began to bother me that I couldn't really talk to him, not about anything personal. He never shared his feelings and neither did I. We were always running to the opera, or the theater, or socialite parties, and we'd have a good time, but instead of feeling closer to him, I felt more and more distant. By the time I broke the engagement, I didn't even want him to touch me. He was so hurt. . . . If only I had tried harder to make him see . . ." Dani didn't want to continue. She was experiencing the same sense of failure all over again.

"It's hard to get through to someone who's perfect."

Dani looked across at Ty, startled by his comment. "But he *was*. Always charming, never moody, always confident, never unsure of himself. Even when he lost a case, you just knew that nobody could have won it. He married a year later. They have a little girl."

Ty didn't answer. He simply sipped his coffee, a brooding look on his face, and then finally shook his head. "It's no good. Everything you've told me only convinces me that if I took you to bed, you'd wind up badly hurt. You can call me a male chauvinist, but I put women in two categories, just like most men do. Some you fool around with, and some you're serious about. You don't get involved with the second type when you know it's going nowhere —not if you have a conscience, you don't."

The words hurt. Part of Dani wanted to escape before this conversation became any more painful, but if she ran away now, she would never understand why he was ruling out a serious relationship, maybe even marriage. If he liked her, why not try?

"But you said you wanted to settle down. You told me you like me, you're attracted to me, and I don't understand . . ."

"All that's true. But the fact is, Dani, that you've got more money than Midas and you own the club I play for. I'm pretty confident, but I don't think my ego could take being married to the boss. Even if it could, I'm not going to play forever. I told you I want to be a general manager when I retire. Normally you work your way up to g.m. You know how I'd feel, automatically replacing Mack because my wife happens to hand me the job? I can't handle that. Working for another club would be out. I would end up doing something completely different, and I'd resent you for being who you are, for standing in my way."

"And if I were somebody else?" Dani asked. "Or if I sold the club?"

"The fact is, you're *not* somebody else, and you can't sell for five years. The situation is impossible. I don't like it either, but it's a fact and I can't change it."

Dani tried to convince herself that it was a good thing they had had this talk now, before things went too far, but she couldn't be coolly logical like Ty was. She didn't want to stop seeing him.

"Dani." He said her name gently, as if he understood how disturbed she was. "You'd better go now. Will you find your way home okay?"

"Yes. I'll be fine." Dani got up and started walking to the door. She didn't look behind her.

Her depression quickly gave way to anger. Blast her father's bloody money! Why did it have to come between her and the first man she'd met whom she could really talk to? She hadn't trusted him completely, of course, but she felt that she might have . . . eventually.

Later, getting ready for bed, she acknowledged to herself that if it hadn't been for who she was, she never would have met Ty Morgan in the first place, and he never would have found her company so enjoyable.

She finally had absorbed what he had explained that afternoon. He had strong drives to dominate, to control any situation he was in. While she didn't doubt he could compromise, she understood that it was difficult for him. When he had perceived her as too powerful, every instinct had told him to cut her down to size.

Besides, as a professional athlete, he had to prove himself every time he walked out onto the field. He was accustomed to earning everything he got, a fact of life which suited both his needs and his personality. He wasn't the type of man who could live with gifts, or accept second place in a woman's life.

Given his feelings, an impasse was unavoidable. As for her own feelings, they were too new to be deep. The fact that Ty would now disappear from her life did not cause the horrible pain that had overcome her when her mother had died. She was far too cautious to allow herself to fall head over heels, which was just as well. She might have been tempted to press for an affair, but Ty was right: the happier he made her, the more badly hurt she would be when it ended.

She told herself again and again that she was lucky he was so sensible, so honorable, but somehow, lying awake until early the next morning, she simply couldn't quite accept the truth of that.

Chapter Eight

$\mathcal{T}$he dejection Dani felt over her stillborn romance with Ty precipitated a re-examination of just what she wanted out of her life. Her situation had changed irrevocably, but up until now she had refused to adapt to her new circumstances. But what was she supposed to do with herself? She was qualified to run a boutique or specialty store, but was not about to take orders from someone she could buy and sell ten times over. Her degree in Fine Arts seemed useless to her. She wanted the freedom to travel with the Condors, or fly to France to see her aunt, or drop everything to run off to a ball game at Clement Field. An eight to five position with a museum or auction house was out.

For the last two weeks, she had purposely avoided the office in downtown Los Angeles which had once been her father's and was now her own. The excuses she had given herself—her lack of experience in real estate development and management, the competence of her employees—were in fact rationalizations for her unwillingness to confront her change in status. Even her extravagant spending was a twisted type of denial. By acting as she had, she was pretending that she had no responsibility for the money, either in how it was earned or how it was spent.

All that was finally clear to her. It was more difficult to discover the reasons for her behavior. Was it a way of punishing her father for his short-comings as a parent, or for wishing her to move here? Was it fear of making decisions which might turn out to be mistakes? Or was it simply a defense mechanism against the upheaval in her life, a reasonable insistence on time to adjust?

Whatever the causes, she was ready to stop running away. At the very least, she would arrange a briefing on her late father's business interests. Once she had some information, there would be time to think about a future course of action.

On Thursday morning, she phoned Edward Reed to tell him that she wanted to meet with the people who managed what was now her money. He seemed pleased to hear from her, remarking that he hadn't wanted to push her, but reminding her of her father's expectations. As a rule, he said, people handled their own money more judiciously than someone else's. She should remember that thousands of people worked in the buildings managed by Korman Properties, and in a sense, they were her responsibility.

Dani took no offense at the lecture. She already looked upon Edward as part-mentor, part-father figure, and was pleased that he had so much confidence in her. He called back that afternoon, telling her that he had arranged a series of meetings for the following day.

Dani attempted the freeways with considerable trepidation, but arrived unscathed, parking her car in the garage beneath the Wilshire Boulevard building housing both Korman Properties and the Korman Foundation. Edward was waiting for her in the lobby.

"You just missed your aunt," he told her. "She must have called you a few minutes after you left. When you weren't home, she tried my office. She's coming to California in two weeks."

Given Dani's subdued mood, it was just the kind of good news she needed to hear. "I really miss her. I'm glad she's coming," she replied.

"Her timing is perfect. Things are moving on the Beverly Hills location—faster than I thought they would, much to my personal satisfaction."

"You'll have to plan your campaign, won't you?" Dani teased.

"That's exactly right, young lady. And now, let's talk about *your* business, which is why we're here. As you know," he said as they stepped into the elevator, "your father's money was invested in four areas—Galaxy Films, the Condors, commercial real estate, and securities. His forty percent interest in Galaxy Films is being sold back to the surviving partners, and I have some papers with me today for you to sign. When that's wrapped up, we'll be taking a look at what you owe in inheritance taxes, and figuring out how you want to pay it."

The elevator stopped; they stepped out into a carpeted corridor, the walls of which were papered in a taupe grass cloth. "I hear you and Mack Harmon are getting along fine—Teddy tells me you're even doing some negotiating around Clement Field these days." He winked at her. "Mitch Ellison is still in shock. He told Teddy he never should have left the room."

His comment gave Dani's ego a much-needed boost. What had happened with Ty, although the result of outside factors, made her feel less desirable as a woman. Success in business helped compensate for that.

They stopped in front of a set of double oak doors, the chrome lettering reading, "Korman Properties, Inc." and "The Korman Foundation." The reception area beyond was furnished in typical California contemporary: a jungle of plants climbed up the walls, and the furniture was all glass and wood and earthtones. Framed posters from George Korman's many films hung on the walls, announcing the late boss's primary occupation. Two doors opened off this central room, one leading to the offices of Korman Properties, the other to the Korman Foundation.

The pretty blonde receptionist rose, greeting them by name. Dani noticed that the girl sounded unsure of herself, perhaps a reaction to Dani's own appearance. Dressed in a black designer suit and dusky pink silk blouse, her hair pinned into a French knot, Dani looked very European, very formidable.

"They're waiting for you in the conference room, Miss Ronsard," the receptionist said. "We're all, uh, very happy you've come today."

"A polite lie if ever I heard one," Edward chuckled as soon as they were out of earshot. They were walking down the left-hand corridor now. "Your father was busy making movies, so he spent very little time here. One of my partners keeps an eye on things. The people here are capable, but they're not used to day-to-day supervision. You can bet they're less than thrilled to see you, but they won't give you any trouble."

Two men, both of them in their forties, were seated in the conference room. The first was the vice president of Korman Properties, Alex Panessa. The second was the controller, Doug Fong. They rose as soon as Dani walked in, and when Edward introduced her as "Miss Ronsard" she checked her usual invitation to informality. If she were ever going to exert any authority over these people, it was better to keep things formal at first.

The three-hour briefing continued through lunch, a superb Chinese meal served to them in the conference room on English bone china and French crystal. As she ate, Dani was once again reminded of her father's predilection for going first-class.

In a few hours, she could absorb no more than an overview of the business. The two men took each investment in turn, sometimes showing her blueprints, and listed construction costs, estimated present value, average income and operating expenses, tenants, and so on. While Korman Properties did not own one hundred percent of these projects, the other investors were silent partners who paid the company a management fee. Many of her employees, Dani learned, worked out of offices situated in the enterprises they supervised. Alex concluded his presentation with a summary of possible future investments.

Dani's afternoon meeting, which concerned the Korman Foundation, was scheduled for two o'clock. She and Edward spent the intervening half-hour in her office, which was located between the two suites and connected to both of them, just as the conference room did. Although beautifully decorated with a mixture of Victorian and more modern pieces, the room offered no evidence of George Korman's occupancy. Dani decided to personalize it by bringing in some of her favorite pictures and knickknacks.

"I feel like I'm back in school," she told Edward. "I think I should set aside a few mornings a week and study each project in turn. Maybe Alex Panessa could suggest some general reading on commercial development in this area."

Edward replied that the business pages of the daily paper would be a good place to start. "But don't feel you have to do everything at once. Give yourself six months to get a feel for things, Dani. It will take at least that long to get the estate straightened out."

Edward was still elaborating on this statement when a knock on the door reminded them of the time. Lewis Burnside, the executive director of the Korman Foundation, escorted them back across the hall to the conference room, where he began to explain the workings of the foundation to Dani.

The previous year, he said, they had given away three and a half million, but the amount would increase due to George Korman's additional twenty-million gift. Although there was a five-person board of directors, in practice they had done little more than rubber-stamp his own decisions. He handed Dani an annotated list of the previous year's grantees.

She studied it, unimpressed by the projects he had chosen to support. He favored established performing companies and artists with influential business or political recommendations. She would have preferred to set aside some money for the avant-garde and the experimental, selecting artists for what they did, not who they knew.

As they rode back down to the lobby, Dani asked Edward, "Is there any way for me to influence the foundation? I think I'd like to see it take a different direction."

"No problem," the attorney said with a shrug. "The board of directors hires the staff. They're all friends of your father, serving as a favor to him. He was the chairman and fifth member. I'll arrange a special meeting to elect you the new chairman, terminate Lew Burnside's contract, and take care of the necessary paperwork to enable you to become executive director. Awards are made in January and June, so it's a good time to make a change."

Dani was taken aback by Edward Reed's nonchalance in reeling off these steps. It was daunting to think that she had the power to change peoples' lives merely by uttering two brief sentences.

"I don't like the idea of firing anyone, but I don't agree with the way he does his job," she explained defensively.

"It's your father's money; why shouldn't you run the show? Lew's contract runs through July 30th, so we may have to buy up the remaining six months. Don't worry about him; with a little help from you, he'll land on his feet."

"You're going too fast," Dani said. "It would be better if he stayed through the end of his contract, Edward. He could help me break in. Do you think he'd be willing to do that, knowing I wanted to take over?"

"Dani, we're here to do anything you want, and that includes Lew Burnside. Just make your decisions and give us your instructions," Edward answered smoothly. "If you need any advice, my partners and I will meet with you any time you want. And now, if you can follow me back to my office, Teddy would like to take you to dinner."

An hour later, Dani was sitting in a homey Italian restaurant with Teddy Reed and telling him all about her plans. "I can't believe everything is falling into place so perfectly. I majored in Fine Arts in college, and I also took courses in drama and, of course, in filmmaking, because of Daddy. I felt so lost at first, almost resentful of the money he'd left me. I certainly don't want to dedicate my life to making even more of it, and that's why the foundation is so perfect. I feel like I'm making a real contribution, Teddy, and in an area I really care about. Of course," she added impishly, "negotiating baseball contracts is pretty interesting, too."

"You did fine with Ty," Teddy assured her. "Mack and Mitch would have squabbled for a week with pretty much the same result."

He went on to explain the details of the contract, then raised the subject of Jeanne Ronsard. His father, he said, was already clearing his schedule for Jeanne's visit. Dani could see that Teddy was curious about the woman who had made such a powerful impression. She told him that Jeanne had made a crusade of independence, and was sure to prove elusive.

She called her aunt that night, casually mentioning that Edward had been a very great help to her, and then adding teasingly, "He can't wait to see you. But he's no pushover, Aunt Jeanne. You'd better watch your step."

Jeanne ignored the baiting comment. "Now that you are settled, I will admit that I have been worried about you. As I told you, I felt it necessary for you to be on your own, but it was such a big change—to a new country and such great responsibilities. Still, we Ronsard women are intelligent and independent, and I had confidence in you. You have done very well, *ma chère.* I think perhaps I miss you more than you miss me."

"Never. I can't wait until you come."

"Will you meet me at the airport?" Jeanne asked.

"Edward will be with me," Dani answered with a giggle. "He would make a wonderful husband, Aunt Jeanne."

"Enough, Danielle. You are turning into a dreadful nag. I am going to say good-bye now."

"*Je t'aime. Au revoir,*" Dani replied.

Dani spent most of the next four days in her downtown office. On Sunday morning, while trying to make sense out of page after page of numbers from Korman Properties' annual report, she recalled her aunt's scolding, "You work too hard and play far too little." The fact was, she was more of a workaholic in Los Angeles than she had ever been in Paris.

She supposed that her initial motivation had been the desire to put Ty Morgan out of her mind, but other, more positive reasons had taken over. She genuinely enjoyed studying the early records of the foundation, reading the grant applications and periodic reports from grantees. Obscure artists supported by the foundation ten years ago were now well-known, if not by the general public, at least in the art world. Nothing could be more gratifying, she thought, than to nurture talented newcomers. Only during the last three years, under the tenure of Lewis Burnside, had the foundation taken such a conservative direction.

Dani talked to Lew on Monday, and found that he was eager to make the transition as smooth and easy as possible. She knew his attitude was the result of her potential influence: she would be giving away millions of dollars a year, and if she picked up the phone and called a theater company or university to say that Lewis Burnside was a pleasure to work with, it would mean a great deal. Nonetheless, she appreciated his cooperation.

As far as Korman Properties was concerned, California real estate was leaving Dani less than spellbound. She gained satisfaction from remedying her ignorance, but found it a struggle to keep her mind on the reports she was trying to read. Her plans for self-education seemed much too ambitious now, and only her sense of responsibility kept her turning the pages.

By Tuesday afternoon, she admitted defeat. What she needed, she realized, were verbal reports from the people who managed each of these projects. The figures might then have more meaning for her. She called in Alex Panessa to explain the problems she was having, and the two of them set up a briefing schedule. Over the next four to five weeks, each of her managers would come to the office to meet with her.

Late Wednesday morning, Dani's intercom buzzed. She was somewhat startled; her employees had the habit of knocking on her door when they wished to speak to her. Then she glanced at the flashing light on the phone, and realized she must have a call. It was the first one she had received here.

She picked up the line. "For me, Ellen?"

"Ty Morgan, Miss Ronsard."

Dani didn't know her palms could moisten so rapidly. She managed a husky "Thank you" and clicked down the button.

"Ty, how nice to hear from you!" She hoped that she sounded enthusiastic, not utterly besotted.

"How's everything going, Dani?"

He sounded very cool, very controlled. Dani was shaking with tension, wondering why he had called, but answered the question at length. Her response contained nothing personal, merely a detailed description of her progress in acquainting herself with Korman Properties and the Korman Foundation.

"You sound busy. Do you have time for lunch today?"

Had the sun risen that morning? "Yes, sure. Where and what time?"

"In an hour." Ty named a restaurant which he said was only a few blocks from her office, then added casually, "By the way, Dani, Mitch Ellison will be with me. It's strictly business—about the ski area."

Dani's instinctive reaction was to hide her disappointment with coolness, but then she thought, He's so big on honesty—why shouldn't I tell him how I feel? "I wish it weren't," she said softly.

There was a pause of several seconds. When Ty replied, his voice was just as matter-of-fact as before. "I'll see you at noon, Dani." He said good-bye and hung up.

Dani took the hint. Ty was telling her that nothing had changed, and she had no choice but to accept that. Besides, she had never chased a man in her life, and wasn't about to start now.

When she walked into the restaurant, Ty and Mitch were talking with the hostess. Or to be more accurate, Dani noted, Ty was talking, and the hostess was staring raptly into his eyes. The woman ceded possession only reluctantly.

Determined to be businesslike, Dani shook hands with both men, and once they were seated, immediately asked Ty why he had wanted to see her.

"Give me two minutes to look at the menu first," he said. Dani was sure he didn't mean to embarrass her, but that was the result of his comment. Her discomfort had made her rush things, whereas he seemed totally at ease. She picked up her own menu, holding it in front of her face long after she had decided on a chef's salad.

Once they had ordered, Ty explained that he had spent the previous weekend at Lake Tahoe, and had met with Carl Andersen, who owned the ski area he wanted to buy. At that point, Mitch Ellison pulled out a map of California and another of the ski area itself.

"As you can see, the property sits on the border," he said. "Eventually we might add a casino-hotel on the Nevada side, but only once your money is out of it, and only if Ty leaves organized baseball. The Commissioner's Office frowns on mixing baseball and gambling."

"Whatever you want to do is fine with me; I have lawyers to check the fine print," Dani replied.

She was wondering if this geography lesson were the sole reason for the meeting when Ty said, "I have a favor to ask, Dani. Andersen wants to meet you."

"Me? What on earth for?"

"The ski area is his baby. He developed it himself and he still runs it, even though he's in his late sixties. He says the winters are getting too hard on him now, so he's going to retire to Arizona. But first he wants to make sure his business will be in good hands. I told him you were only putting up the money, but he's something of a character—he wouldn't budge."

And you're not too happy about that, Dani thought. You don't want me up there. Aloud she said that she would be happy to let Carl Andersen inspect her, and asked about travel and hotel arrangements.

"If you can get away Friday morning, we can meet with Andersen in the afternoon. Jess and I are going up for the weekend on a private plane; I checked and there's room for you. You can stay with my parents and get in some skiing."

Dani glanced at Mitch. If the attorney hadn't been present, she might have questioned the wisdom of this arrangement. It was obvious to her that Ty's invitation stemmed solely from good manners; certainly he had no desire to sleep in the same house with her. But then, what problems could it create? His parents, his sister, and presumably his brother would be there, too. Nothing would happen.

So she politely accepted, and said she would look forward to meeting his parents. For the rest of the meal, conversation stayed impersonal. It was difficult for Dani to believe that the man sitting across from her had once kissed her so passionately, or shown frustration over ending their relationship. She tried to emulate his manner, but doubted she succeeded.

On Friday morning, Dani packed casual winter clothing and skiwear into a large suitcase and went outside to wait for Ty to pick her up. She was dressed quite formally, in heavy leather boots and a fur-trimmed suit which felt ungainly in the seventy-degree temperature. The ski equipment she carried seemed even more out of place.

They drove to John Wayne Airport in Jessica's Mercury. The plane was an eight-seat Learjet belonging to a wealthy California businessman who, Jess told her, wished to procure Ty's services as a corporate spokesman. Dani sat across the aisle from Jess, talking about college courses and boyfriends. Other friends of the absent host filled the rest of the seats.

They stepped off the plane into crisp, smogless air. Dani looked around at the snow-capped Sierra Nevada Mountains, which ringed the airport, and thought of the Alps. Although not so awesome, the Sierras were quite beautiful. She would enjoy skiing up here.

A tall, husky young man approached, kissed Jessica, and shook Ty's hand. "This is my little brother, Greg," Ty told Dani. "Greg, this is Miss Ronsard, Mr. Korman's daughter."

"Call me Dani." She smiled, thinking that "little" was a strange choice of adjectives for someone who was a good 6'5" tall and must weigh in the neighborhood of 225 pounds.

"Your *little* brother looks like he could flatten you with one well-aimed punch," she remarked.

"Let's just say that I wouldn't want to be an opposing quarterback," Ty answered with a smile.

They piled their luggage into Greg's car and set out toward the Lake, pulling into the Morgans' snow-packed driveway some twenty minutes later. Ty's parents were waiting in the doorway of the brown, two-story home. After an exchange of kisses, Ty introduced Dani to Jim and Connie Morgan, who seemed genuinely pleased to welcome her.

Jessica was detailed to show Dani to her room, which had once belonged to her older sister, Ellen. She explained that Ty and her father had built a two-story addition to the original house after her own birth, and assured Dani that her parents enjoyed having company. "Only Greg lives at home now, and they say they rattle around in all this space."

Ty and Dani were meeting with Carl Andersen at his house, which turned out to be a beautiful, chalet-style building that sat nestled into a hillside overlooking Lake Tahoe. By the time they left, Dani had decided that the man was an utter eccentric.

Business was never mentioned. He wanted to know about her childhood, and seemed especially interested in her job as the manager of her aunt's boutique. His parting shot was more of a barrage: ten full minutes of advice about the Condors.

"That man could rival my father," Dani said as they got back into the car. "He's certainly . . . unusual."

Ty grinned at her. His amusement was the first real emotion he had shown since the night they had had dinner, and Dani was grateful for the lowered barriers. It was difficult to talk to someone so relentlessly imperturbable.

"You don't know the half of it," he said. "I think he only agreed to sell to me because I'm a native of Lake Tahoe, and because I play for the Condors. You noticed he's a fan. We talked for three hours last weekend, and most of it had nothing to do with business."

"Don't tell me," Dani giggled, "that he was telling you how to pitch!"

"Close. Actually, it was how to bat!"

Ty's friendly mood carried over to dinner, when family news was exchanged. He told his parents about his new contract with the Condors, admitting with a quick wink at Dani that he wouldn't have taken less than eight million. Jim Morgan seemed to like the idea that his son's salary would be one of the highest in the game, whereas Connie cared only that Ty would be staying in California. Dani suspected that, as her oldest child, he was particularly special to her.

Connie told Ty and Jessica that their sister Ellen's two children were sick with flu, as was Ellen's husband. She had been helping out as much as she could. Christine, she went on, would be arriving the next day with her latest fiancé. The twenty-eight year-old skier had already broken two engagements, and her siblings wondered aloud just how long the latest flame would last. Jessica announced that she felt sorry for the man already.

Jim Morgan told Ty about the universities which had offered football scholarships to Greg. Two schools were still in the running, and father and son were aruging about which to accept. From the disapproving frown on Ty's face, it seemed that Jim Morgan was in for some straight talk from his oldest son about letting Greg make his own decisions.

Afterward, everyone gathered around the fireplace in the wood-paneled family room to continue talking. The three women sat in one group, the men in another. Dani was finding this visit with Ty's parents a revealing one. Jim Morgan was an old-fashioned patriarch, very much the head of the house. He was very ambitious for his children, and although sometimes such parents robbed their offspring of initiative, Jim seemed to have imbued them with the feeling that they could do anything they wanted to, and that the only failure was not to try.

Connie Morgan was gentle and steady, the type of woman who gave strength to her family and derived comfort and joy in return. Like her husband, she was a school teacher. Although soft-spoken, Dani could easily imagine her interceding on behalf of her children when her husband became overly tyrannical. Ty was an interesting blend of the two—sensitive, supremely confident, and perceptive; Dani had also experienced his arrogance, egotism, and sardonic humor. He was quite right to look for a self-sufficient, self-assured wife, because anyone else would be smothered by his success and the force of his personality. He was also right to doubt that such an independent woman would put up with his dominating instincts, and to recognize the necessity for compromise.

Jessica shook her awake the next morning, telling her that breakfast would be on the table in twenty minutes. Stifling a yawn, Dani pulled on a robe and staggered next door to the bathroom which she shared with Jessica. Just as she was closing the door, she caught sight of Ty, heading toward the staircase, dressed in navy ski pants with a gold stripe down each leg, and a gold turtleneck shirt. If those clothes meant what she thought they meant, she would have a few choice words to say to him about a certain clause in his contract.

Somehow she managed to shower, dress, and pin up her hair in the required amount of time. Jessica had just placed a platter of bacon and eggs on the table when Dani walked into the dining room. She was wearing yellow ski overalls and a white turtleneck.

She sat down next to Ty. "Those look like ski clothes," she observed blandly.

"Yup."

"You going skiing with us this morning?"

"You got it."

"But you aren't allowed to do that," she reminded him in an even tone of voice. His family shot her a collectively puzzled look. "It's in his contract," she explained. "No skiing, no motorcycles, no sky diving . . ."

". . . no making love because I might fall out of bed or injure my back," Ty finished acidly. "Look Dani, just for this weekend, could you forget you're my boss?"

Dani clamped her mouth shut. In the first place, Ty looked really annoyed with her, and in the second, he was a grown man, and could decide on his own what risks he wanted to take. He knew the contract would be void if he injured himself.

She tried to put the matter out of her mind as they put on her boots and skis almost an hour later. They had come to Carl Andersen's ski area, which was of moderate size and featured a good selection of trails calling for differing degrees of skill. When they reached the lift area, Ty and Greg headed for the most difficult run. Dani felt a dull queasiness in the pit of her stomach. Why did he have to risk his career this way?

As Jessica had mentioned, she was the non-athlete of the Morgan clan. They skied all morning, choosing runs of low to average difficulty. After a light lunch at the lodge restaurant, they set out for the slopes again. Jessica suggested that Dani might like to go off on her own, but Dani assured her that she was happy to relax and enjoy the unseasonably warm weather. Both women had shed their parkas, and wore only overalls and turtlenecks.

In the middle of the afternoon, Jessica spotted two friends from high school on the lift line, and by four o'clock all four women were sitting in the restaurant, drinking hot chocolate and reminiscing about old times. Half an hour later Ty and Greg clomped in. Dani was relieved to see the pitcher all in one piece, and perhaps it showed on her face.

Ty fixed her with a moody frown as soon as their eyes met. "You want to examine me, boss?" he taunted. "Make sure there are no broken bones?" He held out his left arm, and swung it back and forth in a wide arc. "See? It still works!"

Stung by the unwarranted attack, Dani snapped back, "I didn't say a word. It's *your* career!"

Ty gave a low grunt. "Yeah, you're right. Sorry." Dani had no idea why her show of concern had goaded him into such an uncharacteristic loss of control, but mercifully, it didn't happen again. When they got back to the house, they found that Christine Morgan and her fiancé, Rich McCurry, had arrived, and were talking with Ty's parents in the living room. The rest of the family joined in the conversation.

After half an hour in the same room with Christine, Dani decided that she was a female version of her older brother, as her Olympic medals indicated. Rich seemed very sweet, but much too unassertive for her. As the group was leaving to go out for dinner, Jessica caught Dani's eye, started to giggle, and clapped a hand over her mouth.

Their meal was sporadically interrupted by autograph seekers, who held out their pieces of paper not just to Ty, but to Christine as well. Ty was once again friendly, even warm, and seemed eager to hear Dani's impressions of the ski area. Among other things, she praised the efficiency and helpfulness of the staff, and criticized the T-bar tow at the beginners' area.

After dinner, Rich, Ty, and Jim Morgan headed for the blackjack tables at one of the casinos, while the underage Greg and the four women took in a show. The men, having donated a substantial sum of money to the pockets of the hotel owner, rejoined them toward the end of the performance.

Although Dani was never alone with Ty, she felt his physical impact whenever he was in the same room with her. There was no indication that Ty felt the same way, no sign that he was struggling to keep his distance. He was such an expert at controlling his emotions that perhaps he had simply banished her from his consciousness.

Back at the house, he walked her to her bedroom door, saying that Jessica would be with friends the next day, and Greg had to study. "I hear you were bored today. My sister and her boyfriend are skiing tomorrow, and I'm going along. Want to come with us?"

"I'd love to." Dani smiled up at him, trying to disregard the warmth that was spreading through her body, making her slightly breathless.

"Good. Can you manage an early start—say eight o'clock?"

"You're a glutton for punishment, but I'll try," Dani promised.

"I'll send Chris in after you if you're not ready. G'night, Dani." He turned back toward the steps, leaving Dani with the unproductive thought that she would have preferred Ty himself to roust her if she overslept.

After a day of vigorous exercise, she fell asleep almost immediately and woke early. The sun had not yet risen above the mountain peaks, but even if it had, low, gray clouds would have hidden it from view. There was no trace of blue sky this morning.

Chris and Rich, who planned to spend part of the afternoon with Ellen and her husband, had left in a separate car. They were already on the chair lift by the time Ty and Dani skied into place. Very few people were out on the slopes this morning, perhaps because of the threatening weather and the early hour, and there was no line at all.

At the top of the run, which was one of the most

difficult, Dani paused to admire the view. The trail was heavily shaded, but she could make out the valley through the trees, and could see the peaks of the Sierras disappearing into the clouds above. Rich and Chris were below, the latter skiing at a breakneck pace, but no one was behind them.

Only the moguls made Dani uneasy, but her concern was for Ty, not herself. She wasn't about to irritate him with her fears, and merely observed that it looked rather challenging.

He frowned. Dani knew what that moody expression meant: he had seen straight through her remark, and he hadn't much cared for it. But all he said was, "I'll go first. The snow ices up overnight, so be careful. Wait a minute, then follow me down."

Dani adjusted her goggles and nodded. Ty pushed off, making tight, graceful turns, skiing the moguls with professional skill. He really was good, Dani thought, attempting to follow in his wake. Now she understood why he refused to give up skiing. Not only did it keep him in shape, he obviously loved the sport.

He was flying over a particularly bumpy section now, skiing faster than Dani would have dared. Suddenly she realized that he looked slightly awkward, out-of-control. And yet when he began to fall, it was as though the accident was happening in slow motion. One leg skittered out at a crazy angle, and then all his limbs sprawled wildly. He wound up face down in the snow, well away from the center of the trail. His skis, automatically releasing from his boots, continued on a bit before their brakes caught in the snow.

Panic-stricken, Dani snowplowed to a stop right next to him. She hurriedly removed her skis, stuck them in the snow, and kneeled down beside him. Her heart was racing so erratically that she felt like it was pounding in her throat. No one seemed to be around.

"Ty," she whispered. "Are you all right?"

His only answer was a low moan. Thank goodness he wasn't unconscious. She felt so helpless, all alone up here. "Can you get up?" she asked, placing a gentle hand on his back.

He started to turn, uttered a thick curse. "Help me," he groaned.

Dani put both hands against his right shoulder and applied steady pressure, pushing him onto his back. His features were distorted with pain. "My arm . . ." he muttered.

Dani was numb with horror. His left arm—he hadn't moved it—it looked utterly lifeless. "Oh, Ty!" she murmured miserably, raising her goggles to the top of her head. She slipped off one of her ski mittens and removed his goggles, then brushed the snow away from his neck and face. "I'll . . . I'll get some help. Will you be . . ."

The question was interrupted by a resounding gust of laughter so unrestrained that at first Dani simply stared at him. Were such sounds really coming from the ever-so-controlled Ty Morgan? Within moments her temper began to simmer, heating up until it boiled over with fury.

"You dumb jock!" she raged. "You must be the stupidest man who ever lived! Do you realize what could have happened, taking a spill like that? And just to play an idiotic, juvenile, *stupid* joke on me?"

He couldn't seem to stop laughing. He lay sprawled on his back, hysterical, tears running down his cheeks. Dani was so livid that she took a fistful of snow into her bare hand and rubbed it right into his face. Then she yanked her mitten back on and started to get up.

"You little wretch!" Ty jackknifed up and abruptly shoved her down onto her back, grabbing a handful of snow at the same time. "You're going to pay for that!"

Dani put her hands in front of her face, "No, Ty, don't . . ." she said, beginning to giggle in spite of her anger. Her wrists were seized in an unrelenting grip, the snow sliding harmlessly to the ground. Although she tried to squirm away, Ty easily pinned her hands above her head, rendering them impotent with one of his own, and stared gleefully down at her. He very deliberately picked up some more snow. "Guess where this is going?" he taunted.

Dani closed her eyes and turned her head, resigned to her punishment. Icy snow teased her cheek, her chin, her lips. She tried to free her hands but Ty wouldn't permit it. When the snow came into contact with her neck, she wailed miserably, "Stop torturing me! You're horrible."

He obligingly tossed the snowball aside and released her hands. Dani opened her eyes and shot him a baleful look, only to find him staring at her with unmistakable intensity. Aroused by his scrutiny, she reached out a hand and slid it up his arm to his shoulder.

Ty eased out of his crouched position and stretched out half on top of her. Neither of them was aware of the icy snow underneath. For a few moments he played with her hair, which she had left loosely hanging out of the bottom of her ski hat. His leather-gloved hand was clumsy against her skin, but played havoc with her respiration in spite of it.

Then he lowered his mouth to kiss her—a kiss that

fulfilled the promise of his hungry stare. His tongue explored the softness of her mouth, wandering at will, seeking a passionate response by means of its leisurely yet dominating movements.

Dani slid her arms around his neck and kissed him back, her tongue rubbing seductively against his, tasting his mouth. Exquisitely hot sensations rippled through her body, and yet mentally she maintained a certain wariness. This was the man who had told her their relationship was going nowhere, and her brain couldn't respond to him as quickly as her body.

Ty broke the kiss and raised his head. Dani opened her eyes, then thought in confusion, Why does he look so angry?

She had no time to search for answers. Ty mounted a merciless assault on her resistance, nibbling his way from her temple to her neck, arousing her with the slight pain he inflicted. When he began to toy with her lips, the teasing, stroking movements so frustrated her that she reached behind his head, seeking to force him into a closer embrace.

He complied, his mouth rougher now, and shifted his body to lie fully atop her own. Although their hip-length parkas separated them to some extent on top, their ski pants were a much lighter barrier. The seductive movements of Ty's body sought complete submission from her, and Dani realized that he wasn't simply making love to her—he was waging psychological warfare. Had the two of them been naked together in bed, she would long ago have surrendered to his unspoken demand to let go completely. But the layers of clothing between them enabled her to keep some emotional distance from him.

Ty raised his head again. "Okay," he muttered, "we'll try it one more time."

He resumed his teasing, making her crave the sharpness of his teeth, and then the softness of his lips. He used his mouth like a weapon, endlessly tantalizing but never satisfying. His tongue repeatedly probed her mouth, always withdrawing when he felt her respond. The more he toyed with her, the more aroused she became, until she was conscious of nothing but his mouth and body, and of the hot longing which seemed to pervade every inch of her. Inevitably, she stopped fighting and gave in to the need to melt invitingly, to offer whatever he wanted to take. She shivered, then relaxed completely, her eyes closed and lips softly parted.

Ty sensed his victory immediately, taking her mouth with utter confidence. His kiss, although just as passionate as before, had a gentleness not previously present. Dani, oblivious to the cold and the wetness of the snow, wanted it to go on forever. She had never felt like this, not even with Paul, and had never imagined that a man's sexual domination could be so wildly pleasurable.

They were interrupted by a slowly fading chorus of whistles, hoots, and cheers. Dani stiffened; Ty rolled off her and sat up. "We'd better finish the run; I'll help you get your skis back on," he said calmly.

Dani couldn't believe the coolness in his voice. Where was the determined, insistent lover of only seconds ago? Wasn't he going to say anything about what had just happened? "But Ty . . ." she protested.

"Later," he said firmly. "Both of us are soaked."

The run was a difficult one for Dani; she had to concentrate on skiing the bumpy, icy terrain and forget about Ty's demanding lovemaking. He said nothing as they made their way into the lodge, and it was impossible to judge his mood. While Dani was annoyed about his dangerous prank and embarrassed by her own wanton response, Ty seemed neither disturbed, nor amused, nor guilt-ridden.

Only when they were seated at a table for two in a quiet corner of the restaurant, sipping their coffee, did he break the silence. "I'm sorry about what happened up there. It was entirely my fault."

Dani stared into her half-empty cup, saying nothing. Was she supposed to tell him to forget it? Maybe he could, but she couldn't, not when he had demolished her defenses that way. Where was his blasted sense of honor, up on that mountain top?

"Just for the record, Dani, it got to me when you kept harping that I would damage the merchandise. It made me feel like a left arm, not a human being."

Ty had misinterpreted her motives so completely that Dani was stung into a heated retort. "That's not fair! I didn't *harp*, and I wasn't worried about you because I own the team. I just know what it would mean to you if your career was ended prematurely. I happen to *care* about you!" She paused, startled by her own vehemence, then muttered, "Anyway, it was a stupid thing to do, just to get back at me."

She picked up her cup and sipped, watching a puzzled look take over his face. "You know, I don't think I wanted to see that," he told her.

"See what?"

"That you care about me, that what you feel isn't just physical. It's pretty obvious, so why did I tell myself that you were worried about your investment? Now I feel guilty about scaring you."

Dani was so exasperated that she felt like throwing her empty cup at him. "You're impossible!" she exclaimed. "Never mind scaring me—what about the risk you took? Suppose something had happened?"

He seemed amused by her outburst. "I was never out of control, even though I made it look that way. I purposely landed way over to the side so no one would crash into us."

"Clever, weren't you?" Dani asked acidly.

"Not very. I should have known we would wind up in a scuffle, and what that would do to me, and that I wouldn't be able to keep my hands off you. Hell, it's probably half the reason I set this up. What I didn't expect was my reaction when you held back. It's happened with other women and I didn't give a damn. But with you, it was all-out war. I would have kept at you all morning if I'd needed to."

His tone was bemusedly analytical. Under other circumstances Dani would have been blushing to the tips of her ears by now, but Ty had a way of burying his emotions so deeply that he might have been talking about two strangers. Instead of being embarrassed, she found herself pondering his motivations.

"Maybe it's because you still resent the authority I have over you." She caught his skeptical look, and quick shake of the head. "Just listen a minute, Ty," she insisted. "Last Tuesday, you purposely maneuvered things so that *I* ended up negotiating with you, and giving in to your demands. And that was after you talked about your feelings and supposedly had worked them through. I don't think you like having a woman boss. It threatens your masculinity."

She was irked when Ty burst out laughing. "I've been accused of a lot of things, but never of being insecure about my masculinity."

"But look how you behaved," Dani pointed out. "You needed to—to conquer me, to use your metaphor. You wanted to be in control."

"Sure. I've admitted I have strong drives in that

direction. I never met a star athlete who didn't. But it has nothing to do with your being a woman."

"Did you act that way with my father?" Dani asked.

"Push him down in the snow and make love to him?" There was a definite twinkle in Ty's eyes. "No way. I wouldn't have enjoyed it. But maybe there's something to what you say. If I promise to think about it, will you forgive me?"

Dani found herself murmuring the words she had earlier withheld. "Of course. Forget it."

She cursed herself for being a coward. She was sitting there, aching to bring up the subject of their relationship, yet too afraid of rejection to do so. But then, what was the use? If Ty's feelings had changed, he would have said so. Nothing was different.

"I won't forget it," he answered. "I'll just make sure it doesn't happen again. Let's go home, Dani. I'm beginning to feel pretty clammy."

Or perhaps you just don't want to be alone with me, Dani thought as they walked back to the car.

She spent the rest of the day with Jessica and her friend Susan, shoping for après-ski wear. She found Jess to be delightful company—good-tempered, irreverent, and sophisticated beyond her years. She would pursue the friendship when both of them were back in southern California.

As they said good-bye to the Morgans, Connie invited Dani to visit again soon. But she knew that if she did so, it would be as Jessica's guest, not Ty's. There was an understanding between them, no less clear because it was unspoken. The attraction between them was too strong to stay buried under a platonic relationship. Ty would avoid her in the future.

She sensed his withdrawal on the airplane. "I called Andersen while you were out with Jess," he told her, "and meeting you reassured him. I'll make him an offer, and I suppose he'll come back with a counter-offer within a week or so. When we come to terms, I'll give you a call. We'll set up a meeting to work out the financing."

His tone was all business—crisp and to the point. He seemed to be looking through her, not at her, and Dani was relieved to turn her attention back to Jessica. Later that night, she thought to herself that their meetings were becoming increasingly less intimate. She could picture the next one clearly: a stilted, formal affair, perhaps held in her downtown office, complete with Edward Reed, Mitch Ellison, and a cast of thousands. She was not looking forward to it.

Chapter Nine

By midnight Dani gave up trying to sleep and went out into the living room, where she stood at the window, looking out over the moonlit ocean, depressed almost to tears. Why couldn't she have chosen someone like Teddy Reed to get involved with? She had been in California less than a month, and it felt like a lifetime. Would she ever feel settled and happy in this place?

By early morning, however, her natural spirit had reasserted itself, urging her to stop thinking about Ty Morgan—cursing him for his stubborn, dominating nature, missing his company, re-experiencing his passionate, devastating kisses. A Ronsard didn't let a man twist her inside out this way; she kept herself busy however she could and forced him out of her mind.

She returned to bed, repeating that message to herself, and finally fell into a heavy sleep. When she woke up late that morning, she wasted no time before throwing herself into work, driving to her office where she sorted through the foundation files for the most interesting project folders she could find; several concerned experimental filmmakers, a few were on conceptual artists, and the last (and most fascinating) contained reports from a southern

185

California artist specializing in constructing giant works of art visible from the air.

Every time Dani's attention flickered, she coaxed it back to the papers on her desk. And when her concentration ultimately rebelled, she reminded herself that Jeanne would be coming on Thursday. Her aunt would cheer her up.

Just before she left the office, Mack Harmon called to ask that she come over to Clement Field Wednesday morning. She had important decisions to approve, he said, including the award of the contract on broadcast rights. If it was convenient, club executives would brief her on various aspects of franchise operations at that time.

Dani wrote it down on her calendar. She had Tuesday and Thursday morning meetings with people from Korman Properties, and now the Wednesday meeting with Mack. Edward would be driving her to the airport Thursday afternoon to pick up Jeanne. A full schedule had never been so welcome.

Dani arrived at Clement Field on Wednesday to find half a dozen men waiting in the V.I.P. lounge with Mack Harmon and Teddy Reed. Her executives for player personnel, scouting, minor league teams, and public relations offered concise summaries of their activities, as did manager Marv Richardson. The business Mack had spoken of took less than half an hour; Dani simply accepted his recommendations and signed the appropriate papers.

The last item on the agenda was spring training, which would open in about two weeks, on February 21st. The Condors' camp was located near Tarpon Springs, on Florida's Gulf Coast. After checking her schedule, Dani decided to join the club in early

March, and instructed the team's traveling secretary to book her a suite at the hotel. The players, Mack told her, would spend the first three weeks on general conditioning: getting back in shape, sharpening old skills, working on weaknesses. The "Grapefruit League" exhibition season followed, and the results were often disappointing.

"The players know it doesn't count," Mack explained. "They play like pros, but something's missing—the spark, the hustle. Marv doesn't waste his time pushing. He knows they'll do the job on opening day."

After the meeting, Teddy and Dani walked out to the parking lot together, talking about Jeanne's upcoming visit. Edward was hosting a dinner party for her on Saturday, and taking her to the theater Monday night. "If you're not careful," Teddy said, "he's going to monopolize all your aunt's time."

"I'd love it if she married him and moved to Los Angeles. But Jeanne doesn't believe in marriage or even in commitments. He has his work cut out for him."

"My money's on my father," Teddy insisted. "He doesn't win cases by being shy and retiring. When he wants something, he goes after it. Jeanne doesn't stand a chance."

Dani said that she hoped Teddy was right. Both Edward and Jeanne were unusually strong-willed types, and their conflicting desires were bound to cause fireworks.

The Thursday morning meeting went well, as had the Tuesday session, confirming Dani's feeling that talking to her employees would teach her more than reading pieces of paper. She was finding California real estate somewhat more palatable, and would certainly continue to educate herself. Given the fact that her time was limited, however, she doubted that she would ever play more than a peripheral role here. Her real interest was in the Korman Foundation, and to a lesser extent, the Condors.

She and Edward left for the airport in a driving rain. Since they would be going directly back to Newport Beach, Dani had taken a taxi to work, an extravagance that once might have appalled her. She told herself that hiring a cab was far less expensive than maintaining a full-time chauffeur, as her father had done.

The stormy weather caused the inevitable traffic accidents, which in turn caused tie-ups that left the Los Angeles freeways looking like parking lots. As a result, Jeanne was already off the plane and through Customs by the time they finally arrived.

The moment Dani spotted her, she broke away from Edward's side and ran straight into her aunt's arms. Jeanne was delivering the latest family news in her staccato French by the time the attorney caught up with them. "Let's get you back to Dani's house," he said. "You two have all day tomorrow to catch up; I didn't schedule anything until Saturday."

It was past midnight Paris time when they reached Newport Beach, but Jeanne assured Dani that she had slept on the plane, and was too keyed-up to go to bed. Dani was soon describing everything that had happened during her first month in California, her voice becoming low and hoarse as she told Jeanne about her feelings for Ty.

"I can't accept the situation, Aunt Jeanne, even though I try. It's wrong to complain when I have so much, but I really care about him. I just wish we had a chance to find out . . ."

Jeanne put her arm around Dani's shoulder and hugged her. *"Pauvre petite,"* she murmured. "You were never like this with Paul—so vulnerable. The same as your mama, you fall in love"—she snapped her fingers—"like that."

Dani immediately corrected her. "I didn't say I loved him. I hardly know him. It's just . . . I can really talk to him. And then there's the physical part of it. But you're right about Paul. I'm falling a lot harder a lot faster with Ty. I'm more off-balance with him than with any man I've ever met."

"Ty has many pressures on him, and if he is afraid to commit himself . . ."

"It's not like that," Dani interrupted. "If you got to know Ty, you would see that he's not the kind of person who runs away from commitments. He just has a strong need to be in charge, and to earn what he gets, and the idea of working for me . . ."

"Nonsense!" Jeanne waved her hand dismissively. "If he is married to you, people will assume that he is the boss. After all, *ma chère,* he is the professional in this field, not you. They will expect him to take over."

"Maybe that's true, but if it is, Ty will have to figure it out on his own. If there's one thing I've learned about him, it's that he hates to be pushed. I told you how angry he got over that whole skiing business."

"But look at the result," Jeanne teased. "Perhaps you should make him angry more often."

Dani shook her head. "No, I won't play those games with him. He doesn't like them. And speaking of commitments . . ." She let the rest of the sentence hang, staring pointedly at Jeanne.

In the past, Dani had always avoided the subject

of her aunt's social life, but tonight she felt more like Jeanne's equal, and less like her *petite nièce*. Part of the change was due to Ty, but most of it was the result of being on her own.

Jeanne merely smiled knowingly. "You fall in love and suddenly you are an expert. My life suits me very well, Danielle. I have no need for an overbearing male in it."

"But don't you ever get lonely, Aunt Jeanne?" Dani asked.

"Not often enough to suit the convenience of a husband, Danielle. When a man is your lover, he admires your independence and success. Marry him, and the same man is suddenly annoyed by these qualities and jealous of the business that keeps you working nights and flying all over the world. His possessiveness makes him seek to change the very things that first attracted him."

Only on the subject of men did Jeanne Ronsard indulge in such sweeping generalizations. "There must be exceptions," Dani objected.

"Perhaps among men of your age, *ma chère,* but men of my age are quite impossible." Jeanne yawned, obviously an excuse to end a disagreeable conversation. Dani took the hint and showed her to her bedroom.

Friday afternoon, she drove Jeanne over to Clement Field to show her the ball park and introduce her to the Condors' front office staff. Later they went for a ride past Disneyland and other Orange County tourist attractions, returning after lunch so Jeanne could recuperate from jet lag.

Saturday was reserved for business. Edward Reed called at nine, and although Jeanne pointed out to him that she could easily inspect the store near Rodeo Drive on her own, he was determined to accompany her. Dani dropped Jeanne off at his office, declining her invitation to join them. Edward Reed, she thought with amusement, would never forgive her.

She spent the day in her own office, working on foundation business. She had assigned one of the foundation's two part-time administrative assistants the task of putting together a report on promising new artists, and was now looking through some preliminary information. It had occurred to her that if she traveled with the Condors, she would have a perfect opportunity to visit galleries and colleges in cities all over the country. She was excited by the idea of reaching out to groups and individual artists who would never think of competing for foundation funding without her encouragement. It was an enchanting fantasy—to imagine herself the discoverer of some future Rodin or Cézanne.

Edward's dinner party for her aunt was at his Hancock Park residence. When Dani arrived, she found her aunt and the attorney sitting by the pool, drinking wine, eating cheese, and chatting like the oldest of friends.

"Your aunt's in the middle of her life story," Edward remarked. "You've just come back from college in Boston."

Dani hoped that her smiling nod had covered up the astonishment she felt. How on earth had Edward Reed persuaded her close-mouthed aunt to discuss anything more personal than that day's smog level? It was true that they had spent the last six hours together, but Jeanne Ronsard had known people for years without offering the slightest confidences.

Eventually, Jeanne switched the subject to business, telling Dani that she had liked the store and the general area, and would sign a lease on Monday. The space became vacant on April 1st, so next week she planned to meet with local designers and architects in order to choose people to help her renovate and refurbish for a late spring opening.

Teddy joined them at about six o'clock, and the moment he was settled with his scotch on the rocks, Dani stood up and held out her hand. "Show me through the house," she said.

Teddy was apparently puzzled by her abrupt request, but he took her hand and led her inside. "I wanted to get you alone," Dani admitted to him. "My aunt *never* discusses anything personal except with the family, but when I walked in, she was telling him the story of her life. How does he do it?"

"I told you she wouldn't stand a chance." Teddy was smiling at her. "Dad knows how to draw people out. Clients lie to their attorneys all the time, but not to him." He led her up the stairs and pointed to the brass headboard in the master bedroom. "What do you want to bet that inside of one month, your aunt is sharing that bed, and redecorating the entire house?"

"But she's *never* impulsive! Even when she gets involved with someone, she takes forever to . . ." Dani cut herself off in mid-sentence.

"My father wants more than that," Teddy drawled, putting a friendly arm around her shoulders. "I saw the way he was looking at her. He may seem relaxed, but don't you believe it. He's nuts about her. I said a month. If I'm wrong, I owe you a dinner."

"And vice versa," Dani said, laughing. "What is it about California that embroils me in all these bets?"

"You're a natural. You grew up in Nevada, didn't you?" Teddy teased.

The doorbell rang just as they were coming back downstairs, prompting Dani to ask who else would be coming tonight.

"Most of the people are old friends of Dad's, people he wanted Jeanne to meet," Teddy told her. "He also invited some of your employees."

"From Korman Properties, you mean?"

"That's right. And also from the foundation and the team. Your old friend Morgan is coming. Just warn your aunt not to ask him why a curve ball curves. He's been known to go on for twenty minutes about it."

"Why *does* a curve ball—"

"Nobody really knows," Teddy interrupted with a grin. "Not even him."

Dani was torn between pleasure and nervousness. She wanted to see Ty again, but doubted her ability to make casual conversation with him given the events of just one week ago. When he walked in with Mike and Diana, she was engrossed in a conversation with some of Edward's friends. At one point their eyes met and Dani smiled uncertainly. Ty merely nodded in response, his expression more blank than cool.

She was talking with Mack Harmon when a disagreeably familiar voice reached her ears. "I hope you don't mind my crashing your party, Edward darling. When Ty mentioned it, I just had to drop by and see how my little stepdaughter was doing."

The stepdaughter you could happily have strangled on more than one occasion, Dani thought furiously. She craned her neck, looking around several bodies, and spotted Ty, Mike, Diana, and Viveca standing next to Edward and Jeanne. Viveca had taken possession of Ty's arm and was clutching it so greedily that Dani longed to march over and tell her that she was going to destroy his circulation.

She took a moment to compare the two actresses. Diana was wearing a black and rust knit dress with a matching sweater coat, and looked elegant and beautiful. Viveca's purple wrap dress, on the other hand, had apparently been chosen for the provocative amount of rounded flesh it exposed. Whether in person or on the screen, Diana had a charismatic star quality that Viveca couldn't begin to compete with.

Pasting a smile on her resistant mouth, Dani made her way to the door. When she reached Viveca, she greeted her with a Hollywood kiss—cheeks almost touching, lips pecking at the air. "How nice of you to think of me," she said, all but choking on the words. She proceeded to greet the other three, then asked Viveca ingenuously, "Did Ty tell you that I was up at Tahoe with him last weekend?"

For a moment, Ty allowed his annoyance to show, but he immediately recovered. "You and Jessica really hit it off, didn't you?" he asked, very neatly implying that her visit was at his sister's invitation. "Been working hard this week?"

"As a matter of fact, I have." Ty was looking straight through her again, his expression almost goading her into remarking that he'd been much more attentive on the ski slopes. Instead she complimented Diana on her dress.

"I was just admiring yours; it fits so beautifully. Did you buy it here in Los Angeles?"

Dani's crewneck cashmere dress was baby blue with buttons from neck to hem. "Jeanne designed it," she said. Diana immediately tried to charm

Jeanne into designing some gowns for her new Vegas act.

Edward's cook had prepared a lavish Mexican buffet for dinner. People served themselves from casserole dishes set out on the dining room table, carrying their plates and drinks back into the living room or family room. Dani was seated with the Reeds, her aunt, and some close friends of Edward's. Viveca and Ty were across the room, sitting with Mike, Diana, and two other couples from the team. Perhaps influenced by the margaritas she was drinking, Dani joined them for dessert.

All through dinner, she had surreptitiously watched Ty laughing and talking. As soon as she pulled over a chair, he seemed to switch off. He didn't precisely ignore her, but the occasional comments he directed her way were delivered in an impersonal tone of voice. He was far warmer to Viveca Swensen.

Dani took some satisfaction in the knowledge that Viveca was totally outclassed by Diana, but it didn't compensate for the jealousy she felt when she looked at Ty and Viveca, sitting side by side. As the evening wore on, she became increasingly subdued, barely listening to those around her. Even if Ty weren't serious about Viveca, it hurt to see them together, and to admit that the two were probably lovers again. She knew the actress appealed to him.

Eventually she slipped outside, escaping the noise and smoke of the party, but not her own somber thoughts. She observed Viveca's approach with a sigh of resignation.

"You've done very well for yourself, Deedee," Viveca said with a venomous smile. "I've been hearing about you all night long."

Dani refused to be drawn into an argument. "I could say the same about you," she lied. "I hear you're wonderful in your new film."

Viveca loved to talk about herself. For the next five minutes Dani pretended to listen while Viveca described the brilliance of her performance, and the certainty of an Oscar nomination.

"Now that George is gone, my career comes first," she breathed in her best dedicated actress tone. When had it ever occupied any other position? Dani asked herself. "That's why Ty and I are so perfectly suited. We understand each other. Our relationship is so . . . satisfying."

Dani dearly wanted to ruin that saccharine smile of hers by knocking out a few of the other woman's flawlessly capped teeth. "I'm sure it is," she agreed. If Ty Morgan was stupid enough to sleep with a viper like Viveca, he deserved to get bitten.

The actress, content that she had made her point, slithered back inside. Dani took a few minutes to control her anger, then rejoined Edward and Jeanne. She tried to tell herself that if Viveca were really secure about Ty, she wouldn't need to issue warnings, but she still felt a numbing pain when she saw the two of them leave together.

Jeanne, perhaps sensitive to her feelings, announced with a yawn that she was tired, and wished to go home. Edward walked outside with them, waiting next to Jeanne while Dani went for the car. If her own evening had been something of a disaster, the same was obviously not true of Jeanne's. Dani's headlights interrupted a fervent embrace between her aunt and Edward Reed.

"He is very insistent," Jeanne murmured after Edward walked away from the car.

"You didn't seem to mind," Dani said.

"For the first time in years, I am tempted to do something foolish," Jeanne admitted. "But enough of me. Your Ty is very charming. And not nearly so controlled as you think, *ma chère.*"

Dani reminded her aunt that Ty belonged to no one, least of all her—except in a business sense. Then, unable to help herself, she asked, "What do you mean, not controlled? He was as cold as a slab of marble all night long."

"I saw the way he looked at you when you were not aware of it. It is true that his eyes were cold, but if that is so, why did they return to you over and over again?"

Jeanne's teasing tone failed to improve Dani's mood. "I know he's attracted to me. But he doesn't want to be, and he's determined not to do anything about it."

"And you?"

"I told you, I'm not going to provoke him. It wouldn't change anything, and he would only end up angry at me for trying to manipulate him."

"So you will leave him to that creature Viveca?" No language but French, Dani thought, could quite convey such outraged disgust.

"He's a grown man," she snapped back. "If he's upid enough to be taken in by that . . . that female, he deserves her!"

Jeanne merely smiled and shrugged, changing the subject to their plans for the following day. The rest of her stay would be so busy that she wanted them to spend at least one full day together, relaxing, talking, perhaps sight-seeing. In fact, the two women never left the house on Sunday. In the morning, they brought two lounge chairs out onto the redwood deck in back of the house, along with light blankets to protect them from the sea breeze. After the cold of Paris, Jeanne welcomed the winter sunshine and the ocean view. She entertained Dani with gossip about difficult customers, details of a buying trip to London, and news of the latest family crises.

By the next morning, Jeanne was eager to get back to work. She asked Dani to spend a few hours window-shopping with her in the stores and boutiques on exclusive Rodeo Drive, looking at the merchandise they carried, and studying their marketing techniques.

As they visited store after store, Dani became increasingly fascinated by the way the salespeople instinctively separated the tourists from the serious shoppers. It was not simply a matter of the labels on one's back, but of a certain style, a confidence which proclaimed, "I belong here." Dani was wearing a plaid skirt and sweater, Jeanne a simple beige blouse and brown slitted skirt. Perhaps some of the salesmen recognized Dani, but it was Jeanne's chic and sophistication that set their antennae aquiver.

They were plied with charm and coffee, and even offers of drinks in the stores which had bars. The styles of decoration ranged from Bauhaus to Baroque, the prices from expensive to outrageous. Jeanne took pages of notes, frequently asking Dani for her opinions, and when they had finally left the last boutique, announced that she couldn't wait to begin making some sketches for her own shop.

Dani dropped her aunt off at Edward's about five, stayed for a drink and a snack, and then started home. One of her father's last films had recently been released, and was playing at a movie theater near her home. Impulsively, she exited the freeway at the Huntington Beach cut-off in order to ask Jessica Morgan if she wanted to come out with her.

When she pulled into the drive she spotted Ty, dressed in torn jeans and a U.S.C sweatshirt, standing on a ladder. He was pruning some bushes in the front yard, and glanced up when he heard Dani's car. His eyes registered no emotion at all.

Dani got out and walked over to him. She found it impossible to act naturally when he looked through her that way, and her voice was stilted as she asked if Jessica were home.

"Inside." He turned his attention back to the pyracantha.

Jessica had seen Dani's car through the kitchen window, and appeared at the front door just as Dani opened it. "Hi," Dani began quickly. "I thought I'd go see *Lucifer's Darling* tonight. My father produced it. If you don't have a date, do you want to come along?"

"Love to." Jessica looked up at her brother, about to ask whether he wanted to join the party, then thought better of it. "I don't know why he doesn't let the gardener do that," she muttered. "I'll go grab a coat."

Dani waited, listening to the snapping noise of the shears as they bit viciously into the bush. Good grief, was Ty trying to prune the pyracantha or murder it? As Jessica closed the door behind her, he stopped and glanced over his shoulder. "Enjoy the movie," he said, then neatly amputated another branch.

The two women stopped for hamburgers and shakes, arriving at the theater just as the opening credits were rolling. Dani sobered as the words "Produced by George Korman" flashed onto the screen. Those heavy black letters seemed even more final than the funeral. There would be no more movies, no more madcap visits. The film itself was a comedy/fantasy with a wittily sophisticated tone and a few real bellylaughs. By the time it was over, Dani's wistful mood was long forgotten.

She ran Jessica home, accepting an invitation to come inside for coffee. Ty was sitting at the kitchen table, reading the latest issue of a sports monthly and eating a piece of chocolate cake. Dani wanted to tease him about putting on weight, but one look at his face told her he wouldn't be receptive to her humor. His eyes were blank, just as though his head were stuffed with wire and nuts and bolts, not living tissue.

"How was the movie?" he asked.

"Really good. Is there any cake left?" The question came from Jessica.

Ty picked up his plate and put it in the sink. "Enough for two pieces." He walked out of the kitchen, grabbing his magazine on the way.

"Well, don't be friendly or anything!" Jessica said to his back. To Dani, she added, "He's probably wound up in some dumb article. When he's concentrating, he puts the rest of the world on 'hold.'"

Dani assigned a different motivation to Ty's behavior, but said nothing to Jessica about it. It was almost eleven o'clock when she got home, but she was far too restless to sleep. Ty's attitude was only part of the reason for her mood. She was dying to know the outcome of Jeanne's date with Edward Reed; indeed, after that passionate kiss on Saturday night, she had to wonder if Jeanne would come home at all.

She turned on the TV to watch one of her father's old movies. It was past two o'clock when Jeanne Ronsard slammed into the house, flung herself into an armchair and began to describe Edward Reed in terms usually reserved for unscrupulous tradesmen or customers who failed to pay their bills. Dani was totally bewildered. The polished, gentlemanly Edward Reed, *un cochon, un rat?*

"What on earth did he do?" she asked incredulously.

"He asked me to marry him!" Jeanne spat out.

A proposal of marriage hardly seemed a grievous insult to Dani, and she said so.

"You know I am not promiscuous. I must be in love, always!" Jeanne told Dani in the same volatile manner. "And that—that louse! I tell him this. I keep saying I need more time. But does he listen? No! He takes me back to the house and tries to make love to me on the couch!"

Dani couldn't believe what she was hearing. "Are you trying to tell me he—he wouldn't take no for an answer?"

"Who said no? I did not say no! I said yes. *He* said no!"

"But—but you just said . . ."

Dani's sputterings were interrupted by peals of laughter from Jeanne. At first she was afraid that her aunt was becoming hysterical, but then she realized that Jeanne's fury had passed, and that she was laughing about what had happened. "I was furious with him, *ma chère,*" she said with a giggle. "We did not speak one word all the way home. You see, first he overcomes all my objections by caressing me until he knows I can think of nothing but him, and then, when I finally say yes, he asks when we will be married. I tell him I am not interested in marriage. He says he will not make love to me until I agree to become his wife." She gave a Gallic shrug. *"Eh bien!* An unusual situation, no?"

Dani gave Edward full marks for a unique approach. "Uncle Edward," she teased. "I like the sound of that."

"I do not believe in marriage—not for myself. I will admit to you that I find him terribly attractive, but I will not become his wife. He would turn out to be a possessive and dominating husband, just like all the rest."

"Are you going to see him again?"

"Of course. He will stop this childish behavior. You will see."

Privately, Dani thought that her aunt was the one who was behaving childishly. It was true that Edward was rushing her, even that he had behaved unscrupulously, but Dani refused to believe that he would change into an overbearing ogre the moment his ring was on Jeanne's finger. She remembered the first time she had met the attorney—how she had sensed all the determination of a shark. The irresistible American force, it seemed, had now met an immovable French object. Since the French object was obviously wild about the American force, Dani had to wonder which would prevail. Would Teddy be taking her out to dinner in a month, or, she asked herself with amusement, would *she* be the one picking up the tab?

Chapter Ten

$\mathcal{D}$uring the next week, while Jeanne was busy with the new boutique, Dani worked on foundation business. She met with Lewis Burnside and the rest of the staff on Monday and again on Wednesday to develop new guidelines for funding and a revised rating system for proposals. By Thursday she was ready to think about how much money should go to each artistic field.

She had just set down her pocket calculator when Edward Reed phoned, saying that he had received a call from Mitch Ellison. Ty Morgan and Carl Andersen had reached an agreement on the purchase price of the ski area, he told Dani, and Mitch and Ty wanted to meet with her before Ty left for Florida on Saturday. They settled on two o'clock Friday, in Dani's office.

Ordinarily, she wore suits or tailored dresses to work, pinning her hair into a bun or French knot. Knowing that she would see Ty on Friday, she shed her executive image for something more feminine. The V neck of her long-sleeved dress was all the more provocative for what it merely hinted at; the predominantly violet print complemented her complexion, while the fabric itself clung just enough to accentuate her curves. With her hair in loose waves, she looked delicately beautiful.

After the trouble she had taken with her appearance, she was disappointed and a little irked when Ty walked in and greeted her with a cool handshake and a formal hello. After all, she told herself, she was meeting with him at his convenience, doing him a favor by financing his blasted ski deal. The least he could do was acknowledge her existence.

She said very little as the men began to negotiate, merely nodding her understanding each time Edward's partner Bob Schultz, an expert in contract law, interrupted the discussion to explain something to her. She had maneuvered Ty into sitting next to her on the couch, and when he slanted her a disapproving look and proceeded to ignore her, her annoyance got the better of her. Though she refrained from blatant flirting, she set about capturing his attention in more subtle ways.

From time to time she recrossed her legs, or leaned forward to listen to some important point, or adjusted her body to a more comfortable position. And if a thigh or elbow occasionally brushed against Ty, it was certainly not her fault. If he became increasingly taciturn as the meeting progressed, that was not her fault, either.

"I'll have the contracts ready early next week," Bob Schultz was saying. "I'll send them to Florida first, Ty." He looked at Dani. "Are you going down to spring training?"

"Not for a while."

Ty stood up. "I'll mail them directly to your office after I sign them." He shook hands with the three attorneys and thanked them for their help, adding that he wanted a few words alone with Dani.

Her heart immediately began to thump erratically, but she was smiling as she smoothly escorted the other three men to the door. "I'll see you later," she murmured to Edward Reed.

When she returned to her office, Ty was standing in the middle of the room, his expression anything *but* distant. Dani pulled the door shut and sat down on the couch.

"Was there something you wanted to ask me?" Although his angry scrutiny unnerved her, her voice was cool and businesslike.

"Yeah, there's something I wanted to ask you! Just what the hell were you trying to do to me today?"

Dani's eyes slid to his chest. "I don't know what you mean." Lord, he sounded furious!

"You weren't dressed like that the last time we had a business discussion, and you didn't keep playing with your hair, and squirming around, and rubbing up against me. So what were you trying to prove?"

"I have a dinner date tonight. I'm not going home to . . ."

"With who?"

Dani was taken aback by the curt interruption. What did he care who she went out with?

"With Teddy," she said. She didn't add that Jeanne and Edward would be joining them.

"Yeah? Well let me give you a piece of advice, lady. If you're not going to go along, stop asking for it. Teddy Reed's had a lot of women in that Topanga Beach house of his, and they weren't there to talk about their wills!"

By now, Dani's face was flushed with shame. She really *had* behaved badly. "Teddy's not a rapist," she mumbled.

"Neither am I—normally," Ty snapped. "Look, when are you coming to Florida?"

"On March 7th." Dani managed a quick upward glance, and found Ty regarding her with a mixture of anger and sexual hunger. Her eyes dropped in embarrassment, and she heard him curse softly, then drop into a chair.

"I pitched the fifth game of the play-offs in the Astrodome this year." There was no trace of emotion in his voice now, and he was staring straight into the middle distance as he spoke. "It's enclosed. The roof magnifies the noise from the crowd. The fans were cheering, screaming—they went wild every time I gave up a hit, a walk, even a damn foul ball. I had to keep blocking it out. I couldn't concentrate if I let myself hear it. But I won the game, and I figured, after that, that I could block out anything."

He paused, his eyes flickering back to Dani. She could see that he was upset now, and his voice was hoarse when he continued, "I was wrong, Dani. I can't block it out when you sit four inches away from me and wiggle around for two solid hours. I've been straight with you. I'm trying to be . . . honorable, I guess you'd call it. So what are you trying to do to me? Seduce me? Or just drive me crazy?"

"Oh, Ty." Dani felt lower than a third-string catcher. "I'm sorry. You've been so distant, so cold. You treat me like I don't exist, and it makes me angry."

"So you were punishing me. Look, do you want me to admit I can't be in the same room with you without wanting you? Okay, I admit it. I handle my feelings the only way that works for me. But if you're going to pull that kind of stuff at spring training you'd damn well better rip up my contract."

"I won't; I'm sorry," Dani repeated miserably. By now she was awash in guilt. Ty Morgan was the most decent man she had ever known. He was keeping his distance because he didn't want to hurt her, and how had she reacted? Like a spoiled brat, throwing the adult version of a temper tantrum in order to provoke his attention.

"Okay." Ty stood up again. "I'm glad we understand each other. I'll try to be more human, but it's not easy. My thoughts take off in the wrong direction. And thanks for financing the deal with Andersen. It means a lot to me."

He started toward the door, with Dani hastily following. "I'll see you in a few weeks," she said.

Ty stopped and turned around. "You can show me that fast ball I paid a million dollars for," she added, a tentative smile on her face.

To her relief, he grinned and winked. "That early in the season, it's only worth five-hundred grand, boss. It'll take 'til late April to really heat up." He opened the door and let himself out of the office.

When Dani checked her watch, it was almost five. She had been sitting on the couch for over an hour, thinking about Ty, trying to come to terms with his attitude. There was a painful sweetness to loving him—and she did love him, she knew that now. It hurt that they weren't together, yet brought her poignant satisfaction to care so deeply. She had admired Paul, even idolized him, but had never really loved him as an equal.

On some level she was furious with Ty for rejecting the possibility of a deeper relationship, given the strong attraction between them. She understood his point of view, but still she couldn't accept it. Only this time, instead of trying to put him out of her mind, she reminded herself that people could change. Ty could change.

She ran into heavy traffic on her way to Newport Beach, and arrived half an hour late for dinner. Jeanne and Edward had been together constantly all week, and Dani wondered what was happening to the man's law practice. Although he had seemed as smooth and relaxed as ever today, she also wondered what was happening to his peace of mind. He and Jeanne were fighting a no-holds-barred war. She refused to consider marriage, and he refused to become her lover unless she made a commitment.

Jeanne was furious, frustrated, intrigued. She had dumped half a dozen admirers for the most trifling offenses, and Dani knew there could be only one reason why she would continue to subject herself to Edward Reed's nightly torture: she was just as infatuated with him as he was with her.

Teddy was waiting outside when Dani pulled up in front of the restaurant. She handed her keys to the parking attendant and took his arm, asking, "What's the score, Teddy?"

He began to laugh. "I'd say it's nothing-nothing, in the bottom of the ninth. My father can't take too much more of this, Dani. Your aunt is driving him nuts."

"He's driving *himself* nuts," Dani corrected.

"True. But his ego just can't take the idea of being her California lover." They walked inside to find Jeanne and Edward seated side by side on a banquette, almost touching, talking in husky whispers. The sexual tension between them was unmistakable, and although they conversed politely enough throughout dinner, Dani felt rather relieved when the meal was over and she could escape.

Edward and Jeanne went off to visit some of his friends, and Dani assumed she would be spending another quiet evening alone. She was curled up on the couch with a book when Jeanne stalked into the house and continued straight to the kitchen phone. It wasn't quite 9:30. She punched the buttons, then stood silently for the next few minutes, her foot tapping impatiently. Finally the reason for her call became evident: she was changing her airline reservation from Monday to the next morning.

"Will you take me to the airport tomorrow?" she asked when she hung up.

"Of course." Dani was not about to question her about what had happened. Obviously she and Edward had quarreled bitterly.

By the next morning Jeanne's temper had cooled enough so that she could offer explanations. The argument had started in the car, when Jeanne had asked Edward to take her away for the weekend. He had countered by refusing to see her at all, telling her that he wasn't going to waste his time with a man-hating spinster who was afraid of love and commitment. Jeanne, in turn, had called him a blackmailing prude with a chauvinist need to run a woman's life for her. "And that," she admitted, "was only the beginning of it."

Dani said she was sorry that things hadn't worked out, but privately, she rather sympathized with Edward. He wanted commitment, not blind obedience. His tactics were questionable, but then, Jeanne was exceptionally stubborn. In any event, she would be returning in early April to supervise progress on the boutique, and Edward knew it. Dani was sure that the present stand-off was only a temporary cease-fire, not a cessation of hostilities.

With Jeanne back in Paris and the Condors in Florida, California seemed very quiet. Dani spent most of her time working in her downtown office, occasionally meeting Teddy for lunch or going out to a film, party, or lecture with Jessica and her friends.

Sometimes these evenings proved amusing. On one occasion Jess invited her to attend the screening of several short films directed by a professor at the university. Dani recognized his name at once; he had submitted a proposal for a foundation grant.

The man was quite young, in his late twenties, and clearly enjoyed the attention he received at the party held afterward. He pawed every female who came near him, and kept leering at Dani, who wasn't interested.

Slightly inebriated, he finally strutted up to her. "What's your name, baby?" he asked.

She smiled provocatively, thinking him a fool. "Danielle," she purred.

"And what do you do? Go to school?"

"I work, like most people."

"Well, Danielle"—he seemed to have trouble getting the name out—"how about some coffee later? At my apartment?"

"How sweet of you to ask me." Dani supposed he expected her to stammer with gratitude. "We could talk about my funding your next experimental film— through my foundation. That's the Korman Foundation. Or maybe you're a baseball fan? We could talk about my ball club."

She had never seen a man sober up so fast. He stared at her, turned exceedingly red, and stammered out an apology. Dani put him out of his misery; she wouldn't hold his crude behavior against him. His films *had* shown some merit.

Though she allowed herself to enjoy the influence she wielded, she still thought about Ty much too often. Thumbing through the entertainment section of a Los Angeles paper, she came across a picture of Ty, Viveca, and several other ball players from the team. Viveca, the accompanying article noted, was starring in a light comedy at a Florida dinner theater, and would soon be leaving for England to begin work on her next movie. Dani made herself sick wondering what had happened after the curtain came down. She knew it was stupid to care who Ty fooled around with, but given her feelings, it was equally inevitable.

By the time she stepped onto the wide-bodied jet which would take her to Miami, she missed Ty so much that the flight seemed interminable. She caught a connecting flight to Tampa and was met by Mack Harmon, who drove her to the Condors' hotel and handed her the keys to a rental car which was waiting in the parking lot for her. Her father had always stayed in this same two-room suite, he told her, but George had rented it for the entire six weeks, just in case he decided to drop by for a few hours.

There were fresh flowers on the table, expensive brands of liquor in the bar, and citrus fruits in the small refrigerator. George Korman, Dani once again recalled, had always gone first class.

Mack Harmon's office was located in a trailer parked in a lot adjacent to the ball park. The next morning Dani drove to the field, easily following Mack's directions. She poked her head into the trailer to say hello before proceeding through the gate.

"I'll come with you," Mack said. His eyes ran down the length of her body, which was encased in close-fitting blue jeans with a prominent name on the back pocket, and a blue and white knit blouse. "Uh, I have a present for you."

Dani noticed a pink flush on his cheeks and wondered just what kind of gift this was. "I promised the guys I would give it to you. I just want you to know it wasn't my idea."

He walked over to the closet and took out a yellow and orange Condors jacket, holding it up for her inspection. The back read, "RONSARD," and above her name was the designation "10!"

"I'm glad they rate me that highly." Dani giggled. "I'll pretend this is a comment on my talents as an executive. Who do I have to thank?"

"I don't know. Mike Jones gave it to me, but he's the team captain, so it's logical they'd stick him with the job."

They walked into the park to find several dozen athletes jogging methodically around the outfield. "C'mon Taylor!" manager Marv Richardson was yelling. "Move your—" he spotted Dani and Mack "—legs!" he concluded.

"Some of these guys are lazy as an old hound on a hot day." Mack laughed. "Hate to run, even though they need to get in shape."

"I'll say hello when they take a break." Dani and Mack sat down in the stands, and watched the players run through a series of strenuous calisthenics. One of the coaches was barking orders at them, ignoring the good-natured back-chat about his own overweight torso.

The men were sweaty and grass-stained as they trotted to the water cooler. Most of them glanced at Dani as they ducked into the dugout. She kept a pleasant smile on her face, and to her delight, Ty smiled back, detouring over to say hello.

"You're wearing the jacket," he said with a grin. "Was it your idea?"

"Nope. But I told them you wouldn't mind." He

opened the gate to let her on to the field. "Come and meet everyone."

She recognized about half the athletes from the party nearly two months before, but the rest of them had been acquired in post-season trades, or via the free agent market, or were minor leaguers who had been invited to camp.

"Thank you all for the jacket," she smiled. "Whose idea was it?"

The question was greeted by dead silence and sheepish expressions.

"And I was going to give him a five-thousand-dollar bonus," Dani drawled. Two dozen men immediately claimed authorship of the gift.

She then greeted each of the players, Mack standing by her side to give her information on those new to the team. Afterward she took Marv and Mack out to lunch, and received a report on the first two weeks of the season. Most of last year's starting line-up was back and healthy, and there were four or five hot newcomers as well. The pitching, which many professional baseball men considered to be ninety percent of the game, looked as good as last year.

"Of course," Mack noted, "it's early days yet." Dani supposed that he didn't want to promise her a winning team, only to wind up with mud in his eye in October if the Condors didn't take the National League pennant.

By the time they got back to the field, batting practice had started. Kenny Green, the young right-hander she had danced with at the banquet, was throwing to one of the minor leaguers. He pitched to two more batters and then walked off the mound, to be replaced by Ty Morgan. Mike Jones stepped up and promptly smashed what Mack told Dani was a curve ball deep into center field, over the head of the outfielder.

"Give me a few fast balls, low in the strike zone, on the inside corner," the catcher called out. "I need to work on 'em."

"Can he really do that?" Dani asked Mack.

"More or less. This early, he's still working on his speed and his control. By May, he'll be able to spot the ball—put it where he wants it—as good as anybody in baseball."

"I'm beginning to see why his earned run average was less than two runs a game last year," Dani observed dryly.

Mike Jones stood in the batters' cage for several more minutes, slamming into his teammate's carefully placed pitches. Then he stepped aside for the next batter.

"Hold it a minute, Hal," Ty yelled, taking a few steps toward home plate. "I promised the boss a few swings."

"Oh, no," Dani said. "You're not getting *me* up there."

"Get her the lightest bat we have, would you, Mike?" Ty ignored her protest as if she hadn't made it.

The catcher loped over to the batting rack, a big grin on his face. Dani looked dubiously at Mack. "You're sure I won't get killed up there? I *am* curious about what it feels like."

"Ty won't hit you," Mack assured her. With a shrug, Dani stepped onto the field and took the bat from Mike.

"You'd better show me what to do," she said. "I haven't tried this since I was a little girl in Vegas."

He stood behind her in the batting cage, his hands

over her own, helping her swing. "Now try a few without me," he instructed, "and when Ty throws, don't lean in too far, or change anything you're doing."

With Mike out of the batting cage, Dani took a few practice swings, thinking that her arms were going to drop from the weight of this allegedly light bat. When Ty went into his wind-up, she tensed, ready to swing. The next thing she heard was a loud smack, as the ball landed in the catcher's glove.

"You didn't swing," Ty shouted, laughing at her.

"I never saw the darn thing," Dani called back. It was almost true. By the time her eye had picked up the ball, it was nearly at the plate.

"Fast ball," Mike observed. "Come on, Morgan, stop fooling around. Throw the lady something she can hit."

The next few pitches were probably lobs by major league standards, but Dani missed all of them. By now, everyone except the fielders was standing around the back of the batting cage, shouting encouragement before every pitch. "Just keep your swing level and watch the ball," Mike told her. "He'll throw it where you're swinging."

It took three more pitches for Dani to connect with the ball, which skittered anemically across the infield to the shortstop. The impact made her hands sting fiercely, and she quickly dropped the bat to massage her palms together. Whistles and cheers greeted her debut as a major league hitter, which would also be her swan song, she decided.

When she looked up, Ty was halfway to home plate, an expression of concern on his face. She picked up the bat and walked out to meet him. "You okay?" he asked.

"My hands feel like I slammed into a wall. If that's what a slow pitch feels like, I'd hate to hit your fast ball."

"Fortunately, there's no danger of that, since you can't even see it," he teased. He took the bat from her and tossed it to the sidelines. "Want to try again?"

"Thanks for the offer, but I think I'll pass," Dani told him. Her whole body was stinging by now, and it had nothing to do with batting practice. She returned to the stands, ostensibly to watch the next few players take their turns, but her eyes never left Ty.

That day set the pattern for those which followed. Dani came out to the park every day, learned such things as the difference between a curve ball and a slider, and gradually absorbed the finer points of the game. Occasionally she spoke to one of the players, including Ty, but there was never anything personal about these brief exchanges. She ate dinner with various club executives, and was lonely only at night, when she retired to her suite and fantasized about Ty. Just watching him work out and joke with his teammates was enough to intensify her longing, especially given the snug way his uniform fit.

A few of the players' wives had come down to spring training, but most of them remained at home, tied to jobs or small children. Dani soon realized that there was no possibility of friendship with these women. Most ball players' wives, she found, seemed to live in a state of perpetual fear: fear that their husbands would be traded, or sent down to the minors, or that someone more talented would win their jobs, or that they would be injured. Dani was the boss, and even if Mack ran the team on a day-to-day basis, she had the ultimate power to change these men's lives.

Although an equal relationship with the wives might be impossible, Dani's position didn't preclude kindness. One of the women in camp was Judy Green, who was married to Kenny Green. Perhaps because Ty had promised to help him with his slider, Dani felt a special interest in the boy's progress and would often sit adjacent to the sidelines when he and Ty practiced together. One day she felt someone's eyes on her, and quickly turned her head to catch a look of sheer misery on Judy Green's face.

Dani walked over to Judy and sat down. The girl was obviously nearing the end of her pregnancy, and Dani asked if she were uncomfortable.

Judy shook her head, saying nothing.

"Is something the matter?"

More silence.

Wanting to comfort her, Dani placed an arm around her shoulder and gently coaxed her to talk. "Tell me, Judy. Maybe I can help."

She wasn't surprised when the girl burst into tears—only astonished at the cause. "He's in love with you," she sobbed. "You're all he ever talks about. The doctor says I'm carrying a big baby and I'm really scared, but he doesn't care about *me* at all."

"Judy, Kenny is only twenty. I think of him as . . . a kid brother." Dani was striving to cloak her amazement with reassurance. "Maybe he has a crush on me, but he'll get over it. You know, he may be just as scared as you are—it's a big responsibility to be a new father, especially when you're worried about your job. You just tell him that I said Mack thinks the world of him, and then sit him down and explain how you feel. I promise I'll do everything I can to make sure he's with you when the baby is born, even if it means flying him back to L.A."

Judy was sniffling her thanks and rubbing away her tears when Kenny noticed what was going on and walked over. Dani told him in a stern but gentle voice that his wife needed some love and attention, and then left the two of them alone. She felt so much the mother hen that she might have clucked.

Diana Kendall arrived four days after Dani for a two-week stay with Mike. She and Dani ran into each other in the elevator on Saturday morning and wound up having breakfast together. Diana, Dani realized, was as out of place among the women down here as she was. The actress was no ordinary ball player's wife, both because of her own profession and because her husband was one of the game's true superstars. The other wives were somewhat in awe of her, but Dani found her a delight—intelligent, down to earth, amusing. The fact that Dani was George Korman's daughter gave them something additional to talk about. By Sunday the two were inseparable. They ate breakfast together, lolled around the pool together, watched practice together, and lunched together.

That night, Diana invited Dani to join a group of players for dinner at a Tampa steakhouse. Since Mike Jones and Ty Morgan had been roommates and best friends for the last four years, it was natural to assume that Ty would be one of the group. Terribly in love, Dani couldn't help wanting to wear something more attractive than the jeans and knit shirts he always saw her in. Her side-buttoned strapless white cotton jumpsuit was entirely appropriate given the warm weather, but by the end of the evening, she wished she had chosen a gunny sack. Ty frowned moodily when he saw her, and totally ignored her for the rest of the evening. Since he couldn't possibly consider her mere presence an unwarranted provocation, it must be her attire which offended him.

No one seemed to notice the tension between them. Dani was determined to be vivacious and charming. Ty appeared to be relaxed, his withdrawal applying only to her. When he refused to even look at her the next day at practice, she thought dejectedly that they were right back to Square 1.

The Condors played their first exhibition game on Monday, in Bradenton, the winter home of the Pittsburgh Pirates. Ty started the game, worked six innings, and gave up two runs. Over the next week the team won only half its games, but Marv Richardson was apparently pleased by what he saw.

Dani was staying for one more week of the exhibition season. She continued to spend her days with Diana, dining with a different group of people each evening. After two more meals in Ty's company, she tactfully refused Diana's subsequent invitations. The pitcher was the epitome of gregarious charm with everyone but her, telling stories, signing autographs, and apparently enjoying himself. It wasn't that he was rude to Dani—he simply tuned her out. She understood that his behavior was a defense mechanism, but couldn't help the pain she felt that he was able to dismiss her from his life this way. She would never have been able to do the same to him. She had been in love with Ty even before Florida, but over the past few weeks her feelings had deepened still further. She wanted to share any part of his life he chose to offer her.

The night before her flight to California, the Condors played a game against the Detroit Tigers in Tarpon Springs. It was Ty's third start; the second time out he had pitched seven scoreless innings. Tonight, however, he was constantly in trouble. Every inning he got into a jam, and every inning he weaseled out of it. Only a single run was scored against him over the first four innings, but in the fifth, he loaded the bases with one man out. Dani and Diana, sitting side by side, watched Mike trot out to the mound, talk to Ty, and then trot back to the plate.

Ty walked the next batter on six pitches, forcing in a run. Now manager Marv Richardson walked slowly out to the mound. Mike joined them, there was another powwow, and both Marv and Mike walked away.

"Why is he insisting on staying in the game?" Diana muttered.

"How do you know he is?" Dani asked her.

"There's no other reason why he's still there. Marv must be humoring him."

Their conversation was interrupted when the next batter hit a sizzling line drive down the right field line for a double, scoring three runs. Ty shook his head in disgust and started off the mound even before Marv motioned in a relief pitcher. Dani noticed him flex his left arm, rub his shoulder, then wince. Marv was standing on the dugout steps and slapped him on the back as he passed to go inside. Since the manager was standing only a few feet away from her, Dani was able to get his attention while the reliever warmed up.

"What happened?" she asked.

"He says his arm is tight. He figured he could work it out if he kept throwing, so I let him pitch to another batter. I knew he'd get pounded, but the game doesn't count."

"Is he okay?"

"Sure. Same thing happened two years ago." He paused. "I know Ty. If I let him do something stupid in Florida, he doesn't argue with me when the season starts. Go talk to him if you want to. Nobody's around except Lem."

Dani knew that personal conversations with Ty were out, but trainer Chuck Lemon would be inside. She was worried about Ty; he had seemed to be in pain when he left the game. After five minutes of agonizing, she managed to convince herself that her interest was purely professional.

She walked down a corridor into the locker room, passing the trainer on the way. Maybe she should have turned back, but she had already spotted Ty in the adjacent training room, lying on a table, his eyes closed. He was stripped to the waist, his shoes on the floor, and to Dani's horror, his bent left arm was submerged, elbow down, in a small plastic tub. A wet towel was wrapped around his shoulder.

She came just close enough to look inside the tub. It contained ice water. "Did you hurt yourself?" she asked hoarsely.

His eyes flickered open. He seemed both annoyed and weary, but at least he wasn't pretending she wasn't there, although he said nothing.

She took a few steps forward, trying to ignore the sight of all that exposed flesh. If the man was handsome with clothes on, he was devastating half-naked. His chest and arms were perfect—strong, solidly muscled, covered with a light layer of still-moist hair.

"I thought Mack said you did something stupid. Is that why you're soaking your arm that way?" she asked.

Although his laughter was subdued, there was no doubt that her question had amused him. "I always soak my arm after I pitch. It always hurts, it always swells up, and I always soak it, just like most pitchers. But yes, I did something stupid. I should have left the game when Mike told me to. But I was too damn stubborn."

"But you're okay."

"Sure I'm okay. My arm is healthy. It hurts a little more than usual, but I'll live."

They stared into each other's eyes. Ty looked exhausted, and was obviously in pain. Dani longed to touch him, to comfort him. "Do you know," he mumbled, "that you look absolutely sensational in those things?" She was wearing wheat-colored jeans and a black turtleneck top.

"You look pretty sensational yourself."

"You've got to get out of here, Dani."

"Only if you want me to go."

The exchange was conducted in husky whispers. Finally Ty muttered, "I can't take this," an ambiguous response which became clear when he lifted his arm out of the ice water, shrugged off the towel, and swung himself into a sitting position. By now, Dani was standing flush with the edge of the table, her face tilted up to his.

The kiss was different from any of the others they had shared: sweet, lingering, gentle. Ty slid off the table, leaning against it. Dani lifted her hand to smooth his unruly hair, her caress instinctively soothing. She held back nothing, seeking only to comfort him, to convey her love.

She was barely aware of his right hand pulling her shirt from the waistband of her jeans and sliding up her back to unfasten her bra. All sensation was focused on her mouth—the warmth of Ty's lips against her own, the hardness of his tongue as it probed, withdrew, teased. An icy wetness settled itself against her stomach and she started, her entire body jerking with shock.

Ty laughed against her mouth. "Cold, huh?" he murmured.

"Uh-huh." But his hand hadn't been soaking in the ice water, and it wasn't cold at all. His fingers were warm and firm and wonderfully calloused as they cupped her breast, playing with the hardened nipple, massaging the sensitive flesh in a way that made her forget any notion of comforting. The contrasting coldness of his forearm was painfully erotic, and when he began to kiss her again, his mouth had all the insistent passion which had been absent earlier.

His tongue was still skillfully dominating her mouth when his hands dropped to her waist, lifted her up, and set her on the table. By the time he shoved up her shirt and bent his head to her breasts, she was weak with excitement, her body arching eagerly against his lips. His tongue and teeth teased and nibbled until Dani was making unbidden little moans, digging her nails into his shoulders. When Ty pulled her back into his arms to kiss her again, she clung to his waist, rubbing her breasts against his chest like an ecstatic kitten. He was still in uniform from the waist down, and she felt a flash of frustration with the protective equipment he wore.

Both of them were breathing raggedly now, the kiss out of control, their hands moving restlessly over each other's bodies. Then Ty abruptly pulled his mouth away and buried it against Dani's neck, offering hard kisses to her hair and shoulder. For a moment more he stood motionless, still holding her tightly in his arms. When his breathing had settled into a regular, even rhythm, he straightened, gently putting her away from him.

"Put yourself back together," he ordered hoarsely. "A training room isn't exactly private."

Dani hooked her bra and tucked in her shirt, her hands clumsy with tension. She was afraid that Ty would berate her for coming here, or reject her yet again. "Go back to California," he said. Dani looked up at him, feeling herself go pale. "I want you to think this over," he continued.

"Think what over?"

"Whether you should start sleeping with me. You know how I feel about marriage. If I was a nice guy, I'd throw you out of here. But I want you so much I feel like stripping you naked and throwing you onto the training table."

He smiled just slightly, making Dani realize that his control was not as tenuous as he implied. As far as she was concerned, there was nothing to think about. She was wildly in love with him. If she couldn't have him as a husband, she would settle for having him as a lover. It would hurt when the affair ended, but that was far in the future, and thus unreal. She knew only that it was tearing her to pieces to be without him right now.

"I'll come to your room tonight," she murmured.

"No, you won't." His tone brooked no argument. "If you do, I won't let you in. You're going back to California, and you're going to think things over for a few weeks. Are you coming to Houston for the opener?"

"Of course."

"I don't want to see you first—I have to pitch. Come to my room after the game, and we'll talk. Now get out of here before one of the guys wonders what we've been doing in here."

"I wouldn't care if they knew," Dani said.

"But I *would*. You don't know how ball players

talk about women. I don't want them talking about *you*." He settled himself back on the table, stuck his elbow into the ice water, and closed his eyes. "Houston," he murmured. "Do what I tell you."

Dani leaned over and kissed him good-bye. "Yes sir, boss," she teased. Smiling to herself, she quietly left the training room.

Chapter Eleven

$\mathcal{A}$ week later, Dani was sitting in her living room, looking at the quarterly income statement for Korman Properties, but thinking about that evening's dinner with Teddy Reed. He had paid his debt cheerfully enough, taking her to an unpretentious but excellent seafood restaurant, and informing her with a smile that his father had gone to Paris the day before to be with Jeanne. After six weeks of frustration, Edward had decided to convince her that she couldn't live without him.

"Another month," Teddy had said confidently. "Next time, you'll be taking *me* out."

But when Dani phoned Jeanne that weekend, there was no hint of a forthcoming marriage. It was true, Jeanne said, that she and Edward were having a marvelous time together, and that she adored him. He was an exquisite lover, a delightful companion. She would be wretchedly lonely when he left. Her solution was a pragmatic one, though; she would arrange to spend more of her time in Los Angeles, and cajole Edward into frequent trips to Paris.

Dani held her tongue, but silently wished that Ty would chase across thousands of miles to propose. Instead, he made it seem a major concession that he was willing to have an affair with her, and instead of resenting it, she couldn't wait to see him. She knew he cared for her deeply, and although that was not quite the same thing as loving her, it would have to do.

She arrived in Houston five days later, dining at the home of a local businessman who had been a friend of her late father's, and then driving over to the Astrodome to watch the game from his private box. Someone handed her an after-dinner drink and a pair of field glasses. She sipped the first and scanned the stadium with the second, stopping when she came to the visitors' bull pen. Ty was warming up, oblivious to the bevy of seductively clad women who surrounded the area, flirting with the other pitchers.

By the time Ty walked out to the mound to pitch the bottom of the first inning, Dani had accordion-pleated the cover of her program and done Origami with half the inside pages. Ty had pitched well in his remaining exhibition starts, but that didn't count, and this did. The first batter slammed the ball deep into the outfield. The crowd exploded, and was still buzzing after the center fielder coralled the shot. Dani was physically sick with nervousness. How was she going to sit through nine innings of this torture?

Ty's first three innings continued on this shaky course, but the Astros managed to score only a single run off him. In the top of the fourth the Condors took the lead, and Ty seemed to settle down. He breezed through the next five innings, only getting into trouble with one out in the ninth. Marv Richardson called in the team's ace reliever, who got the next batter to hit into a double play, ending the game.

There was a private party afterward, but Dani left as soon as she decently could, taking a taxi back to the hotel. As she walked inside, she realized that she had no idea what room Ty was in. The woman at the desk was polite but firm.

"I'm sorry, ma'am," she drawled. "We're not allowed to give out that information."

Having seen the women who swarmed around the players, Dani could understand the reason for this policy. "I'll ring him later, then," she murmured.

"I'm sorry, ma'am. Mr. Morgan doesn't take any calls, except from his family."

"How about from his boss?" Dani snapped, suddenly exasperated.

The clerk smiled. "I have to say that's the first time any of you gals have come up with *that* one!" she said.

Dani supposed she would have to call the club's traveling secretary to find out Ty's room number. She was about to turn away when inspiration struck. "Look, do you have a copy of today's paper?"

The clerk reached under the counter and pulled it out. Dani took it, flipping through the sports section to find the profile of Ty that she had read while waiting for the game to begin. The accompanying photo was a wire-service shot of Ty and herself, taken at the Condors' banquet last January. She silently pointed it out to the clerk.

"Oh, I *am* sorry, Miss Ronsard," the woman apologized, mispronouncing her name, "but we *do* have to be careful." She punched something into a computer terminal, then announced, "He's in room 906, with Mr. Jones."

Dani went up to her own room to wait another half-hour, giving Ty time to shower, dress and get back to the hotel. She had been so nervous about how he would pitch tonight that she hadn't thought about what would happen when they were alone together. Now she did, and apprehension began to mingle with her eagerness. This wasn't something she made a habit of.

By the time she knocked on his door, she was actually trembling. "It's open," he called out.

Dani went inside, shut the door behind her, and locked it. She was trying to carry this off with some degree of sophistication, but she felt awkward and tense. Ty was lying on one of the beds, shirtless, propped up against several pillows. He wore only a pair of gray slacks; a navy blazer, blue shirt and striped tie were slung over a chair back. His left elbow was wrapped in a wet hotel towel, and rested atop a plastic laundry bag which protected the supporting pillow underneath.

"You pitched a good game," Dani said. "How's your arm?"

"Okay."

He didn't look particularly happy to see her, Dani thought nervously. Maybe he was tired. It was past 11:30, and he had had a rough few innings at first. She hesitated, thinking that this might be the wrong time to be here.

"You staying or leaving?" he asked, a curt edge to his tone.

"Staying," Dani mumbled.

"So come here."

If Ty had lost the game tonight, Dani would have understood his black mood. Given his performance, it didn't make sense. She slowly approached the bed, sitting down to his right. She didn't want to jostle his pitching arm.

"Is something wrong?" she asked. "Your arm . . ."

"I said it's fine," he snapped. "Look, are you

229

going to take your clothes off, or just sit there all night?"

"Just . . . just like that?" Dani stammered. "I thought . . ."

"What did you expect me to do? Seduce you? You're here. You came to go to bed with me. So get undressed."

Why was he so angry, so cold? "Do . . . do you have to treat me like . . . like . . ." She couldn't get the word out. "You make me feel . . . dirty."

"What do you think this is, a Sunday School picnic?" he barked. "Either play ball or get out!"

Dani stared at him, tears running down her cheeks, too stricken to move. "Why are you doing this?" she sobbed.

His only answer was a loud curse. Dani turned away, her composure destroyed. "You said . . . I came here . . . and I love you . . . and I don't understand . . ."

"You think I feel any different?" he muttered.

The disgruntled statement was enough to stop her tears. "You mean . . ."

"I mean I feel like a heel," he interrupted. "But I want you so much it's killing me."

He pulled her halfway across his body, kissing her with a brutal passion so sudden and so intense that she instinctively stiffened. Ty released her and she wiggled off his chest and onto her side, watching him remove the compress from his arm and drop it onto the floor. Finally he stroked her hair, and tipped up her chin, and kissed her gently on the mouth. "You wouldn't believe how mixed up I am," he admitted softly.

Dani didn't know what to say. She settled on, "I love you, Ty."

It must have been the right response. Ty took her into his arms, holding her close against the length of his body. His mouth was more controlled now, but burningly demanding for all its gentleness. Dani helped him unbutton her blouse and unsnap the front closing of her bra. He ran a hand lightly over her breasts, teasing the hard nipples, then eased her onto her back and covered her body with his own.

For several long minutes they clung to each other, the kiss increasingly savage. Dani's skirt presented no barrier to Ty's exploring hands, his fingers grazing her thighs and hips. She arched pliantly against him, her hands around his neck, running over his muscled shoulders and back, her body adjusting itself to his movements. She made no protest when he unbuttoned her skirt, sliding down the zipper and slipping a hand intimately against her skin. But only moments later he tore his mouth away and sprawled onto his back.

Dani turned on her side and reached out a hand, starting to unbuckle his belt.

"Wait a minute." He clamped a hand over her own. "I'm going to wind up raping you at this rate."

She pulled the edges of her blouse together as she watched him master his emotions, and then, after another few seconds, smile. "I don't like rushing—remember?" Without another word he pulled her to her knees to finish undressing her.

He removed each garment so slowly and so sensually that the process was a seduction in itself. By the time he was done, Dani was the one in a hurry. She wound her arms around his neck, only to have them removed.

"My arm hurts," he whispered. "I can't use it anymore."

She took the hint. She wasn't as expert as he was, but managed to accomplish her goal just the same. Afterward, Ty lazed back against the pillows, his hands clasped behind his head.

"Turn off the light," he said.

Only one light was on in the room: the lamp on his end table. Since it was switched to the dimmest setting, Dani was surprised he wanted it off.

She moved to the edge of the bed, ready to walk around to Ty's side of it, but he caught her wrist to stop her. "Not that way. Reach over me."

"So that's the kind of game you want to play, is it?" Dani arched across him in the most provocative manner imaginable, but just as her fingers made contact with the switch, Ty's hands clamped around her waist, and flipped her onto her back so that she was lying on top of him.

She laid her head down, using his shoulder for a cushion, giggling. "The light's still on, Ty."

"Sure it is. You're so damn beautiful, I want to look at you while I make love to you."

Dani started to turn into his arms, but was stopped by one well-placed hand. "Not so fast, lady," he said. His other hand had started to explore again, feathering down her side to her hip, caressing her breasts, slipping downward to touch her intimately, insistently. At the same time, he was nuzzling her neck and shoulder with his lips.

Dani turned her head, seeking his mouth. From the way he kissed her, it was obvious that he wouldn't be able to continue his teasing. He was breathing as rapidly as she was, his mouth devouring her own. Somehow they wound up side by side, their legs tangled together as Ty took possession. Dani, her nails digging into his back, knew there was no way she could wait—not after the last fifteen minutes. And neither could he.

"I thought you never rushed." Dani, lying contentedly in Ty's arms, teased him in a gentle, husky tone.

"I was never in love like this. And I've never had to wait so long for something I wanted so badly."

"You've been spoiled, then."

"You can spoil me some more, then," Ty told her. "There's some beer in an ice bucket in the bathroom. Bring me a can."

"Please," Dani said.

"Please," he repeated.

She obediently went off to fetch it. "You know," he said when she handed him the can, "I was looking at the local paper, and there's a show at the Museum of Fine Arts. I thought we could go together. Native American—" he cut himself off. "What's so funny?"

"I'm not laughing," Dani corrected, "I'm happy." Ecstatic might have been closer to the mark. That he wanted to share that side of her life with her—she was thrilled. "I'd love to go . . . in the morning?"

"Umm. We could meet for breakfast." He flexed his arm. "I think I twisted something, honey. Would you mind wrapping some ice in a damp towel and bringing it in here?"

"Of course not. I have to protect my investment," Dani teased. She grabbed her purse on the way and shut the bathroom door behind her. It took her a few minutes to brush out her hair and repair her makeup. She was putting ice into the towel when she heard someone open the door.

Since she had locked it, that had to be Mike Jones. She wasn't embarrassed; Ty and Mike were very close friends, and Mike undoubtedly knew what was going on.

"We brought you a sandwich and a copy of . . ." The voice had been Mike's, but he stopped in mid-sentence. Then other voices took over.

"Who's the chick, Morgan?"

"Hey, look at all that lace and silk. Classy."

"She in the bathroom? Can we have a look?"

Other comments were even more crude. And then Mike was speaking again, sounding angry. "Okay, you guys, just get the hell out of here. Now."

There was a brief pause, and then the sound of a door being shut. "I'll bunk in with Mack," Mike said.

"It's okay. Give us half an hour." A few seconds later the door opened and closed again.

Dani wrapped a towel around her and opened the bathroom door just a crack.

"You can come out. They're gone," Ty told her.

She wanted to seem matter-of-fact about what had happened, but her face was already flushed and she reddened even further when she noticed her clothing, scattered over the foot of the bed. After hesitating briefly, she started to dress.

Ty looked both weary and disgusted, and when he spoke, he used that distantly cool tone Dani had come to detest. "I had to talk to someone, so I talked to Mike. I told him I couldn't do it—that I loved you too much to subject you to gossip and dirty jokes. I . . ."

"I don't care," Dani interrupted.

"The hell you don't. Look in a mirror. I took a bellyful of locker-room ribbing the last time we saw each other. A couple of guys came close to being hit. So I decided I would tell you to leave tonight, but when you came in, I couldn't do it. I was angry with myself and I took it out on you. You were supposed to run out of the room, not tell me you love me."

"I *do* love you. I want to be with you."

Ty shook his head. "You heard those guys. There are kids on the team who are half in love with you, Dani. How do you think they're going to feel when they find out that you play house with your star pitcher?"

"They'll think I love you, that I'm human." Even as she said the words, she knew they weren't true. They would snicker behind her back and lose respect for her. The double standard was still alive and well.

Given that fact, Dani saw an obvious solution. "Okay," she went on, "you're right. But you've got to be logical about this, Ty. I don't run the team, and you can't seriously consider me your boss. I'll sell in five years, and then the g.m. thing won't be a problem. If you love me, marry me."

"You think I could live with myself? Baseball has enough lousy owners. We need people like you."

"It's my decision," Dani insisted, becoming frustrated by what she considered his stupid, obstinate attitude. "I want to spend my life with you."

"You wouldn't sell if it weren't for me. And maybe it's not just your position, Dani, or even the g.m. thing. Maybe I can't handle being married to all your money."

"What am I supposed to do? Let Viveca have it?" Dani paused, knowing that her thoughts were irrational, but so upset that she voiced them anyway. "Is that what this is really all about? You'd rather sleep with Viveca, but you don't have the guts . . ."

"That's a hell of a thing to say!" Ty broke in. His voice was every bit as heated as her own now. "I've just told you I love you. There's nothing between her and me, and you damn well know it!"

"Then let's get married!" Dani shouted.

"You're sure as hell good at proposing! What will the license say? Mr. and Mrs. Danielle Korman?"

"That's not fair!"

"It's exactly the point, though," Ty snapped. "What will you give me for a wedding present? The Lake Tahoe ski area? No thanks!"

Dani burst into tears, screaming, "Fine! Be a pigheaded male chauvinist, then. I don't know what I ever saw in you!" She fumbled with the buttons of her blouse and ran out of the room, to the accompaniment of Ty's, "Well it's damn well mutual!"

It was dawn before Dani finally admitted to herself that Ty was not going to call her on the phone, and that he was not going to appear at her door to whisk her off to a minister. Originally she had planned to travel with the team for the entire eleven-day road trip, but now all she wanted to do was go home and hide.

Somehow she maintained her composure as she checked out, leaving a message for the team's traveling secretary that she had been called back to L.A. on business. For the next two days, she scarcely got out of bed. She seesawed between tears and numb depression. Her occasional efforts to shake herself back to life failed. When she tried to eat, she got nauseous. When she looked at herself in the mirror, she was too disgusted with her own haggard appearance to do anything about it. She didn't even bother to go through her mail, much less open a paper or turn on the TV. Her only contact with the outside world was the telephone, which she answered in the vain hope Ty was calling her.

One of those calls was from Jeanne. "Darling, I

tried to reach you in Houston," she said. "Why are you . . ."

Dani started to cry as soon as she heard her aunt's voice, causing Jeanne to interrupt herself with a distraught, "Dani, what is the matter?"

"It's Ty. Everything's all wrong. I can't talk about it."

"You quarreled?"

"It's over," Dani sobbed. "I can't—I don't want to talk about it."

The more Jeanne coaxed and soothed, the more upset Dani became. Ultimately her aunt ended the conversation, saying she would call again in a day or two.

Dani was lying in bed on Monday, half-dozing, when the doorbell awakened her. She tried to ignore it, but the caller kept ringing and knocking until she pulled on a robe and went to the door. "I don't want any," she said dully.

"Darling, it's Jeanne. Open the door."

Dani did so, fleetingly ashamed of her stringy hair, and of the rumpled nightgown she had worn since Friday. Edward was standing beside her aunt. "I'll call you later, honey," he said, kissing Jeanne on the mouth.

Jeanne gathered a tearful Dani into her arms, maneuvering her inside to the couch, stroking and holding her until she quieted. At first she asked no questions, concentrating her persuasive powers on getting Dani to bathe and wash her hair, and then eat the omelet she fixed.

Dani felt a little better afterward, and with a minimum of prompting from Jeanne, related everything that had happened. "And I feel so ashamed of myself, falling apart this way," she finished.

"You are entitled to fall apart," Jeanne scoffed. "It was hard enough for you to adjust to such a different life, so far away from home, with your father's money to cope with. It was the wrong time to fall in love, especially with an impossible man like Ty."

"He may be impossible, but I love him," Dani wailed.

"And you should be proud of yourself, not ashamed. So many rejections, and each time you went on. It will be hard for you to believe this, but your Ty will come around."

"After what we said to each other?"

Jeanne simply smiled. "You were both angry. He is simply mixed up, just as he said. He loves you too much to let you go, especially if you handle him properly."

"What do you know about it?" Dani burst out. "You and Ty are just the same. Stubborn, overly self-sufficient, and determined to control everything. It doesn't do any good to tell either of you . . ."

The tirade was squelched when Jeanne wiggled her left ring finger under Dani's nose. "One sees reason when the right person comes along," she said.

Dani stared at the diamond ring. It must have weighed a good two carats. "You said yes? I never even noticed it."

"I forgive you. It is why I called yesterday—to tell you Edouard and I were getting married. It was excellent timing, *ma petite,* because I can see that you need me. I will devote myself to feeding you and cheering you up. You need some decent French food. This California junk food—*incroyable!"*

"But what made you change your mind?" Dani asked. "And when are you getting married?"

"As soon as you are settled, *ma chère*. You see, I finally understood that I can do as I please with my shop, and have Edouard also. You may call me perverse, but once I understood that he was asking nothing of me other than that I marry him, I was willing to move to Beverly Hills. I wish to make more time for our relationship, so perhaps I will add a buyer to my staff, and concentrate on designing. Edouard is not like most other men. He is secure enough to delight in my success, and could love no one but an independent woman. Your Ty, I think, is the same. He is simply younger, and perhaps has not yet realized his own strengths. There is, after all, no real conflict between you, is there?"

"My money . . ."

"Men marry rich women all the time. Besides, your Ty is not exactly destitute. And as for this so-called problem of your owning the team—is it really a problem, darling?"

"Not as far as I'm concerned. I enjoy owning the Condors, but I don't want to run things any more than Daddy did. I'd rather spend my time on the foundation."

"Exactly." An impish gleam lit Jeanne's eyes. "You will see. Your husband's only problem will be to deny that he is the boss while he is still a player. Poor Mack Harmon!"

"I don't even want to think about it," Dani moaned. In truth, she felt very much better, and every time her doubts returned and depression set in, Jeanne was there to give her a pep talk.

Ty pitched twice more during the road trip—on Tuesday in San Francisco and on Sunday in San Diego. Dani watched both games on television. He struggled through seven innings of the first game, giving up three runs, and left in the fifth inning of the second game, with two men on base and two runs already in. Usually cooperative with the press, he refused to grant any interviews. The local sportswriters, mortally offended, attacked both his silence and his performance. They cross-examined his manager, his catcher, and even Dani herself, who answered their calls with a terse, "No comment." It was appalling to her that yesterday's hero could so quickly become today's whipping boy.

The team came back into town on Monday, having won six out of ten games on the road. Dani hadn't planned to go out to the ball park, but Jeanne insisted. "Humor me," she said. "Let Ty see you there. Edouard and I will come along with you."

They sat in her father's favorite spot, just to the right of the dugout. Ty preferred to watch the game from the bull pen in right field, an eccentricity which his manager indulged. During batting practice, Mike Jones came over to Dani and asked how she was feeling.

"Okay." She knew her cheeks were flushed; it was impossible not to think about what he had almost walked in on. "Uh, Mike, this is my aunt, Jeanne Ronsard. Mike Jones, our starting catcher."

"Ah. Ty's good friend, *non?*" Jeanne asked ingenuously.

"Maybe not. I'm trying to talk some sense into him, but he doesn't want to listen. All the same, he'll come around. He's crazy about you, Dani. Sooner or later, he'll stop torturing himself." He winked at her and trotted back to home plate to take his turn at bat, leaving Dani's mood much improved.

After the game, Ty walked back to the clubhouse with the relief pitchers, but kept his eyes off Dani and didn't join in the friendly greeting offered by his companions. This treatment was repeated again on Tuesday.

Diana called Dani on Wednesday to invite herself to the game. Like Mike, she was supportive, reminding Dani that she herself had gone through similar problems, and assuring her that Ty was too rational not to take his own advice eventually.

Shortly before game time, Marv Richardson trotted out of the dugout to the stands. "We've got a bit of a problem," he said to Dani. "Maybe you can help."

"Sure. What's wrong?"

"Judy Green just called the ball park. She had a few contractions and panicked. She wants Kenny home, but he's starting tonight."

Dani told Marv that she had promised Judy that Kenny would be with her for the child's birth, and asked if someone else could pitch. The problem, she learned, was that Kenny refused to leave. It was his first home start of his career, and he maintained that his wife would still be in labor long after the game ended.

Dani, who knew nothing of such things, looked at Diana for guidance. "He has a point, Dani. Jeremy took fourteen hours, and that's not unusual."

After a few moments of thought, Dani told Marv that she thought she could settle things to everyone's satisfaction. She went inside to call Judy Green, and then, pleased with the results, had Mack summon a cart to take her out to the bull pen to talk to Kenny.

He was loosening up, throwing to the team's utility catcher. Ty was leaning against the wall, talking to one of the relief pitchers. Dani smiled at him, but received only a vacant look in return.

She told herself that it was better than a cheerful

hello; it proved he was upset. She walked over to Kenny, calling his name to get his attention. "We sent a car to bring Judy to the ball park. Diana and I will sit inside with her, and watch the game on TV. But I want your word that if things go faster than we expect, you'll come out of the game." Dani was careful to keep her voice soft and sympathetic. "Your wife is very young, very scared. I know that's tough for you to handle, Kenny, but she needs you now. There'll be lots of other starts, I promise, but you don't become a father every day."

"Yeah, sure. Thanks." The words might have been brusque, but Kenny's eyes were eloquent. Dani read relief and gratitude in them, but mercifully, no infatuation.

Several other women were in the wives' lounge during the game. One of them coached Judy in how to breathe, and all commiserated with her on the woes of being married to a ball player. By the time Kenny left the game in the seventh inning, she was quite relaxed.

Her contractions were nine minutes apart when he walked into the lounge. "Go shower and change," she told him calmly. "I want to watch the rest of the game, make sure your two-run lead holds up. There's plenty of time to get to the hospital."

The two left arm-in-arm forty-five minutes later. The next day, Kenny called Dani to thank her, and to tell her that Kenneth Green, Jr., who had weighed in at a whopping ten pounds, fifteen ounces, had been born at 3:01 in the morning.

Thursday was an open day and Ty was pitching Friday. "We have decided," Jeanne told Dani that afternoon, "to give your pitcher a little push. Teddy is taking you to the game tonight."

Jeanne didn't have to spell out what she had in

mind. "That's a horrible thing to do," Dani protested. "I can't put him . . ."

"Of course you can," Jeanne scoffed. "For once, listen to me."

Dani did so, but not without misgivings. From the time Ty stepped out onto the mound, it was all she could do to maintain her composure. The Astros were pounding the stuffing out of his pitches. For the first few innings he got away with it, because the Condors' fielding was absolutely dazzling, turning base hits into double plays and home runs into outs. A few times Ty glanced over at Dani, and Teddy somehow chose just those moments to whisper into her ear, or touch her, or smile tenderly at her. Ty gave up two runs in the fifth and two more in the sixth before Marv Richardson finally picked up the phone to the bull pen and summoned a reliever.

"Let's get out of here," Dani said as Ty walked off the mound. "I've had enough of this."

"You won't get an argument from me," Teddy replied. "I don't like the look on his face. When my father volunteered me for this, he didn't mention that I could wind up dead!"

In spite of his laconic tone, Teddy was obviously amused. It was the first time he had alluded to the reason for his presence, and he was gentleman enough not to pursue the topic. He took Dani out for dessert and coffee, then dropped her at her house.

Jeanne was out with Edward, so Dani turned on the TV just in time to hear Ty dissected on the post-game show. "The million-dollar arm was worth about a dollar nighty-eight tonight," one of his opponents joked.

When Dani heard a car pull up, she wondered if it was Edward, bringing Jeanne home early. She opened the door to greet them, but there was a Ford in the driveway, not a Continental, and Ty was the one striding up the walk. There was a grim expression on his face. "Is Teddy still here?" he asked.

Dani shook her head, wondering whose car he was driving.

"He's lucky I didn't let loose with a fast ball, straight at his head," Ty snapped.

"The way you pitched tonight, you probably would have missed," Dani retorted.

"Real funny, Dani. You should have been a sportswriter!" He paused. "Are you going to let me in?"

Dani stepped aside.

"I wasn't kidding, Dani. I didn't like the way he was touching you."

"He's only a friend," she assured him.

He shot her a hard look. "You little wretch! You were trying to make me jealous."

She couldn't help the smile on her face, seeing how well she had succeeded.

"So you finally found out what you saw in me, huh? Where's the bedroom?"

Up until now, Dani had rather enjoyed this moment of triumph, but she began to wonder just what Ty had in mind when he stalked through the living room and down the hall, opening doors until he found the right one. She didn't believe he was capable of violence, and yet he *had* looked incensed with her.

"Nervous?" he taunted. "You should be. I was coming to see you tomorrow. You didn't have to put me through six innings of hell tonight."

"What are you going to do?" Dani asked huskily.

"Go get a suitcase."

"Not until you tell me . . ."

"Just do it!" Ty barked.

His tone was so intimidating that Dani scurried into the guest room, fetched a suitcase from the closet, and brought it back to her bedroom. Ty was rummaging through her drawers, pulling out clothing and tossing it onto the bed. Dani stood by, watching helplessly, as he shoved everything into the suitcase and snapped it shut.

"Where's your aunt? When is she coming back?"

"With Edward, and probably not for hours. Honestly, Ty, I never meant . . ."

"To bed, Dani," he interrupted. "Now." He pointed at the now-rumpled covers.

No man treated her this way, not even the man she loved. "Just you wait a minute, Ty Morgan. You can't barge in here and start giving me orders and expect . . ."

"The hell I can't!" Moments later Ty had snatched her up and dumped her onto the bed, pinning her down with his body, holding her hands above her head. At first she struggled out of instinct, squirming furiously to get away. Then she noticed that Ty had started to smile, and fought him a little less enthusiastically, and for quite a different reason.

"You're beautiful when you're angry," he teased, nibbling at her ear and neck.

"*You're* a bully!" Dani craned her head away from his foraging lips.

His response was to unbutton her blouse, exposing her breasts to the provocative movements of his hands, which began to move lightly over the sheer lace of her bra. "Maybe," he murmured, "but if I am, you might as well enjoy it."

It was impossible to do anything else. He made love to her with such thoroughness and deliberation that she marveled at his control. When she would have rushed, he slowed her down. They caressed each other, kissed, stopped. And took feverish pleasure in denying and being denied ultimate satisfaction.

And after the waiting segued into a wild finale, they lay clinging together for minutes more, coming slowly down to earth.

"I think," Ty said when they finished dressing, "that you'd better leave your aunt a note and tell her you're with me."

"Where should I say we're going?" Dani asked, already complying with his suggestion.

"Las Vegas. Where else would we go?" He picked up the suitcase and started toward the door.

Dani followed, thinking that she liked that destination very well indeed. "Have a sudden urge to gamble?" she asked.

Ty reached into his jacket pocket and tossed a small jewelry case at her. "You could say that, couldn't you?"

Dani caught it and opened it up. There was a beautiful marquise-cut diamond ring inside, which she slipped onto her finger.

"I should have taken you to a motel and kept you in bed for two days before I gave that to you," Ty said as they got into the car. "That was a lousy thing to do to me, bringing Teddy there and making me watch him paw you when I was trying to pitch. It tore at my guts." He started the engine and backed out of the driveway.

"I'm sorry." Dani was very contrite. "Jeanne said . . ."

"I don't like being manipulated, Dani," Ty broke in.

His tone was very firm. Dani had already apologized; she didn't know what more she could say. An uneasy silence filled the car as they traveled on the main road toward the freeway. Dani gave him some time to cool down, then asked who the car belonged to.

"It's rented. We'll leave it in Vegas and fly home. I figured if we took a plane *there*, we'd have half a dozen reporters waiting for us when we landed."

The explanation was delivered in a slightly more promising tone of voice, prompting Dani to ask if he were still annoyed with her.

"Only when I think of Teddy groping you," he said.

Dani decided to try a different approach. She unfastened her seat belt and slid across to him, nuzzling his neck and caressing his thigh. "Didn't I make it up to you?" she purred.

Ty shook his head, laughing now, and put his arm around her. "Like no one else, ever," he said. "Now behave yourself before you get me into an accident."

"Were you really so angry when you came in?"

"Half-angry, half-joking, and dying to make love to you. If my arm hadn't hurt, I never would have lasted that long," he admitted.

"I'm not complaining," Dani giggled. "Except maybe about the suitcase. You packed all the wrong clothes."

"It doesn't matter. I have a lot of frustration to work off. You're not leaving the bedroom until Sunday."

"Only until Sunday?" Dani drawled.

"I pitch on Wednesday. We have to get back to L.A."

"So I'll give you the week off."

It was the wrong thing to say. Ty pulled over onto the shoulder of the freeway and switched off the ignition. "Let's get something straight, Dani. *I* run my career. You may own the team, but don't make the mistake of thinking you can tell me what to do. Only Mack and Marv have that right."

"I was only joking," Dani said defensively.

"I know that. I just want you to understand that this wasn't an easy decision for me. I'm not a pigheaded male chauvinist. I'm only realistic about the problems we'll have."

Dani didn't want to hear about problems, not just yet. "I'm sorry I called you names, but you were very sarcastic to me. I was upset."

"I know." His tone was gentler now. "I've had a miserable two weeks, Dani. I've been pitching like something out of the rookie leagues—lousy concentration, worse control. I never imagined that could happen to me. For the first time in my life, I couldn't block out everything but the game. I think that, on some level, I didn't want to, because my own attitude toward you didn't feel right. I was raised to go after what I want, accept challenges, and here I was, deciding in advance that something I wanted very much wouldn't work. You were so terrific with Kenny the other night—I stood there, watching you, loving you. And I finally realized that the money was irrelevant. It would only matter if it affected your life-style, but it doesn't."

"And the general manager job?"

"I want it when Mack retires. I really don't care what people say. Nothing could be worse than the stuff I've had to read for the last two weeks."

"And suppose you have a disagreement with the owner?"

Dani meant only to tease him, but he took her question very seriously. "I've been around baseball all my life, Dani. I'll explain everything I do to you, and listen to your opinions, but until you know as much as I do, I run the show. Do you have a problem with that?"

Dani reminded him that *he* was the one with a problem. "There was all that talk about earning everything you got, and being the boss. You're very arrogant at times."

"Don't marry me if you can't live with that," Ty replied. "I know myself well enough to know that I have to come first. I have a huge ego and a dominating streak to match it. During the season I'll want you to come along on the road trips, seduce me out of my rotten mood when I lose, and cater to my schedule, even if it means we never go out the night before I pitch. I'm selfish. I want you to adjust your life to mine so we can be together. I've talked a lot to Mike, and Diana's turned down movie roles and club dates just to be with him."

"Are you finished telling me all your faults?" Dani asked teasingly. "I said you were arrogant *at times,* but I fell in love with you because you were sensitive, and sweet, and open, and you put my feelings before your personal desires. Sometimes, Ty, I think you look for problems where they don't exist. I'm *relieved* you'll be running the team eventually. I only worry that everyone will assume you're running it now."

"Don't. Mack would resign, and everyone knows it." He grinned crookedly at her. "The only one who wraps him around her little finger is you. But you have other commitments, Dani. And you're very strong-willed yourself."

"I'd better be, married to you!" she retorted. "My work with the foundation is important to me, but fortunately, it's flexible, Ty. And speaking of flexible, it seems to me that Diana mentioned that Mike was on location with her last winter. And you *did* offer to go to the Houston Museum with me."

"So okay, I was overstating the case," Ty admitted, a sheepish look on his face. "I want to share that part of your life with you, and during the off-season we'll be able to do much more of it. But I know I can be overbearing at times—like at Tahoe. I was falling in love with you, and I was furious when you held back on me. I forced you into giving me the response I wanted. When I was a kid, I couldn't cope with my own intensity, and I used to explode. I've settled down, especially since my accident, and I've learned to control my temper instead of losing it. But it's still there."

"I accept that. Sometimes I like it when you lose control of yourself. Like at Tahoe," Dani teased. "And in the training room, and your hotel room, and my bedroom . . ."

"And now." Ty reached out to circle her waist with his hands, pulling her onto his lap. After a preliminary nuzzle of her neck, his mouth captured her lips for a searing, probing kiss that made her melt against his chest. "We'll fight," he muttered against her mouth. "Sometimes I'll push too hard, and you'll push back."

Dani nibbled at his lips. "I think you like me this way."

"Umm. Love you. And to think I used to avoid women after I pitched." He kissed her even more hotly, his hands wandering under her sweater to explore the softness of her breasts.

For several long minutes the outside world ceased to exist. But then reality intruded in the form of a flashlight, shining through the window into their eyes.

Ty, laughing, put Dani back into her seat, and

rolled down the window. "Was there some problem, officer?" he drawled.

"This is an emergency lane, sir. May I see your license and . . ." The highway patrolman did a comical double take. "Hey, you're Ty Morgan."

"That's right."

"Geez, Morgan, what's wrong with you lately? You pitched one lousy game tonight. They practically torpedoed you off the mound!"

"Insane jealousy," the pitcher answered solemnly, cocking his head at Dani. "She was with another guy. I'm taking her to Vegas to marry her."

"Wait 'til I tell the guys about this. They'll never believe . . ."

"Officer," Dani interrupted. "Would you mind making sure the press doesn't find out? They'll be all over us by tomorrow as it is."

"If there's nothing else, we'd like to get along. It's a long drive," Ty added.

"Morgan, if I thought it would help your pitching, I'd turn on the siren and give you a police escort all the way to Nevada!" The officer chuckled.

"Thanks, but we'll get there on our own," Ty told him. "Look for a shut-out on Wednesday night, okay?"

"You got it, Morgan. And hey, good luck." The patrolman walked back to his car, and Ty started the engine of the Ford.

When they were back on the freeway, Dani asked with a giggle, "Hey Morgan! What *would* help your pitching?"

"You," he replied obligingly.

It was exactly what she wanted to hear.

If you enjoyed this book...

...you will enjoy a Special Edition Book Club membership even more.

It will bring you each new title, as soon as it is published every month, delivered right to your door.

15-Day Free Trial Offer

We will send you 6 new Silhouette Special Editions to keep for 15 days absolutely free! If you decide not to keep them, send them back to us, you pay nothing. But if you enjoy them as much as we think you will, keep them and pay the invoice enclosed with your trial shipment. You will then automatically become a member of the Special Edition Book Club and receive 6 more romances every month. There is no minimum number of books to buy and you can cancel at any time.

Coming Next Month

Tears And Red Roses by Laura Hardy

Carly Newton had made her choice in life: she
wanted a career, not a man, and her position as
editor-in-chief satisfied her in every way. Then
she met Adam Blake, and the storm he
unleashed in her swept away all her resolution.
Could she live without the lightning in his eyes,
the passion in his kiss and the winds that blew
through her at his every touch?

Rough Diamond by Brooke Hastings

Dani Ronsard and Ty Morgan, the spoiled
heiress and the star of the baseball diamond.
What match could be more unlikely? Yet his
muscled body awoke in her sensations that more
cultured men had never aroused and the passion
that lay beneath her veneer of sophistication
drove him to the edge of control—and beyond.
Under the hot summer sun they played a game
without rules, for the greatest prize of all.

A Man With Doubts by Linda Wisdom

Actress Tracey White was tired of playing the
other woman. When she met Scott Kingsly he
seemed all too convinced that the roles she
played reflected the real Tracey. But slowly they
learned to trust, to share a passion and an
intimacy she had dreamed of, though never
found. Together they created a blaze strong
enough to melt the Colorado snows and
keep out the winter's chill.

Silhouette Special Edition

Coming Next Month

The Flaming Tree by Margaret Ripy

Blair St. James was the aspiring songstress who would give anything in exchange for a chance to make music. Dirk Brandon was the famous composer whose fee for collaboration was marriage. He taught her the melody of love, the changing rhythm of desire, the forté of true passion. Her zest for life and his masterful skill, harmonized in a melody as sweet as love itself.

Yearning Of Angels by Fran Bergen

Violet eyed Nina St. Clair was determined to make her own dreams come true—and when she sold her first screenplay, she thought she had found the gold at the end of the rainbow. But the success of one goal led her to a tall, dark prize she'd never expected. In Hollywood mogul Robert Whitney, she found the one man who could hold her heart like a captive bird and teach her body the ways of love.

Bride In Barbados by Jeanne Stephens

Lost in love, Susan married Travis Sennett and followed him to Barbados, land of searing heat and sunsets of fire. But Travis married Susan for a very different reason—a selfish reason—and suddenly time was running out for them. There in that honeyed land, on an island lush and made for love, could they carve out their future and build a dynasty that would survive forever beneath the flaming sun?

MORE ROMANCE FOR
A SPECIAL WAY TO RELAX

$1.95 each